Glitter on the Rocks

a novel by

Frank Allan Rogers

DANCING CROWS
PRESS

DANCINGCROWSPRESS@GMAIL.COM

Dedication

This book is dedicated to Bob McDill and Dan Seals (1948-2009), who cowrote the song, Everything That Glitters (is Not Gold). Dan Seals' recording became a hit song. The inspiring message touched my heart and inspired this story.

Acknowledgements

I am indebted to the following people who helped to make this story better in so many ways.

Eddie Grantland aka Fast Eddie, Skydiver extraordinaire and good friend. My skydive scene would not seem authentic without your help.

Beta readers Debra Watzman and Judy Newberry Moody, for your time, attention, judgment, and sharp eyes that improved the story's impact and appeal.

Ron Frank and Jim Mitchell, aircraft pilots and masters of the air, for your time, patience, and expertise on the speed, cost, and luxury of private jets. And for my first time in a Learjet. Your input improved the story's credibility.

John Frank, for taking time from your busy schedule to help me with rodeo terms.

Bob O'Kelly and Elyse Wheeler for your professional help in formatting, editing, and many other areas.

Don Chance and Mike Bryce, champion bull riders who gave their time for interviews to help my story carry the ring of truth. And Hal Ivey (RIP) their friend and mine, who set up the interviews.

Barry Starr, Abbey Thompson, and the entire team at Stanford Genetics, The Tech Interactive. Your super group did not merely tolerate, but welcomed, my many questions about DNA testing and results. Your time and expertise make my story more authentic.

Acknowledgements cont.

Ty Murray, nine-time world champion cowboy, for your autobiographical story, *King of the Cowboys*. Great book.

Ruthi Pippin, for advice and knowledge on genetics and DNA. Thanks, cousin.

Professional firefighter, Chris May, for your help. Your expertise added true realism and authenticity to the fire scene.

Carrollton Writers Guild, for your comments, critiques, and suggestions as the story developed. I am privileged to be a member of that highly-skilled group.

A special note of thanks to my darling wife, Mary, for all your help. For listening, encouragement, patience, and your artistic sense for cover design.

Chapter One

They stood in the middle of his living room. He kissed her lips, her neck, and her lips again. She arched her back, slid her hands from his shoulders to his waist and pulled him tight. He moaned as her chest pressed against his. He put his mouth to her ear.

"Scrambled or fried?"

Her breath caught. Her brow wrinkled. She held his waist and pushed back.

"What?"

"Just planning breakfast."

Green eyes lit with a sudden twinkle. "Are you … asking me to spend the night?"

"I love how smart you are." He pulled her close and kissed her again. She leaned back, laughed, and shook her head.

"I didn't bring my overnight bag."

"You can borrow mine."

She giggled. His hands eased down her back, wrapped around her hips and squeezed. He kissed her neck again. She whispered, "I didn't bring a toothbrush."

He whispered, too. "I have a new package."

"But I don't have my PJ's. Not even a nightshirt."

His voice grew husky. "I like you more all the time."

Large pupils looked up at him with a sparkle that didn't say yes, didn't say no. But they were curious.

***

The cool morning breeze wafted through the screen into the house, and carried evidence of coffee bubbling and sighing in the pot, and of the mad sizzle from a pound of bacon on the big cast-iron griddle.

Marty and Elly slept little during the night. Yet he woke wide-eyed, smiling, and full of energy. Elly slept now. But she would be awake soon enough. Morning coffee and frying bacon could snap Rip Van Winkle out of a coma.

Marty grinned and nodded as he talked to himself. *I meet the nicest people at rodeos.* Last night, on their fifth date, he and Elly were intimate for the first time. His eyes could not get enough of her, and he loved the smell of her, and ... it was more than physical, an attraction that excited him, made him happy. Yet a bit uneasy. Would he wake up and find that none of it was real?

Champion bull riders and rodeo sweethearts had busy schedules, and both careers required endless travel. How often would schedules put Elly and him at the same event? The next date could be two weeks away. Or three. Or never. Five dates didn't guarantee another. Maybe Elly was a heartache on hold.

Marty scooped the bacon onto a plate, sprinkled olive oil on English muffins and threw them down to make toast. He'd promised his date a big breakfast, though she didn't answer his question about the eggs. He would go ask again.

Bright green eyes stopped him at the door. Last night, Elly worried about her overnight bag. Now, she stood in the doorway wearing a good-morning smile and Marty's heavy work-shirt she stole from his closet, her hair wild, her face undone. The woman still qualified as a knockout, and bore no resemblance to Rip Van Winkle.

Marty wanted to say, *Stay forever and then you can go.* Instead, he filled a heavy mug with coffee and held it out.

"Black?"

Elly nodded and took the coffee. Marty angled his head at the grill behind him.

"Hungry?"

"Famished."

"Scrambled or fried?"

She cocked her head and smiled. "Yes."

An hour later, he pulled her to him, kissed her, and gazed at her up close. "You have the sexiest green eyes I've ever seen."

She grinned. "That's why you made me breakfast?"

He nodded. They laughed.

A lump grew in Marty's throat when Elly said she had to go. He scoured the grill. Elly walked to her car, blew him a kiss, and drove away.

***

Not many Saturdays made Marty enjoy cleaning the barn. This one did. Not many April days in northern New Mexico were perfect. This one was. Seventy degrees and sunny.

3

A light breeze puffed through the doorway in easy gusts, and scattered loose hay about his boots. Marty caught the hay with a pitchfork and threw it back on the stack.

A hammer, a shovel, or a pitchfork can be a tool or a shackle, his uncle once told him. *Hard work, or therapy. User's choice.*

Marty chose therapy. Let the wind tease him. He would gather and stack hay scattered by the wind and horses, and focus on the best parts of his life. An old proverb came to mind. *Home is where the heart is*, another of Uncle Clarence's favorites.

Working in the barn often reminded Marty of his uncle. The hundred-acre estate Marty inherited two years ago was a small tract of land compared to ranches around the small town of Cimarron, but the right size for him. It became his *happy place.*

Uncle Clarence bought the property years ago, took down the crumbling adobe home, and built a modern home in its place. That home burned five years before Uncle Clarence passed, and the property sat vacant for a long time.

Marty built a new home. The old barn stayed. Massive wooden beams creaked with the slightest wind. The block-and-tackle for lifting hay to the loft. The corroded windcock on the roof. They gave the building character he could never get in a new barn.

The estate also came with a rooster Marty named Hobo, a part-time resident or frequent guest, and the only one of his kind that hung around here. He'd stay for an hour or two, disappear, and show up again two or three days later.

Marty figured Hobo had a harem of hens somewhere on a nearby farm, and wouldn't stay away from them for long. A man couldn't fault a rooster for that.

Even so, Marty scattered shelled corn near the barn, hoping the rooster would stop by and crow every morning. But a murder of crows turned Hobo's treat into a quick snack.

In the barn, Marty's mind was free to think about anything it liked. Today, his mind liked Elly.

Yesterday after breakfast, Marty and Elly sat by the grill, sipped coffee and talked about rodeo people. He asked her about announcer, Charlie Harmon. Everyone in the circuit knew about their off-and-on affair. By the time Marty finished the question, he was sorry he asked. None of his business. But Elly didn't seem to mind.

"That ended a few months ago," she told him. "Did you ever notice when a married woman fools around, her husband is the last to find out? Well, it works the other way around, too. Seems I was the last to find out Charlie Harmon is married."

Was that affair really over? At shave time this morning, Marty resolved that question talking with the mirror. *Elly was done with the announcer.* If a man debated with himself, one side or the other would win, almost always. Mirror talks, truck talks, and barn talks helped him make the right decisions. Although he had to admit, he was a bit biased in discussions about Elly.

Rodeo competition could be a sport, show-business, or both. It didn't matter. But a name did matter if you wanted to be remembered. Charlie Harmon – most folks called him *Charmin' Harmon* – had an ideal name for an announcer. When Elisa shortened her name to Elly, Elly Kelly became unforgettable. Being gorgeous also helped. For Marty, she was unforgettable with *any* name.

A car door slammed and brought Marty back to the present. He stood his pitchfork against the big square post and took a step toward the house, but changed his mind. Probably another witness preacher woman. Or worse, the same one. Besides, whoever it was would come to the barn when no one answered the door at the house.

Marty cleaned up more hay with the pitchfork. But Buck Naked's ears pricked, and he whinnied. The horse showed a cranky mood all morning. Marty took him out the back of the barn to the corral. When Marty stepped back in, boot heels thumped near the front of the barn, and startled him. He spun around, pitchfork in hand, and stared.

A woman stopped in the doorway, pushed back her cowboy hat and rested her hands on her hips. The breeze caught her hair. She swept it out of her face and nodded at the pitchfork. "You really make a girl feel welcome."

Marty laughed. "Sorry, Elly. I didn't know it was you. Didn't know you were coming. But you've been on my mind all morning."

With a mock smile, she angled her head toward a pile of manure. "Oh, how flattering. Shoveling horse crap made you think of me."

Marty laughed and shook his head. "When I think of you, I see only you."

"Oooh, smooth talker." She grinned and looked around. "I like your barn, Marty. Mine serves the purpose, but yours ... it's got real personality." She nodded at a big brass spittoon. "Yuk. You use that thing?"

Marty's nose wrinkled. He shook his head. "I found it on the porch of my uncle's house after the fire. So I cleaned it up and brought it out here."

With big eyes and a bigger grin, Elly jerked her head toward the wall. "A picture of a chicken? You put that up?"

Marty smiled and nodded. "My friend, Hobo. He posed for the picture, and I built a frame for it. He fits right in out here, don't you think?"

Elly nodded and looked around again. "Lots of special things. What's your favorite?"

He looked around, and back at her. "I like everything in here. But my favorite one is standing right here in front of me." He leaned the pitchfork against the wall, and stepped toward her.

Elly held up her hand to stop him, and grabbed a shovel from the corner. She pointed at a stall.

"I've got work to do." She motioned at the haystack. "And so do you." She grinned. He shrugged, and turned back to his job.

Marty chuckled. "Buck Naked's in the corral. He's gonna strut all day when I tell him a gorgeous woman came to muck out his stall."

Elly stopped and looked at him. "You have a horse named *Buck Naked*?"

"When he's wearing a saddle, I just call him *Buck*."

She rolled her eyes and grinned. "Anyone ever call you *sane*?"

Marty widened his eyes, smiled, and shook his head. "Would a sane man climb on a 2,000-pound bull that wants to kill him?"

Elly lowered her head and stared up at him. "Would a sane woman date a man who does that for a living?"

He shrugged. "Never met a sane woman."

Elly grinned and shook her head.

They worked and talked. Elly asked about Marty's family, and if he'd ever been married. But she didn't probe. He told her he was divorced. She didn't ask for details, but snapped her head around, "You never told me how old you are."

"You never asked."

"I'm asking."

"Twenty-four."

She smiled and nodded. "That'll work. I'm nineteen."

Marty angled his head toward her. "Certainly works for me."

Elly grabbed the garden hose, washed the shovel, and stood it back in its corner. She cleaned her hands with sanitizer, stuffed the bottle back into her jeans, and blew Marty a kiss. "Call me later. I gotta do paperwork stuff but I can talk for a few minutes."

Marty's chin dropped. "Leaving already?" He wiped his hands on a bandanna and tossed it on an empty Jack Daniel's whiskey barrel in the corner. "Not many people come here just to muck out a stall."

She took off her hat and leaned back against the doorframe. "I like you, Marty. When's the last time someone came just to see you?"

"Too long. I don't get much human company out here in the barn."

Her voice grew soft. "You're a fine man, Marty Redman. I'm glad I came."

He stepped in front of her, caught her wrist and wrapped her arm around his waist. "I'm glad, too, Elly. A fine man and a fine woman belong together." He ran his open fingers through the hair above her ears. "When's the last time someone kissed you in a barn?" He flashed a crooked smile, pulled her close, and whispered, "You don't have to answer that." He kissed her, and then again.

She grabbed his waist and backed against the haystack. "When's the last time you had a good roll in the hay?" She pulled him down on top of her.

"Well, I —"

She covered his mouth and whispered, "I didn't come here to *muck*."

Marty was not a man long on patience. Time dragged while he struggled with her boots. His breath came heavy. Pulse thundered in his ears. His lips found hers. His fingers tugged at buttons, hooks, and snaps. Her fingers reached for a zipper.

He pulled at the hems of her Wranglers, and gazed into wide green eyes, only inches from his own. The eyes grew misty.

In the heat of the moment, a rattle or shuffle near the door may have tried to catch Marty's attention. He did not know. He did not care. The something became a distant nothing while the world outside the barn disappeared.

Three minutes later, the long gasp was not Elly's. Marty pushed up, and turned his head. A stone-faced young woman shivered near the doorway. Tears clouded her wide eyes. Her mouth gaped. Her head wagged in slow motion.

Marty laughed. "Oh, my God."

Elly pushed him off and sat up. She raked hay out of her hair with her fingers, and leaned to look out. Marty stood, pulled up his jeans, and Elly found her hat.

Near the door, the woman's feet moved backward in stiff-legged steps. The full dress dragged on the high tops of heavy, black shoes.

Elly caught Marty's arm, and pulled up. The woman by the door gasped once again. Her eyes bulged. Elly stood next to Marty, wearing only a sock, a smile, and a mangled cowboy hat.

The lady wheezed, turned, ran to her car, and scrambled in. The engine revved. The transmission clunked, and the car leaped backward. Tires slung gravel from the barn's driveway. The transmission clunked again. Black smoke gushed from the tailpipe. Marty and Elly watched the old Buick Roadmaster rumble down the road. Marty grinned.

"She comes almost every Saturday."

Elly jerked her head toward him. "For what? Who the hell was that?"

"That witness preacher woman. I been trying to get rid of her for weeks."

Elly grinned. "You think this'll do it?"

He felt his eyes grow bigger while he scanned her up and down. "You better stop by next Saturday. Just in case."

As Marty watched Elly's car grew smaller down the road, Hobo strutted by the open doorway, and crowed loud and long.

Chapter Two

Marty paced through the house, knowing his driveway was still empty before he looked out. He stared at the road, sighed, and checked his watch again. She was a half-hour late. He'd left a message on her cellphone and called again ten minutes later without leaving one. He checked the TV—nothing happening around Cimarron. But, in a village of a thousand people, nothing ever did.

Rodeo crowds were the only crowds Marty Redman liked. When he was not competing, he wanted no part of big-city buzz. Still, he found it ironic. Cimarron, New Mexico had long been famous for its history and old west outlaws. Now the town's biggest news centered on events at the local Boy Scout Ranch.

He glanced at his watch again. Elly was now *more* than a half-hour late. He took a beer from the fridge and guzzled half of it before he turned the bottle upright. He turned on the radio on his kitchen counter, but heard only commercials. A minute later, he talked to himself in the bathroom mirror.

Stop the worry, Marty. Elly is a beautiful girl, but you've had lots of 'em. I am not in ... He could not say what he wanted while he looked into his own eyes. He looked down and said aloud, "I'm not in love with her."

Again, he nodded at the mirror. *There, I said it.* He finished his beer, dropped the bottle into the bathroom trash, and looked again in the mirror.

Could be anything. Ran out of gas? She'd be stranded. If somebody stopped to help, that could be dangerous. Dammit, I'll give her another twenty minutes. Then I'll be out looking for her.

Marty hurried back to the kitchen when he heard news from the radio. At this time of day, radio interference could be a real nuisance, and the local station was not immune to the problem. Marty heard only pieces of the broadcast as the radio crackled and popped. His breath caught when a newsman reported a crash on Highway 58, followed by more static and pops.

Marty grabbed a flashlight, a jacket, two bottles of water, and a blanket, and ran to his pickup in the driveway. Elly would be driving highway 58, the way she always came here, the only decent road that led here from her place. The instant his butt touched the seat, a car turned into the driveway behind him, headlights beaming. The driver sounded two short beeps on the horn and stopped the car.

Whoever was in that car had to get the hell out of his way. He had to find Elly. Marty jumped out and ran back to the car. Before he reached the driver's window, the driver stepped out.

"Hey, handsome, sorry I'm a bit late."

"Elly?" His eyes went wide. "Oh, God. Uhm … I'm so happy you made it." He grabbed her and hugged her, his breath coming in short gasps.

Elly giggled, pushed him back, and looked up. She eased up her hand and wiped a small tear from the corner of his eye. Her face wrinkled.

"Marty, are you okay."

He shrugged. "Oh, uh, yeah. Everything's fine."

"You going somewhere?"

"No. Why?"

She dipped her head forward. "Your truck is running."

"Hah. Oh yeah." He talked over his shoulder, walked to the truck and shut off the engine. "Just checking my emergency stuff. You never know when you might need it." He nodded toward the house. "Come on in."

In the house, Elly pointed to the kitchen radio, still blaring. "I heard that in the car, Marty. Over on fifty-eight, a truck hit a herd of cattle crossing the road. Killed one cow and injured another one."

Marty turned off the radio. "So that's what made you late?"

Elly nodded as she sat on the sofa. "When I heard that, I took a detour down a dirt road. Long and dusty." She nodded toward the fridge. "Got a cold beer for a thirsty girlfriend?"

****

Elly placed her hand on Marty's arm. He woke up and rubbed his face. He adjusted the pillow, and turned toward her, his voice rough from sleep.

"Bad dreams?"

Her answer came in a loud whisper. "No, I've been awake all night."

Marty propped up on his elbow. Elly lay on her back, moonlight through the window reflecting off her wide green eyes that stared at the ceiling.

"Too much coffee?"

She drew a long breath and eased it out. "Just thinking about us."

Marty had a gut feeling. He waited.

Elly angled her head toward him. "When I first got here, you ran out to the car. I saw a tear in your eye, and I—"

"Oh, I had a gnat in my eye a couple of minutes before you drove up, and —"

"Too bad." She turned and faced him. "For a minute, I thought you cared enough to worry about me."

Marty sighed. He wedged his arm under her, lay back on the pillow and pulled her over on top of him. He looked up at her tender, beautiful face.

"Elly, my dear, a few weeks ago, you said, *Don't fall in love. You might get hurt.* So, I'm trying to take your advice."

She lowered her head, her face almost touching his. "I repeated what you said to me a couple months before. That was *your* advice, Marty Redman."

He pulled her down and whispered, "I'm sorry."

She pushed herself up to see his face. "I've been hurt before, but it's not your fault. You told me how much Luna hurt you. I care, but I won't let you take it out on *me*." Elly swung away, and sat on the edge of the bed, her feet on the floor, her back to Marty.

He turned toward her. He loved her face, but she was almost as beautiful from the back, the moon making highlights on the hair she pampered so often. He cleared his throat, reached out and closed his hand on her shoulder, "I don't blame any of that on you. It's not like that."

"Oh, really?" She pulled away and stood beside the bed, her back to him.

"Well, tell me what it's like, Marty." She crossed her arms over her chest and waited. When Marty didn't answer, she turned to him and spread her hands.

"We've been seeing each other for six months. We go places, hold hands, laugh together, have fun. We buy things for each other, go to dinner, come back and spend the night together at your house or mine. We make love, and it's always terrific. But ..." her voice slowed, "not one time have you ever said the words, *I love you, Elly*. So, if you're not blaming me for anything, you must have some other reason for not saying that. For not *feeling* that."

She turned, flipped on the wall switch for the bedside lamp, and turned back. Marty shielded his eyes.

"Let's hear it, Marty. Tell me what it is. Am I ugly? Am I stupid? Am I boring? Or am I just *not* what you hoped for?"

He uncovered his eyes and sat up. "Oh, God, Elly. That's ridiculous." He left the bed and stood in front of her. "You're not stupid, you're not boring, and ... and you're sure as hell not ugly. You're one of the best-looking women I've ever met."

Her eyes scanned him from his feet to his face, and she shook her head. "So, is that all I am to you, Marty ... just a good-looking piece?"

Marty turned his back to her, stared up at the wall, and shook his head. "You've never said, *I love you, Marty*."

"And you won't hear me say it till you say it to me."

He heard her snatching items off a chair in the corner, and turned to look. She disappeared into the bathroom.

Minutes later, Elly made a casual exit from the bathroom, looking calm and in control, with her hair done and her makeup in place. She scanned Marty up and down again as he stood in front of her, still in his underwear, and swallowing the last drop of a beer. She wore a slight frown but did not speak.

Marty dropped the bottle in the trashcan, spread his hands and looked back at her. "What are you doing?"

"I'm going home."

"Home?" His eyes shot to the clock on the bedside table, and back. "What the hell's wrong with you, Elly? It's three o'clock in the morning."

Her words came without emotion. "I'm not spending the night with someone who doesn't care about me."

His face wrinkled. His chest tightened. "How could you think that?"

Her face stayed calm. "How could I *not* think it?" She turned toward the door. Marty caught her arm.

"Elly, please. Give me a minute. Please."

She stopped, looked at him and waited. He released her arm and pulled her hand to his lips. After a gentle kiss, he held her hand to his chest and looked in her eyes.

"Elly, I'm sorry I lied to you when you asked about the tear in my eye. There was no bug. When you pulled up, I was loading stuff I might need in the truck. A minute later, I would've been out looking for you."

Elly looked down. Her face softened as she looked up again. "So, you really were worried?"

A lump grew in Marty's throat. He nodded. "More than you could know."

"Just because I was a bit late?"

"You said a truck hit a herd of cattle. The only part I heard on the radio was, *one killed and another injured*. I didn't know it was cattle. I thought … well, you can guess what I thought. So, I uh …." He took another deep breath. "You're the most precious …." He sucked in a deep breath, and another tear appeared. Marty lowered his head.

Elly pulled up his chin, kissed the tear, and then wiped it away. She squeezed his hand and wagged her head, though her eyes never left his as she whispered. "Why is it so hard for you to tell me you care about me? To tell me how you feel?"

He looked away from her. "Because it doesn't seem …." He shrugged.

Elly turned his face back to her. "Doesn't seem … what?" He turned his face away again. Elly turned it back. "Doesn't seem *what*, Marty? Manly?"

"Well, yeah. I mean, a man's got to feel like a man. I'm a bull rider and—"

"Yes, you are. One of the best ever. You're strong and tough, and you've got a lot of guts. You're a world champion. But you've got it upside down. Riding a bull doesn't make you a man."

Elly looked down and shook her head, and then looked up at him again. "I've seen women bull riders. They don't turn into men. Think about that for a little while. And then decide if you're tough enough—*man* enough—to deal with your own feelings."

Marty stared blank-faced. "I don't know what to say."

"Well, I do. I feel most like a woman when I'm with you, Marty. Not when I'm driving a car or riding a horse. Not when I'm showing off in the arena. Not when some jerk makes a rude remark about my breasts." She caught his arm, stood tall, and looked in his eyes. Her voice grew soft.

"It's when I'm with you, Marty. I feel most like a woman when I'm with you. Don't I make you feel like a man? If I don't …." Her head made a slow wag. Her eyes stayed fixed on his. "This is never going to work for us. If I do make you feel like a man, don't be afraid. Show enough of that manly courage to say so."

She caught his head in her hands and brought his face down close. "Even if it takes a little tear to show how strong your feelings are."

A lump swelled in Marty's throat as Elly led him to the bedside table, took a tissue from the box, and wiped another tear from his face. She backed against the bed and sat on the edge.

Marty took her hands in his, leaned and kissed her forehead, and smiled. "You mean so much to me, Elly. I really care about you, and I want you to know that. I mean that with all my heart, and every bit of manly courage I can muster."

"Thank you, Marty. That wasn't so tough after all, was it?"

He grinned. "Is everything good now?"

The soft, green eyes looked into his. "No."

"No? But, Elly, I —

She pulled him down on the bed and put her mouth to his ear.

"Make me feel like a woman. Make love to me, Marty."

Chapter Three

The big pickup hummed down the highway as Marty headed east on Interstate 10 through Texas. He liked living in Cimarron, New Mexico. Most people there were friendly and sociable, but would leave you alone when you wanted. He also liked to drive fast, and the 80-mile-per-hour speed limit was another reason to like Texas. Besides, the Lone Star State hosted a whole slew of rodeos, and bull riders were always the main attraction.

He won his first competition in San Antonio two years ago, where he kissed the prize-money check, as well as the lady who gave it to him. He signed a contract to promote a line of tires and picked up more money before he left town. Since then, his truck always had new tires that cost him nothing.

Fifteen months and more than two hundred bull rides after that first prize check, he earned the coveted gold buckle, and the title of world champion. Product endorsements came hot and heavy, and they paid well.

He left the interstate and followed a two-lane road to Ted's Texas barbeque, where he stopped last year. Today, the place was closed down. On the way back to the interstate, his thoughts centered on last year. He'd come a long way in his career since then. But scattered raindrops and the intermittent flash of brake lights ahead brought his mind back to the present.

Near the interstate access road, a young man looked *all teeth* each time he grinned and wagged a thumb at a slow-moving car or truck. His grin changed to a worried frown as each possible ride left him standing.

While Marty's truck eased closer to the hitchhiker, the streak and squeak on the windshield reminded him once again he needed new wiper blades. Texas always seemed to get too much rain or not enough. Regardless, it was still better than riding a bus. He hated the monotony of buses. He hated trains more. He liked planes, but getting to an airport, dealing with parking, luggage, tickets, and boarding, often took a toll on his patience.

Over the years, he often competed at five or six rodeos each week. Anytime it was practical, and sometimes when it was not, he drove his pickup truck from one rodeo to the next. This time, his truck was practical. He'd ride at seven rodeo locations in this state before he headed home.

From the driver's seat of his truck, he'd seen a hundred hitchhikers, maybe more while he drove from one rodeo to another. He'd passed by a few and picked up a few too many. Marty liked to help people who deserved it. But his truck was always the cleanest one around. That's how he wanted to keep it. As for the hitchhiker ahead … well, his boots looked muddy, and rain dripped off his cowboy hat. Marty felt bad for him but did not want the mess in his truck.

Traffic slowed to a crawl, the dripping cowboy hat now only two cars ahead. Marty leaned toward the windshield and stared at the wiggling thumb. The little man had hands so large he looked like a cartoon character.

A minute later, Marty flashed his headlights. The hitchhiker dropped his overgrown thumb, shook the water from his hat, and reached for the door as Marty stopped.

The toothy grin returned. Marty's new passenger planted his huge, muddy boots on the spotless floor of the truck. He threw his weather-beaten, wet suitcase into the storage area behind the seat, and slammed the door too hard. He wiped water from his face, tried to dry his hand by rubbing it on his soggy jeans, and then shoved the hand toward the man who rescued him.

"Kyle Kross. That's Kross with a *K*, not a *C*."

Marty reached for his hand. "Okay, Kyle Kross with a *K*. I'm Marty with an *M*." Both men chuckled as Marty steered the truck back onto the interstate.

"Where ya headed, Kyle?"

Kyle held up his thumb. "I'm ridin' this thumb to San Antonio. And I'll be riding a bull when I get there. Hope it's by four o'clock."

Marty nodded. "That's where I'm headed. It's less than a hundred and fifty miles." He checked the clock on the dash. "We've got lots of time. A long walk, but an easy drive."

Kyle's face brightened. "You can drop me off anywhere near Freeman Coliseum if you don't mind. That's where I'll be competing."

Marty's eyes widened. "You said you'll be riding a bull?"

Kyle nodded. "I'm a bull rider. You like rodeos?"

"I do … long as I don't have to sit out in the sun or rain. I'll come and watch you ride."

Kyle held up his hand. "Maybe you didn't notice, but I have big hands and feet. It's a real plus in bull riding. But … sometimes I still get embarrassed when somebody mentions it." He talked nonstop about rodeos throughout the southwest.

Marty's gut rumbled. He pointed at a billboard. *Cracker Barrel, Next Right.* "Ready for some grub, Kyle?"

Kyle blushed, and jerked his head toward the back of the seat. "I got peanut butter and crackers in my suitcase. I uh … I kinda have to watch my money. You know? Entry fees and all that."

Marty wagged his head at the thought of anyone eating peanut butter in his truck. "Lunch is on me." He took the next right. "You can tell me about your bull riding career while we eat."

Marty tried to tell Kyle he, too, rode bulls, but during lunch and all the way to Freeman Coliseum, the big-handed little man talked about rodeos and bulls and how he would do anything and everything to become a champion.

The two men arrived more than two hours before the bull riding competition would begin. Marty had been here several times and appreciated what Freeman Coliseum had to offer. He'd never occupied a standard seat in the crowd, but all ten thousand seats for rodeo spectators appeared to be comfortable, with a good view. He was glad to be back.

Marty and Kyle left the truck, and started toward the arena's back entry. Marty placed his hand on Kyle's shoulder. "Kyle, there's something I—"

"Marty Redman," the rodeo announcer shouted as he too walked toward the rear entry. He stuck out his hand as he approached. "Welcome back, Champ." The two men shook hands.

"Thanks. Glad to be here." Marty had long been proud of his memory for names. He could recall the name of every bull he'd ridden, and where it happened. Now his face grew warm. This man had an easy-to-remember name that rhymed. But it wouldn't come to mind fast enough. Was it *Jack Shack*? Marty motioned at Kyle. "This is Kyle Kross. He's a bull rider."

The announcer extended his hand to Kyle. "Oh, yes. We've been expecting you. Welcome." The man angled his head at Marty as he spoke to Kyle. "You can learn a lot from this man. I've seen him ride many times. He's one of the best I've ever known."

Marty's face stayed red. Kyle's face grew white while he stared with his mouth open. "You're Marty Redman? You didn't even tell me. I saw you ride on TV, but I didn't recognize—"

Marty slapped him on the shoulder. "It's all right, Kyle. I'm just a man."

Kyle shook his head. "Not just a man. A damn tough one."

***

A dozen bull riders showed up to compete in the afternoon event. As reigning champion, Marty had the distinction of riding last. Of the eleven riders before him, three stayed on for the full eight seconds. Kyle got a good bull, rode him well, and had the best score so far. Now, to take first place, Marty had to beat his new friend.

He shook his head and put it out of his mind as he straddled *Fool's Game,* a big, ugly beast of a bull that looked like he could tackle a freight train. But often, the bigger bulls were slower or they tired faster. Marty needed a high score, and hoped this bull would be a real challenge. He tightened his grip on the rope, eased his knees into place, and pulled his hat down low. He scrunched his butt on the bull's spine, and nodded at the gateman.

"Let 'er go."

Fool's Game was no fool, and he was not slow. Marty knew this animal had been here before when it shot past the gate, twisted, turned, leaped, and spun. Marty's hopes rose. He had a

23

true challenge and focused only on the bull's hump while the stadium, the crowd, and the world, spun out of focus around him.

No two bulls were ever the same. Marty knew that as well as anyone. This one was tough, but Marty read him well, and felt confident during the first few seconds. But a quick spin and a heavy buck made Marty's left knee slip out of place. Maybe it moved only an inch, but keeping the knees in the perfect spot was critical. When a knee slid up, the butt moved away from the knee, often throwing the rider off the opposite side of the bull. If a knee slid down, the butt would follow the knee to the ground. End of ride.

Marty's left knee slipped down. A smart opponent like Fool's Game would spin right to throw the rider left, show the pesky creature on his back who's boss, and let him make a splat in the mud. A smart rider would react without having to think about it. Marty swung his right knee out and brought it back hard against the side of the bull. Fool's Game took the bait, and spun left, shifting his rider back to center.

More moves from the bull, and counter moves from Marty, offered the challenge he hoped for. Would it be enough? The buzzer sounded. Marty bailed, grinning as he planted his feet in the mud and manure.

The third-place contestant stood by the announcer to accept congratulations and his paycheck. He thanked the crowd for being there, and he walked away.

Kyle waited while the announcer praised him for a great ride. When Kyle walked away with his check, Marty signaled him to wait, and tried again to remember the announcer's name. *Paul Stall? No, that was not it.*

"Ladies and gentlemen, I'm Ed Shed, and as your announcer, I have the privilege to tell you about this Champion. Marty Redman is a name I could never forget." He lavished praise on Marty, and presented him with the big check of the day while the crowd applauded loud and long. Marty thanked them and then turned and beckoned to Kyle.

With Kyle by his side, Marty took the mic and placed his hand on Kyle's shoulder.

"Mister Ed Shed, ladies and gentlemen, cowboys and cowgirls, and everyone else in the crowd tonight … please welcome my good friend, Kyle Kross. That's Kross with a *K*, not a *C*." Marty waited while the crowd laughed.

"This young man took second place tonight. He missed first place by only two points. Kyle has a lot of heart, a lot of skill, and he has his eye on the prize. I'm forecasting right now he will soon be wearing a gold buckle because he is going to be a world champion bull rider." As the crowd stood, Marty yelled into the mic, "Let's wish Kyle the best, and give him a big hand."

Marty's face burned red while his afterthought kicked him in the butt. *A big hand?*

***

Kyle's next rodeo was in Amarillo, Marty's in Dallas. The two men said goodbye after breakfast next morning, Kyle's treat.

"I'll never forget how kind you are," Kyle said. "And I'll treasure your advice." He nodded. "Every bit of it."

Marty shrugged. "It's the least I could do for a future world champion. Someday, you'll be giving me advice."

Kyle grinned. "I could start right now, Marty. You need new wiper blades for your truck."

After a half hour, and twelve dollars at a do-it-yourself car wash, Marty left San Antonio. While he drove, he thought of Kyle, confident the two of them would compete again at some location in the near future. He could not hope the young man would be lucky. He wanted Kyle to win because of his skills, his determination, his constant effort, and his courage. The little man with oversized hands and feet must win because he needs victory. That victory will define *who* he is and *what* he is. And when that victory comes, he must learn to smile and nod when someone calls him *lucky*.

Kyle showed real promise. He was barely eighteen, yet his career seemed ready for take-off to the big time. Marty's take-off didn't come until he was twenty-two.

He listened to the weather report, switched off the radio, and let his thoughts travel back through his career. He took pride in his success. He had a right. He'd earned it with sore muscles, backaches, sprains, and bruises from New Mexico to New York, from South Dakota to North Carolina. He broke a finger in Fort Worth, and a tooth in Fort Wayne. He busted a lip in Wyoming, left Arizona with a sprained wrist, and arrived in Arkansas with a black eye. He'd lost track of how many rides left him with a bloody nose.

In spite of it all, he was ahead of the game and discovered that everything heals a lot faster when you win. He watched riders suffer dislocated shoulders, broken arms, legs, or ankles. Some left the grounds with injuries that ended careers. Bull riding, the roughest sport on planet Earth, took a heavy toll on the human body.

Some riders left the business after investing hundreds of hours in training and thousands of dollars in expenses. It was *win big or go home.*

Professional bull riding had been a long, rough road from Marty's days as a rookie. Before he won anything as a pro, he invested more money than he could afford, along with credit card debt for travel and entry fees in a business that left no time for a regular job.

He'd banked a few thousand dollars his father left him, and that money helped him survive while he traveled from town to town, from state to state. It kept him in the game, but he lost many competitions, and risked his life along the road. Yet he had to remain dedicated to be the best, to learn how to win.

If luck played a part in his success, it was damn small. Coaches in every sport often said success was ten percent ability and ninety percent effort, and that effort comes from attitude. Marty knew better. It was much deeper than attitude.

Success is a creature of action demanded by a craving that gnaws at the gut, a demand that will not be denied, a passion that rules the heart and soul. An undying need that hangs in the mind and keeps a man awake nights until he proves to everyone, and most of all to himself, he is good enough to be the best at what he does. A turning point where a man knows winning is not a part of his life. It is, instead, a life of its own, as crucial to his existence as breath and heartbeat. He must do everything necessary to win or call himself a loser as long as he lives, because the result of winning or losing affects every part of a person's life.

Marty thought of Elly. She surrounded herself with winners and big thinkers. Marty and Elly were attracted to each other because they both made the sacrifices to become champions. God, how he missed her. He would love to be home with her right now. But she was not home. The sweetheart of the rodeo was working in Arizona. Their time together was limited. But both had discovered that life in the winner's circle made the whole trip worthwhile.

And he'd learned the obsession to win often takes hold of a man after a major loss. Marty knew his major loss, his turning point, came when he lost Luna Long.

Chapter Four

No matter how much Mom and Marty objected, the family moved from Albuquerque to Cimarron when Marty finished eighth grade. He'd been near the top of his classes in Albuquerque schools and made many friends. At a friend's ranch, he learned to ride bucking horses, a real adrenaline rush, and discovered he had a knack for dealing with animals. But Dad insisted Marty could get good grades, make friends, and ride horses anywhere. And Dad believed a small school would be better for Marty's development.

Marty didn't understand the whole concept of development. He couldn't imagine how Cimarron, a northern New Mexico town with barely a thousand people, could help anybody develop anything. But at the end of the first year at Cimarron High, he had good grades, and new friends like Zane and Billy. Besides, the sports teams and friendly girls were a dream come true, and Marty developed a strong interest in Luna. Dad was right about development, whatever it was.

Zane caught up with Marty on a Friday as they left school.

"Hey there, New Kid in Town. Where you headed?"

Marty shrugged. "Home for dinner, and then ... whatever."

"You're good on a bucking horse. Ever rode a mechanical bull?"

Marty smiled and wrinkled his forehead. "No, but I'm game. Sounds like fun."

Zane held up his car key. "There's a bull in Taos I want you to ride. Stay on him for eight seconds, and I'll buy you a steak."

Zane was the only fifteen-year-old Marty knew who had a car and a driver's license. Zane's father knew somebody who knew somebody and got his son a license for emergencies.

At Marty's house, the two friends told his parents what they were up to. Mom said it was too far to drive just to do something dangerous. Dad said it sounded like a lot of fun. Ninety minutes later, Zane and Marty completed their emergency trip to Taos.

Brandon's, a low-slung adobe building looked much larger inside. The noisy, Friday-night crowd laughed, yelled, clinked glasses, and sang along while the sound system offered David Allen Coe belting out, *You Never Even Call Me By My Name.*

While his eyes searched the room, Marty took a deep breath. His stomach rumbled from the mouth-watering aroma of grilled steaks, fresh-baked bread, and fried onions.

A bull skull with horns hung high on the wall. From a dark corner, lights flashed, bells rang, and a noisy pop-pop-pop directed Marty's attention to two young men who laughed and played an antique pinball machine.

But the carpeted circle in the center of the expansive dining room captured Marty's gaze. On the floor, large blocks of foam rubber surrounded a lifelike bull under a spotlight.

Zane beckoned a young lady in a black cowboy hat. She cocked her head, flashed a bright smile and came toward them. A white logo on the front of her black shirt displayed *Brandon's* below a pair of bull horns.

"Howdy, cowboys. Name please?"

"Zane. Table for two."

She nodded at a row of seats near the front window, each one crafted with a leather saddle on a wood frame. "Mount up. Your wait is only about twenty minutes."

Zane nodded at the bull in the center of the room, and grinned. "We'll wait over there."

Marty attracted more curiosity than he wanted as he and Zane reached the bull. He had not told Zane, but Marty heard about this manmade beast at school, from teenage boys who pretended to know everything about it, and from champion bull riders at rodeos, who knew first-hand of this bucking machine's reputation. Most mechanical bulls could deliver a challenging ride, but this one earned his fame. He could imitate the ride of a real bull, with twenty-one bucking programs designed for first-timers, and all the way up to trained professionals.

Most mechanical bulls Marty had seen did not have a head. This one looked real, with a head, eyes, ears, and rubber horns. Real bull-hide, or maybe *cowhide*, covered his lifelike body.

Marty looked it over while he rubbed his chin. Bulls were harder to ride than bucking horses. Bulls twisted more. They were bigger, tougher, and stronger. He rode unbroke horses many times on ranches, but not with a large crowd looking on. Maybe not *everyone* in this dining room watched now, but Marty knew all eyes would be fixed on the rider when this crazy machine came alive.

None of it mattered now. He did not come here to ride a bucking horse, real or mechanical. He came to Brandon's Steak House in Taos, New Mexico to ride the famous mechanical bull named *Buck U.* So, let the crowd look. Let them *all* look if they wanted. Marty would not look at *them*. He swung his leg over, and straddled the iron animal. The room grew quiet. He wiped a bead of sweat that edged down his temple, grabbed the strap, and took a deep breath.

Zane stuck a debit-card in a slot, pressed a few buttons, and then rested his finger on the start button. He turned to Marty. "Say when."

Marty gripped the strap tighter, pressed his knees into place, and nodded. "Let 'er go."

The bull moved high but not fast. The animal's head and shoulders went down while his butt went up. He moved faster, and twisted while his head went up. He turned with a faster twist, and his butt shot up again while his head went down. Marty gripped the strap tighter.

He pressed his knees harder against the sides of the bull to maintain control. He assumed the bull must be at full speed now. He was wrong. The room became a spinning blur. Marty's knees slipped. His butt bounced and then slammed down as the bull's butt came up to greet him. The impact expelled Marty's breath.

He did not ride for the crowd, not for Zane, not for a reputation or recognition. He rode for Marty, for pride in himself, for knowing he did his utmost to stay on this demon as long as he could.

The merciless animal repeated the technique but twisted in the opposite direction, bouncing his rider up again. As Marty's butt went up, the bull's butt went down. Again, when Marty's butt came down, the bull's butt slammed up to meet him. This jolt did not expel the rider's breath from his lungs. It expelled the rider from the bull.

The blurred, spinning room looked like a mountain of grey rock until Marty crashed facedown with his hands spread. That foam rubber saved his nose.

Marty heard no noise while he got to his feet. The scoreboard flashed *Buck U, Buck U* while the young lady in the logo shirt brought a microphone. Zane stared at it, and then at her, and took the mic.

"Ladies and gentlemen, my friend, Marty Redman, came here tonight to ride this bull, although he's never been on a bull before. I told him I'd buy him a steak if he stayed on eight seconds." Zane pointed at the lighted scoreboard high on the wall. "He rode for 6.8 seconds. Should I buy his dinner?"

The diners cheered, clapped, and whistled. Some stood, held up their glasses, and shouted, "Buy the steak, buy the steak."

The chants faded. A young lady rose from a table, and faced Zane. She placed her hands on her hips, and stuck out her chest.

"Honey, if you don't buy that good-looking, young man a steak dinner … send him over here. I'll buy him anything he wants." The crowd cheered.

The noise died. A man with a long nose and big lips held a mug of beer while he staggered up from his chair and braced himself on the table. He stared at Zane, hiccupped, and wiped his lips with the back of his hand.

"Buy that man a …" hiccup "Buy that man a steak …" hiccup "you cheap bastard." The room erupted again.

***

That ride on the famous bull at Brandon's ignited in Marty a spark to tackle every new challenge with all he had to give. His heart pounded with excitement every time he straddled a bull. That unique sport gave him the biggest adrenalin rush he'd ever known. Within a year, the local, amateur rodeo circuit had a new top competitor on bulls, and Marty's father supported him every step of the way.

But girls soon replaced bulls for a favorite pastime. By his junior year in school, Marty discovered Luna. They spent many hours together, and Marty treasured their time at her parents' guest ranch.

A sudden heart attack took Dad's life before the school year ended. Marty grieved and withdrew. Mom did her best to cope with the emptiness and to comfort Marty. His friends gave him the space he needed to deal with his grief. But the support and sympathy from Luna helped him more than everything else. She knew when to cry with him and when to laugh. She was smart and pretty, a high-energy girl with a great sense of humor. When someone forgot her unusual name, she'd tell them her middle name was *Tick*. They never forgot *Luna Tick*. She was his rock.

Chapter Five

Since high school, Marty worked as a wrangler, an all-around flunky, at the Long Family Guest Ranch. The job didn't pay well, but after he and Luna married, they lived in a guesthouse. They paid no rent or utility bills.

On the day Luna filed for divorce, Marty led a column of city slickers on a ride across a pasture so they could be fascinated by watching cows up close, just like real cowboys.

Luna's father showed up on Ahab, his prize Arabian horse, and rode to the front of the line. He held up his hand for the guests to stop their horses. With petrified faces, they leaned closer to their horses' ears and yelled, *Stop, Stay,* or *Halt.* One smug-faced tourist bent forward and said, "Whoa."

Marty knew something was up. He'd lived on this ranch, and worked for his father-in-law, long enough to know Sydney Long was a condescending prick. His daughter, an only child, was classy and gracious like her mother. She had her father's drive and work ethic but not his arrogance.

Today, Syd Long's daughter broke Marty's heart, though it came as no surprise. An hour ago, he received the notice. Luna had filed for divorce. She saw it as the only way to fix an unhappy marriage.

Syd turned to Marty and smiled. "Rhonda will take it from here." He cranked his head around and jerked his thumb toward a lady on the horse behind him. Then with a huge grin, he turned back and dipped his head toward the horse Marty rode.

"Put that horse in the barn. Pack your crap, everything you've got in the house, and pick up your last paycheck from my secretary. And..." he tipped his hat and grinned again "kick up some dust on your way out." That was Syd's way of saying, *you can't get the hell out of here fast enough to suit me.*

Guests looked on. Mouths hung open. Marty shrugged and rode toward the barn. He'd expected to get fired since the day he started here and never heard anybody accuse the boss of being subtle, or even polite.

With the few things he owned in the bed of his old pickup, Marty drove fast down the half-mile, dirt driveway toward the road. Still on his prize horse that cost more than most cars, Syd Long now waited by the gate, perhaps to give his dear son-in-law a proper sendoff. If so, Marty did not want to deprive the man of his eager farewell.

He slowed the truck to a crawl, screamed, "Bye, Daddy," and drove through the gate while he flashed a big smile. Then he poked his arm out the open window and extended Syd a long, one-finger salute. In his mirror, he watched the man's face distort and his eyes bulge. Marty stomped the gas pedal, and yelled, "Here's your wish, Mister Long." Tires spun. Ahab bolted, and left Sydney behind, flat on his ass, choking in the dust he wanted to see.

Marty headed toward home, where he and his parents had lived, where his father died. After Marty married and moved out, Mom moved back to Albuquerque to care for her ailing sister. Aunt Elma died eight months later. Mom inherited her sister's home and stayed in Albuquerque.

The home here in Cimarron sat empty. From time to time, Marty checked on it and knew it was still in good shape and still full of furniture. He could move right in, after a few days of dusting. He'd have a lot to do before he could crawl into a bed with clean sheets.

He could not decide what to do first. Then it hit him. He turned his truck around, headed toward the giant Cold Beer sign in Dawson, and laughed all the way.

"Hey, Marty. Over here." Marty recognized the voice. Across the room, Zane waved him to the corner table.

Where else could they go? Cimarron's night life seemed to go the way of all the famous outlaws many years ago. Now, the after-hours crowd from Cimarron came here to Dawson, a few miles north, though Dawson was hardly a bustling community.

Once a thriving coal mining town, Dawson had a tragic history. On October 22, 1913, residents as far as two miles away from the coal mine felt the tremors of the explosion that ripped through Stag Canyon mine number 2 like a giant bomb. Two hundred and eighty-six coal miners reported for work that morning. Only twenty-three would live to see another day.

Ten years later, an explosion tore through Stag Canyon mine number 1, and put another hundred and twenty-three miners in the local graveyard. Many were sons of the men who died in mine number 2.

The mine disasters sapped the town of its spirit, its will to survive. Within a few years, Dawson became a ghost town. Now, this bar and grill was the only business around.

This had been one hell of a day for Marty. Now he needed action, a party with music, laughter, happy people, and beer, to take his mind off reality when life made no sense. This place had it all, a jukebox, noisy people, and friends like Zane and Billy with their girlfriends, scarfing down pizza and beer.

According to Zane, his grandfather had been a good friend and great fan of Zane Grey, the famous author of westerns. "That's where my name came from," Marty's friend often said. But that didn't keep other kids from calling him *Zany*.

After high school, Zane turned his amateur rodeo success into a pro rodeo career. He won often, earning a respectable living and a reputation as a champion. He often encouraged Marty to concentrate on his bull-riding skills, and to get involved in pro rodeo. Marty liked bulls, and scored well in the amateur class during high school. But after he married, bucking animals couldn't compete with Luna.

"Hiya, Marty." Billy stood, shook hands, and introduced Juanita. Marty saw them together a couple of months ago. Later, Billy told him they were no longer an item. Yet, here she was. Life was full of surprises.

Marty sat, took a long drink from his first beer, and turned to Zane. "What's new, old man?"

Zane angled his head at the girl next to him. She drew Marty's attention earlier when he walked toward the table. Her crossed legs exposed a lot of thigh below a short, black skirt that fought for attention with a low-cut blouse broadcasting a generous cleavage.

Zane grinned. "This is what's new. Her name is Rayne, and I'm crazy about her." He placed his hand on her thigh and said. "Show Marty how crazy I am."

Rayne's tongue pushed out the side of her cheek. She pulled her left hand from under the table, held it up, and wiggled her fingers.

Marty's mouth dropped open. He'd never seen a ring with that many diamonds. He looked at her smug face. "When did this happen?" She smiled. Zane answered.

"Last week. I've been excited ever since. The wedding's only two months out."

Marty looked at her again. "I'll bet you're excited, too." She smiled and nodded. Marty's brow wrinkled. *Could the girl talk?* He held up his bottle.

"Cheers to Zane and Rayne. Sounds like a great combo."

After toasts all around, the conversation changed, and the jukebox played oldies while people laughed, drank beer, ate too much, and talked too loudly. Billy sat across the table from Rayne who stared at him with her lips parted as if lost in thought. When he spoke, she'd cup her ear and lean toward him with her head back as if to hear better, exposing more of her chest.

Zane seemed oblivious to it all. He looked around at the crowd in the room no matter who was talking. Billy's girlfriend, Juanita, seemed aware of everything, but said nothing. Still, her jaw was set, and her hard eyes glared as she shifted her vision from Rayne to Billy and back again. The message behind the glare was unmistakable but lost. Rayne didn't see anyone's eyes. Her eyes never left Billy. Billy didn't see anyone's eyes. *His* eyes had locked on Rayne's hooters.

No one at the table asked Marty how things were going. No one asked about his job or the Long Ranch. No one mentioned Luna. No one wanted his opinion on anything. So, Marty watched everything that happened here without distractions.

While Rayne stared at Billy and leaned toward him, lust hung in the air so thick Marty could smell it. He also noticed Rayne's forefinger stuck in her hair next to her ear, and how she twirled her hair around the finger. A psychologist friend of the family once said to Marty, "When you see a woman do that, it's a subconscious sign. She wants to grab the man she's gazing at, drag him into bed, and screw him into a coma."

Marty nodded. Trouble was brewing.

Chapter Six

Engine noise might have interfered with talk among the passengers, three men and a young woman, in the noisy and boxy Pilatus Porter aircraft as it climbed to 3,500 feet and began to circle. But no one had uttered a word since the plane left the ground. They sat on benches along the walls and stared at the floor or their shoes or the maze of switches, dials, gauges, and signs on the instrument panel. The black and yellow sign, *Warning: Set Correct Trim Before Take-off*, seemed to stare back as Marty read it again and again. He hoped the pilot had set the trim, whatever-the-hell that meant.

A man's fingers drummed nonstop on the wall. The woman's knee bobbed up and down. Deep breaths made stomachs move in and out. In time, each passenger would turn toward a window, look out, and then summon the courage to look down. Three seconds later, the passenger's head would jerk back toward the switches and gauges. But no one spoke.

Marty sat next to the open door, which meant he would be the first student to jump. His stomach knotted as he forced himself to look out. And down. The 20-acre drop zone where virgin skydivers hoped to land looked a lot smaller from up here. And it was surrounded by woods. He tried to force himself to think about something other than a one-point landing in a tree.

Back in Psych 101, he learned to clear his mind of worry by thinking about two opposing events happening at the same time. Now, eating popcorn during a round of great sex flew through Marty's mind. But it was gone before it could distract him from thinking about the final gasp of life with a tree limb rammed—

"You wanna do this?" Fast Eddie, the jumpmaster, stared without blinking. Marty jerked his head around to face him, and realized the man had asked twice. "If you don't want to do this, tell me now. Once your foot's out the door, you don't get back in. Look me in the eyes." Fast Eddie blinked and pushed his face close.

"Yes? Or no?"

Marty's back stiffened. His last yes-or-no question left him married at 19. Luna had been his high school sweetheart, a knockout who had wealthy parents and lots of friends. She could have dated any guy in the school, maybe any guy in the state. Yet Luna was crazy about Marty. Her father was not.

Two years after she and Marty graduated from high school, her father cornered Marty at the Long family ranch.

"I had hopes my daughter would marry a man with potential," Syd Long told him, "not just some horny cowhand. But Luna is twenty years old and can make up her own mind. She wants you but can't get a straight answer. So, tell me, Mister Redman … you gonna marry my daughter?" He blinked and pushed his face close.

"Yes? Or No?"

Syd wanted potential. Luna wanted babies, more than anything else in life. So, for the first year and a half of their marriage, Marty exposed his potential. He and Luna plugged in five or six times a week using every angle, technique, and position they knew and a few they invented. For Marty, life on earth was better than the stuff he'd heard about heaven.

He'd never known a man could love a woman as much as he loved Luna. Still, eighteen months of bliss was not without tension. Sex could be a great stress reliever except when it had a mission. His mission was to get Luna pregnant. When doctors could find no reason for her infertility, she nagged Marty to get checked. The drift between them seemed to begin on the day the test results came back.

A low sperm count did little for Marty's ego. Six months after the test, his ego struck bottom. Utopia collapsed. Luna walked out.

I don't have to prove I'm a man to anyone. Not to Syd Long. Not to Luna. Not to the jumpmaster. I'll just tell him no.

A dry throat wouldn't let Marty swallow. His answer came out in a raspy squeak.

"Yes."

The jumpmaster hooked the overhead static line to the ripcord on Marty's parachute, and nodded toward the wing. Marty took a long breath. His pulse beat on his eardrums. His leg quivered.

He stuck his foot out the door.

From the all-day training class, Marty knew to lean forward, grab the bar that ran along the edge of the wing, and work his way out to the end. But somehow, the trainers failed to mention that the wind and the speed of the airplane might be something to deal with. In spite of that, sliding his hands along the bar took him to the end within seconds that seemed like twenty minutes.

During class, the jumpmaster assured students the airplane they would leave behind in the sky was designed for stability. Fast Eddie knew more about skydiving than all the people Marty ever met ... combined. The man held a few world records and made thousands of jumps. The jumpmaster deserved respect, and Marty was impressed by the man's record, but couldn't force himself to care about airplane design.

Until now.

Right now, it all made sense. He was glad the plane was stable. Because right now, at 90 miles per hour, Marty flew across the sky like a comic book superhero, except the man of steel didn't need goggles and a helmet, nor an airplane to hang on to.

Marty hung on. He was sure his hands clamped the steel bar tight enough to melt it while he watched the man in the plane and waited for the signal to let go. How insane—diving out of the clouds for no sound reason, pretending he could fly and praying a sheet of nylon would save his sorry ass from his own stupidity.

While the knot in the gut found its way to his chest, he hoped his family and friends would forgive him for ending his life this way. Even more, when the parachute didn't open, he hoped he'd have time to forgive *himself* on the way down.

There it was. The signal. Maybe. He had to be sure. Again, the man stuck his arm out the doorway and jerked his thumb toward the back of the plane. *The signal.* No doubt.

Letting go of the bar was not optional. The pilot would not try to land a plane with a coward hanging on the wing. Attila the Jumpmaster, safe and comfy inside his precious Pilatus Porter, could reach out with his bamboo cane and wear a huge, evil grin while he banged a few knuckles.

Marty didn't want to die with bruised knuckles. He let go.

The airplane eased away. The full force of the wind now struck his face, buffeted his helmet and goggles and roared past his ears. Emotions flooded every pore. Countless images raced through his mind in a frantic search for a solution to this sudden dilemma and found ... nothing. Random thoughts invaded the brain, like a fleeting wish that he could have left behind a child of his own creation.

Arms outstretched more than three thousand feet above the earth, Marty flew like a giant condor, a freedom he had known only in dreams. That sense of freedom now collided with a sense of dread. Abandoned by mankind, Marty knew that if anything went wrong, his sorry ass was a goner.

He was supposed to count to ten after he let go of the bar, and the parachute should open.

Should.

But he forgot to count. And this ludicrous flying-human trick warped his sense of timing. Had it been ten seconds? A hundred? He didn't know. There was no one to ask. And he didn't dare look down. With every breath, the trees got closer.

He could hear the minister now… "Our departed friend, Marty Dumbass Redman, bought the farm because he was a world-class idiot and—"

Marty gasped at a loud rustle behind him. Two seconds later, something popped above his head, and the harness squeezed his chest and yanked him backward. Marty swallowed hard. His lifeline flapped and rattled above him, with cords twisted around a chute that could not open.

Oh, shit.

His mind buzzed. Had the trainers covered this during the class? No? Oh hell no. Why not? It didn't seem fair. Oh wait. Yes, they did. Try to think. This is no time to panic. *If I do, the crew will have to scoop me off the ground with shovels and a bucket, or peel me off a tree. And the trees and ground are getting closer.*

Pull the handles wide apart, and kick to make your body spin out of the twist. Yeah, that's what they said. *Okay, I'll do that. But if this doesn't work, it's time to panic.* Marty looked down. The earth spun beneath him, and a sudden pop exploded above.

Now, he looked up. *Pull down the hook-and-loop fasteners to release the handles.*

He laughed aloud and drew a long breath. Many times, he'd noticed cotton-candy clouds against New Mexico's intense, magic-blue skies, how they often created an artist's paradise of brilliant colors and contrast. But nothing could match the color and beauty of the nylon canvas that now flapped in the sky above him. That restored his faith in miracles. The parachute was open.

Skydiving scared him more than anything he'd ever done, Marty told himself. Except … maybe … getting married. Falling out of the sky could be a lot like falling for a woman. Except women didn't come with parachutes.

He reached for the handles to steer the chute. His chest expanded. Would the other jumpers have the cojones to say yes to the jumpmaster? Would they stick a foot out the door? Would they be as brave and proud as me, Marty Redman?

Now, if I can only miss the trees…

Chapter Seven

Elly was ambitious and dedicated. Marty admired that. She worked hard and gave everything she had to put on a great show. Marty respected her for that, but her work kept her away from him. Today, she'd been gone three weeks, and called only twice. Three days ago, she called to say she'd booked a show in Dallas and another in Fort Worth, to follow the Tucson show. She would be gone another week.

Did she really care about him? Did they have a lasting relationship? Did they have a relationship of any kind? Did he have any reason to be faithful to her?

While he brushed down his horse in the corral, Brandi popped into his mind, a rodeo trick rider he met a couple of years ago. He had a crush on her since he ogled her when he saw her first performance. But then again, every cowboy had a crush on Brandi after watching her perform.

Within an hour after he finished grooming Buck Naked, Marty's phone rang. He didn't often answer a call unless he recognized the number – too many telemarketers. But that time, he answered. It was Brandi. He could not convince himself it was just a coincidence she crossed his mind for the first time in weeks, and called an hour later.

He'd watched her perform as lust overloaded every cell in his body. In her skin-tight, black mesh costume, she rode bareback on a black stallion, sometimes standing on his back, her long, silky black hair waving in the breeze, hair that hung down to her beautiful ass when she stood to accept her applause after the ride.

Marty hung up the phone and chuckled. Was Brandi serious? "There's a new movie I really want to see," she told him, "and I'd hate to go alone if I could talk a handsome bull rider into going with me."

Brandi was not the first girl to ask him for a date, one of the perks of being a champion. It was what she said just before she ended the call that grabbed him by his animal instincts.

"I'll bring my overnight bag if you like."

His tongue stuck to the roof of his mouth. He could not remember how long he'd wanted to hear that, how long he'd wanted to ravage that tight, sculpted body, tall and slim with every part the exact right size and shape.

He'd held her a few times on the dance floor and when they stood outside her door making out after a date. She would invite him to explore. Then she'd take a deep breath and stop him five seconds after he started. Now, the teasing was over. She would pick him up, take him to the movie, bring him home and ….

Marty's mind went to the rodeo arena. While they waited to perform, cowboys always talked about the animals, how to avoid getting ripped open by a horn. But a common belief among the cowboys was that rodeo women were the horniest animals in the show. And ... the most dangerous. Was Brandi one of those? Marty wanted to find out. He glanced at his watch. She'd be here in an hour.

After a quick shower and a dash of El Toro cologne, he stood on his front porch trying hard to look casual while he glanced at his watch every three minutes and watched for Brandi's black Camaro convertible.

***

46

She stopped the car in his driveway, turned off the engine, and sat without moving, her unfocused eyes aimed at the steering wheel. Marty waited.

A minute later, she stepped out but folded her arms when he started toward her. Marty stopped. His eyes found hers.

"Elly, tell me what's wrong."

Three days back, she called to tell him she'd be gone another week. Instead, she drove her truck home to Taos, unloaded and groomed her horse, and then washed her truck and trailer, before she came here in her car. Marty knew her routine. She was finicky about keeping everything clean. He liked that about her. But today, something was wrong.

With her arms still crossed, Elly backed against the car and glanced up.

"We need to talk."

Marty swallowed hard but nodded. He'd been through this before more than once. When a woman breaks up with you, this is how it always starts. But, how could she? She'd never made a real commitment. Neither had he, but he was in love with her. Marty spread his hands and shrugged. He cocked his head.

"Okay…let's talk."

She looked down again as she spoke. "I had a doctor appointment yesterday morning and ..."

Marty waited a few seconds. He reached for her hand. "Are you okay?" Elly shrugged but did not look up. He lifted her chin. "Elly, please. Tell me what's wrong. You know I care about you. I'll stick with you, whatever it is."

She caught his arm and looked at him. "How do I know that?"

"Because you're my girl, Elly. That's why. Maybe I don't say it often, but I don't want anyone but you. And I'll stay with you all the way no matter what." He took her hand, pressed it against his cheek and looked in her eyes. "You're scaring me. Is it cancer?"

She shook her head. "No, Marty. It's not cancer. It's something I … something I caught from you."

Marty backed away and glared. "From me? I don't think so. You caught nothing from—

"I'm pregnant."

Marty stared, his mouth open. "Ha! What? You're what? Oh geeze, I thought it was …" Marty's face grew red and then serious. He pulled her to him and lifted her chin, his eyes large. "Elly, are you sure? You and me? We're gonna have a baby?" His eyes dropped to her stomach and then shot up again. His face glowed. He gazed into the green eyes, now more beautiful than ever.

"Am I your only one, Elly?"

Her eyes locked on his. "You are, Marty. You are."

He kissed her and pulled back. "Hey, gorgeous woman, mother-to-be … will you marry me?"

Her gaze wandered as if searching for an answer, and then gazed into his eyes. "Are you sure, Marty?"

"As sure as I've ever been about anything."

"I will."

Marty scooped her up and danced around the driveway. Laughing and out of breath, he sat her on the fender of her car and stared up at her.

Tears filled her eyes. She shook her head. "God, Marty … I've never seen you so happy."

"There's a reason for that. I've never *been* so happy." He laughed. "A couple of minutes ago I was really worried about you. Now … the most beautiful woman on earth, the one I'm crazy about … is gonna have my baby. Do you know how much I want to be a daddy? Do you know how complete that makes me feel?"

Marty forgot about everything else in life because right now nothing else mattered. Nothing until … until a black Camaro slowed as it neared the driveway.

Elly sat on the fender of her car with her back to the road. Marty hoped she did not see the Camaro, but when he glanced up, he knew she saw his face go pale. Elly turned to look, but tires squealed on the pavement and the car leaped ahead and sped past the driveway. Elly jerked her head the other way and watched until the car disappeared in the distance. She turned back, dropped her head and looked up at Marty.

"Who was that?"

Marty shrugged. "A fan of yours, maybe?"

She slid off the fender and rolled her eyes up at him. "More like a fan of *yours*."

"Uhm … speaking of fans, I guess the Dallas event got canceled?" Elly nodded and started to speak. Marty interrupted. "So, uhm … how'd things go in Tucson?"

She told him how much the crowd in Tucson enjoyed the show and presented her with a *Sweetheart of the Rodeo* plaque. She opened her car door, and turned back toward him.

"I have four days off but a lot to do. I'll try to get back over here before I leave for the show in Denver."

Marty stared. "I was hoping you'd stay here." His voice rose. "We just got engaged. We're going to be parents. We have a lot to talk about." He reached for her hand. "Elly, did I say something wrong? You drive all the way here from Taos, stay a few minutes, and drive back?"

Elly shook her head. "What … an hour drive? Besides, I didn't want to tell you about my test results on the phone." She drew a long breath. "And now …" she tilted her head back as tears came … "now I need to go home and pack." Her eyes found Marty's. "Gotta go to Santa Fe tomorrow to see my dad, and …" she pulled her hand away from Marty and patted her belly... "and give him the news."

Marty wondered if Elly had told her mother. Probably not but he did not want to ask. Elly's parents divorced more than six years ago. Elly and Mom had never been close, and when Mom remarried and moved to California, the gap grew wider. Marty remembered the lump in her throat when Elly told him she sent a card for Mother's Day the first year Mom was gone but never knew if it got there. Now they exchange only birthday cards, and Elly always writes, *I love you, Mom* at the bottom. Mom's generic birthday cards to Elly are simply signed, *Mother*.

Elly's father stayed in Santa Fe to run his art gallery. With Dad's help, Elly bought a small ranch near Taos two years back.

Marty spread his hands. "Want me to go with you? We'll just tell your dad we're getting married. Let him find out about the other part later. Wouldn't that be … easier?"

She shook her head, got into the car and stuck her face through the open window.

"That car that came by earlier? I knew who was in it. And *Brandi* on her license plate tells *everybody* who's in it."

Marty's face flushed as he backed away. "I'm sorry, Elly. I didn't see you for three weeks and … well, she called and just wanted to go to a movie, and I—"

"And you splashed on your El Toro cologne. My nose works just fine." She glared at him. "I won't put up with that, Marty. If we get married … and I do mean *if* … it has to be only *me*. I'm dead serious about that."

Marty nodded. The lump in his throat returned as she backed out of the driveway. He whispered *I love you* and threw her a kiss. But Elly did not look back as she drove away.

Chapter Eight

Life made more sense on the road, and Marty most often enjoyed the three-hour drive between Albuquerque and Cimarron. It gave him time to think, to sort out things and give each one the right priority. Today, he had mixed emotions. The list was longer and might be tougher to sort.

He'd been to see Mom. He liked her cooking more than his own, and he wanted to tell her in person that he and Elly were going to be parents. He knew she would not lecture him. Mom was not like that.

Yet on his way there, he remembered driving to Albuquerque a few years ago to tell her Luna had filed for divorce. Mom took it hard, and cried again the next day as Marty left. So, he'd felt uneasy on his way there this time and could not guess what her reaction might be. But this time, Mom acted happy and not at all surprised.

She did not ask if Marty and Elly had wedding plans but said, "I hope you two get married." She did ask if Elly was happy about the baby.

Marty shrugged. "Hard to tell, Mom. I'm excited, but I'm not sure she's ready for this."

Mom offered a slight nod. "Elly and I talk whenever she's around. Sometimes it's a bit personal, but we never get into private stuff. She seems a bit uneasy with that, and that's okay. I like her, but I'm not sure I know her very well."

"It's not just you, Mom." He told her about Elly's family as she grew up and that she and her mother had never been close. "Elly sometimes has trouble trusting people enough to become close friends."

Mom's eyes grew large. "Oh, my. I'm so sorry, Marty. Poor girl. I wish I could give her a big hug and tell her how much I care about her."

Marty felt his chest tighten. "For a long time, I've wanted to be a father, and I'll try really hard to be a good one, Mom."

"You will be, Son. You're gonna be a great father, just like your dad."

Marty nodded. He couldn't ask for a better example than his own father. "Thanks, Mom. I just hope Elly gets excited about our baby. That will make all the difference."

Mom leaned in her chair and caught his arm. "When your dad and I got married, he wanted kids right away. I wanted to wait. We fought about it for two years, and then we separated for almost a year. I got pregnant as soon as we got back together. When you came along, I was happier than I'd ever been." She gave him her motherly smile. "Give Elly time, son. Give her time."

***

On familiar roads in his pickup, Marty's mind drifted back to Mom's words. His parents split up for a year before he was born. That shocked him. Digesting what she told him did not come easy. What was her real reason? Was she trying to tell him more than he heard?

He tried not to think about what his parents might have done during that year. *Date other people?* Somehow that seemed all wrong. And Mom said she got pregnant as soon as she and Dad got back together. *But what if she got pregnant before ... No.* His head shook hard. He refused to consider that.

The harder Marty tried to block unacceptable thoughts, the more determined those thoughts seemed to be. He wouldn't ... he couldn't ... call Mom, and ask for more details. He searched his mind for any clues his mother may have offered in the past, but he found nothing. He cranked up his stereo system, found a rodeo song, and sang along.

At the end of the song, he turned off the music. Maybe his father had said something Marty overlooked. His mind scanned back over the years, but came up with nothing ... except ... blood. When Marty's father died, he left behind a vial of his blood he wanted Marty to keep. It was still at home in Marty's freezer. ... *Could that be ...? No, no, no.*

Chapter Nine

Marty hated hospitals for all the same reasons everyone did. And he had another reason. Hospital disinfectant often made him pass out. But he came today to see a dear friend. Zane took a nasty fall from a horse at the Taos rodeo a couple of nights ago. Landing flat on his back could have left him paralyzed. It didn't. Doctors said his back would be okay. But the bucking horse's foot came down on Zane's belly, and did a lot of damage to his insides.

Marty stopped outside the room and hoped his friend would be asleep. *I can just drop my get-well card on his bed and get the hell out.* After a deep breath, he shook his head and stepped inside, not prepared for what he saw.

Zane lay on the bed, unmoving as he stared at the man in front of him. Yet even now, physically helpless, the expression on Zane's face made him appear to be in control. It made him the great baseball catcher in high school. He could grasp the situation and send signals to the pitcher about what to throw next or signals about a runner on base.

That same skill helped him become a champion bronco rider. Zane could sum up a situation and make the right, instant decisions about most things, but not about women. Marty once told him that may be his greatest weakness.

Zane smiled, and his eyes rolled toward his visitor. His voice was not strong, but clear. "I knew you'd come."

Marty cocked his head. "You did?"

The injured man's head did not move. His clear brown eyes looked down. Seconds later, misty eyes looked up. "That's what best friends are for."

Marty's throat sprouted a lump. He shrugged it off and tried to smile. "So, how's the food in this joint?"

Zane rolled his eyes toward the IV in the back of his hand. "Not much taste."

Marty jerked his head toward Zane's IV bag. "You want me to tell the nurse to squeeze some jalapeños into that stuff?"

Zane's eyes popped wide. His lips parted in a big smile and his chest heaved. He moaned and his eyes grew misty again. "Sorry, I'm not supposed to laugh."

Marty heard a swish behind him, and turned. A large nurse stepped inside and leaned forward. With a slow nod, she looked at the man on the bed and scrunched her face as she checked his monitor. Her head swung side to side and looked at Marty. She stopped and glared, "The patient must rest." Then she was gone.

Shuffling his feet, Marty smiled at Zane. "Hey, I can't stay. Just wanted to come by and check on you. I got a show in Houston coming up Saturday, but I'll get by next week."

"I got surgery next week. Don't know which day."

Marty nodded. "I'll check with your dad to keep me updated."

The brown eyes now seemed intense. "Say hello to Billy for me."

Not sure of what he heard, Marty snapped his head away and then back toward the man on the bed. "Billy? Yeah … I will. Maybe he'll drop by to see you."

"I hope so."

<u>An hour later, Marty sat in Billy's living room and</u> told him what Zane said at the hospital. "Zane wants to see you, Billy."

Billy shrugged. "For what?"

"You know, Billy, I hate to say this, but there's a chance he won't make it. I think he knows that. Maybe he finally let go of the grudge. Just go and talk to him."

Billy wagged his head. "I tried to talk to him a half-dozen times in the past. You know I did. It didn't help, and you know that, too."

Billy took a long breath and let it go. "The last time, I told him only a bad woman could wreck the kind of friendship he and I had and both of us know Rayne Waters was a bad woman. And I said, *I know you can't forget any of it, and maybe you can't forgive her. But maybe, just maybe, you can forgive me.*"

After a minute of silence, Marty looked up. "Well, what did he say?"

"Not a damn thing. It was like talking to a rock." Billy stared at Marty for a full minute. "But … I'll think about it."

****

The rodeo in Houston could not have gone better. Elly was there. She and Marty had time for two dates, and Marty took first place in the bull-riding competition. He accepted a TV interview, got another product endorsement, and came home with a lot of money.

A big check for riding a bull was always a great *high* for Marty. Now, he drove out of the Cimarron cemetery, asking himself why a big *low* had to come so soon after that.

57

Focusing on the road could have helped keep his mind occupied. But there was no need to focus. He knew every dip, crack, and turn in the winding road that led to the Cold Beer sign in Dawson and could drive there while his mind went elsewhere. Right now, he wanted his mind to wander into the past to escape the present.

Marty recalled the mixed emotions of freedom and failure on this road three years ago after Luna filed for divorce. It all seemed crazy now. Luna called him six months after the divorce. She would do anything he wanted if he would spend the night with her. He arranged to meet her at a motel. He didn't show, changed his mind at the last minute. For a long time, he was sorry he turned her down. Now he knew he made the right decision.

While he drove toward the bar and grill, random thoughts offered small relief from today's grief. Mist filled his eyes and he drew ragged breaths. The pain seemed more than his heart could hold.

Marty's knees grew weak today when he and five others carried Zane's coffin. He served as pallbearer a few times before and always considered the job an honor. But it wasn't fair that grief always attached itself to that honorable duty. It wasn't fair that a man so young, with so much potential, so full of hope and determination did not survive the surgery meant to save his life.

The funeral pulled nearly half the people in Cimarron. The awards chairman from the National Rodeo Society read a list of honors and awards Zane won over the years and told of his courage and determination. The chairman delivered a great tribute.

But one man who should have been there … was not.

Zane, Marty, and Billy had been longtime friends and teammates in high school sports. As catcher on the baseball team, Zane could handle a fastball and throw out a man at second like a pro. Marty was the best hitter, and Billy won the award for best pitcher. They hung out together on weekends, played poker, got drunk, skipped school, chased girls, and shared their dreams of the future.

A week before graduation, Zane offered to take Billy home from a party. Both were buzzed. Zane laughed and talked while he drove much too fast on the narrow road that snaked through the countryside. A deer darted in front of the car. Zane jerked the steering wheel to miss the deer. Rear tires slid on the roadside gravel. Zane lost control. His car left the road, rolled over in an arroyo, turned upright again, and slammed into a large boulder.

The impact rammed the steering column through the firewall. The column barely missed the two high-school seniors as it wedged between them.

The engine caught fire.

No matter how hard he pushed and kicked, or how loud he screamed, Zane's door refused to open. Billy got out, ran around the flaming car, and ripped off the door, in one of those super-human feats of strength he'd only read about before. Seconds after Billy yanked him away from the car, Zane's old Ford exploded.

Next morning, the news was everywhere, and everyone believed nothing could destroy the friendship between Zane and Billy.

On the same date three years later, Zane proposed to a beautiful young woman who had moved to Taos from Colorado. He had been crazy over her since the day they met. Her name was enough to make him lose his heart. But his love for her was deep and genuine. Zane used to say Rayne Waters was the sunshine of his life. And she accepted his proposal.

Ten days before the wedding date, Zane's fiancé taped a note on the steering wheel of his new car. There would be no wedding. For hours, Zane drove around in a state of panic and talked to everyone he knew while he tried to find Rayne. He needed help from his best friend, but Billy would be at work and couldn't answer his phone. Zane went to see Juanita, Billy's girlfriend. She gave Zane the news. Rayne left town with Zane's best friend. Billy.

The hot fling between Rayne and Billy had a short life. The damage lived on.

Rayne sold the engagement ring Zane gave her. She moved back to Colorado. Billy moved back to Cimarron. The following month, he got news about Rayne when her father drove from Colorado to see him. In a less-than-polite conversation, Mister Waters told Billy he wanted to knock *down* the punk who knocked *up* his daughter. After the conversation, Mister Waters drove back to Colorado. Billy drove to the Taos hospital to get treated for a battered nose and broken jaw.

***

After an hour at the bar and grill, Marty paid the check for his two beers and for Billy's three and left a generous tip. Marty brought a photo album from home, to share old photos of Zane. Most would know him and appreciate the memories. However, most photos included Billy and Marty, and it all seemed too awkward when Marty found Billy inside the bar and grill. He picked the photo album off the table and walked out. Billy walked out behind him.

"I remember that album, Marty, and I'm glad you didn't open it." Awkward silence hung in the air. Billy shuffled his feet, and called out behind Marty. "If you're not going to bring it up … I will. I guess you think I'm a real jackass for not going to the funeral."

"Yeah, Billy, now that you mention it …" Marty turned toward him … "that did cross my mind." Marty laid the photo album on the passenger seat of his pickup and turned back to Billy. "I really wish you'd gone to the funeral. To tell you the truth, Billy, you pissed me off. But more than that, it breaks my heart."

Billy stopped and stared then shook his head.

Marty spread his hands. "Maybe you two could've worked it out if you'd gone up to…" He stopped, drew a long breath and sighed.

Billy stared at the ground and shook his head. He looked up, rubbed his face, and glared at his friend. "Well, Marty, I did take your advice. I went to see Zane the day before his surgery. The day before he died." Billy's eyebrows rose. "You happy now?"

Marty managed a faint smile and nodded. "That ought to be worth *something*."

Billy opened his truck door, stepped on the running board, and turned to face his bull-rider friend. "Okay, I guess I gotta tell you something you don't want to hear. Something I swore to myself I'd never tell *anybody*. You know what he said to me, Marty?"

Color rushed to Billy's face. He pushed his head forward, and his voice rose. "You know what he said? He told me to go to hell. And said he was glad I came so he could say that to my face."

Billy slammed the door and started the engine. He backed away with his head through the open window. Tears flooded Marty's face as Billy yelled. "So how much is that worth, Marty? How much is *that* worth?"

Chapter Ten

Elly grunted, and pushed herself up from the sofa. "Marty, look at me. My due date is one month from today."

Marty stood, spread his hands, and shrugged. "I know that, Elly. One month."

Elly glared. "You know, but you don't care."

Marty glared back. "What the hell is that supposed to mean?"

"You want to take off for Wyoming. I guess you don't want to be here when your child is born."

"Aw, come on, Elly. I'll be back in two weeks, probably sooner. I won my first gold buckle in Cody. They love me there, and I already paid the entry fee. How would it look if the world champion didn't show up at the rodeo capital of the world?"

She put her hands on the sides of her swollen belly. "How would it look if I have to go to the hospital before you get back?"

Marty walked across her living room and caught her in a big hug. "You're due in one month, not one week. Everything will be fine. Call me every day, please. Or call me every hour if you want."

He squeezed her hand, softened his voice and spoke slower. "You know I want to be here when this big event happens. If there's any good reason, I'll jump on the first plane and come home."

She looked up at him as the stress lines in her face began to fade. "I'm sorry, Marty. I guess I'm just afraid."

"I've never seen you afraid of anything."

"I've never been through this."

"You're gonna be just fine, Elly. The baby's gonna be just fine. And me, too." He held out his hand and made it quake while he made his eyes grow large.

Elly laughed. Marty kissed her, and said, "Two weeks will go by fast, and I'll be back before you know it."

***

Next morning, Marty's flight left Taos Regional Airport after a two-hour delay. But by late afternoon, following a short stop in Salt Lake City, a Western Sky Airlines flight headed for Yellowstone Regional Airport near Cody, Wyoming with only a dozen passengers. Marty sat near the front with empty seats all around him. If he decided to nap, he didn't want to be bothered. But for the first half-hour, he enjoyed snacks and beer while a flight attendant, tall, attractive, with long dark hair, catered to the passengers. Marty noticed the extra attention she gave him. He gave her a smile and a slight nod. But his thoughts were on Elly.

She lived only minutes from the hospital. When he returned from Cody, he would stay at her home until the baby was born, and maybe for another week or so. What would happen after that, he could not guess.

For months, he tried to talk Elly into coming to live with him in Cimarron. She had reasons for staying where she was, and wouldn't change her mind. Now, he hoped she would come to live with him after the baby arrived.

The fifty-two-minute flight to Cody seemed much longer. Marty was bored, and wished it was over. He pulled a handful of

63

magazines from the seat pocket in front of him, and found a copy of Rodeo World. He thumbed through it, stopped on a photo of himself, and laughed at the headline. *Will the Champ Return to Cody This Year?*

He grinned. If the mag had checked with the rodeo office, they would know he was scheduled to be there. But what kind of headline would that make?

The flight attendant came from behind and stopped beside him. He looked up at her. With wide eyes and a bigger grin, she stared at the photo, then at him.

"That's you. You're a champion bull rider?"

Marty nodded. "Yes, ma'am."

She took a step forward, turned and looked at him. Her voice rose to a higher pitch. "Ma'am?" She stood tall and straight with one hand on her hip. "Do I look old enough to be called *ma'am*?"

Marty laughed. "No offense. I don't know your name. I'm Marty."

She shook his hand. "Roxanne." She turned to go, but stopped, took a card from her pocket, and turned back. "Roxanne," she repeated, and nodded at the card as she gave it to him. "It's on there, Marty. Don't lose it."

On the back of her airline business card, he found her first name and a phone number. He looked up when a woman seated across the aisle two rows ahead, turned and glared. She gave Marty a *thumbs down,* and shook her head.

Minutes later, Roxanne stood between the vertical bars near the cockpit while she prepared the passengers for landing. Finished, she grabbed a bar in each hand and pushed out her chest as she leaned forward. Marty noticed she'd undone a button near the top of her shirt. She looked at him and licked her bottom lip.

"So, Champ, how long you staying in Cody?"

Marty shrugged. "A few days, maybe a week."

She cocked her head. "I'll be back here Tuesday. If you need some company, I'll have a room … and a three-day la-y-y-over."

The woman across the aisle turned and glared again. Palms up, she spread her hands apart. Her mouth hung open. Her eyes grew wide while her head wagged side to side.

Marty blew her a kiss and grinned.

***

This year, the Cody competitors were better, tougher, more determined. *They had to be*, Marty told himself. The bulls were bigger, better, faster, harder to ride, a trend that would likely continue.

***

He arrived there last Friday, and rode every night, taking first place twice, scoring second place other nights. This week, the bulls were ranked higher. With a score of 72, Marty took third place on Pit Bull but came in first on Mega Bux and Pile Driver.

This was the famous Cody Stampede, an every-night rodeo that started the first day of June and ended the last day of August. This was the last day, and Marty had one more ride tonight. That ride was about a half-hour away, and Marty kept his mind on other things while he waited. He fumbled through his pockets for something that would distract him, and found the card from Roxanne. He called her the day after she gave it to him but got no answer. He told himself he wanted nothing from her, didn't

65

need to meet her anywhere. He just wanted to talk because she was intriguing … and bold … and beautiful.

****

Ground Pounder gave Marty his money's worth. The bull turned and twisted faster than most and bucked as high and hard as any bull he ever rode. But Marty was at the top of his game, his concentration well-focused. He kept his seat for the full eight seconds, and captured a first-place round with a score of 91.

The announcer gave the totals. Tonto was the winning bull rider of the Cody Stampede, with a four-point lead. Marty lifted his hat and congratulated the winner. Then the announcer told everyone that Marty's earnings for the year totaled $2500 higher than his nearest competitor, a small margin, but enough to keep Marty at number one in the world of rodeo. The announcer thanked all the sponsors and officials and then paid tribute to all the grinning winners as they collected their prize money.

Every year the event drew many thousands of rodeo fans, along with performers, ranchers, reporters, product reps, entertainment crews, cowboys and cowgirls, and women who wanted to spend a night with a champion cowboy. Bull riders were their favorite. While lights went out around the arena, people broke into small groups to plan after-the-rodeo parties. Most would finish the night less than sober and crash in a rented cabin or motel room, some with old friends, others with new friends.

Marty turned to Tonto. "I got a rental car if anybody needs a ride."

Tonto nodded and approached a group of young women near the stage who waited for husbands or boyfriends, or whomever. If women didn't know which cowboy was the champion, Tonto would not tell them. They would flock to the champ. It wasn't ego, it was just fact. Tonto and Marty had been

66

in the business long enough to know. Tonto had a short conversation with the ladies, shrugged, and jerked his thumb back over his shoulder. Three came toward Marty. A tall one with a big smile reached him first.

"Hello, Marty. I'm Roxanne. Remember?"

Marty remembered.

Chapter Eleven

Marty and the three young ladies got acquainted with back-and-forth questions *...Where you from? How long you staying? What's your favorite drink?* They headed for Marty's car.

Roxanne grabbed his hand and hung on tight as they crossed the parking lot. At the car, she opened the doors and made sure Carol and Barbara took the back seat. Roxanne climbed in beside Marty, her face a giant smile.

"Bull Chute," Roxanne yelled as the car leaped forward.

Marty snapped his head around. "Say what?"

She giggled. "Bull Chute. It's a great little out-of-town bar and grill with live music and a dance floor. And they throw together the best steak sandwich and margaritas around." The girls in back agreed on the place, though both said they'd never been there.

Thirty minutes later, the party of four sat at a booth in a noisy crowd wolfing down a late dinner and throwing back drinks while a country-western band kept it all alive at the Bull Chute. Marty and the three ladies danced and laughed and joked. Roxanne stuck a cherry in her mouth, stem and all, and pushed it out a minute later. She'd tied a knot in the stem with her tongue.

Marty's mouth fell open. He moaned and rubbed his chest. "You must be one hell of a date."

Under the table, her hand caressed his leg. She growled, "I *can* be."

Two men approached the table and shook hands with Marty. They congratulated him on being a world champion, and made idle conversation about bull riding. Marty had them figured out and introduced them to Carol and Barbara. The band began the next song, and the men asked the girls to dance. After the dance, Carol, Barbara, and Roxanne had to visit the ladies' room at the same time. Marty smiled. They were scheming.

****

Carol and Barbara caught a ride with the two men they'd just met. Marty and Roxanne walked through the parking lot to his car without talking. He opened the door for her. She reached for him instead of the door, pulled him close and kissed him. She got into the car without talking.

On the highway, she placed her hand on his shoulder and leaned toward him. "You like art?"

His face puzzled. "Art who?"

She smiled big. "Oil paintings. I have something at my room I want to show you."

"Really? You want to show me your collection?" Marty laughed. "No offense, but I've heard that line in a dozen movies. Except it was always the guy trying to get the girl into his apartment."

She turned away. "That's an insult, Marty. It's not a line. I have a painting of you on a bull. I wanted to surprise you, but you ruined it." Hurt showed on her face when she turned back toward him. "Just let me out here. I'll walk the rest of the way."

Marty pulled off the road and stopped the car. "I'm sorry, Roxanne. I really am. I was just making a joke." He took her

69

hand, leaned toward her, and whispered. "I'm sorry." He looked in her eyes and waited.

"You think I'm hitting on you, Marty? I've never had trouble getting a date, and I never have to drag a man into my room."

Marty's eyes swept over her. "I have no doubt." He took a long breath and let it go. "Forgive me?"

She nodded as he steered the car back onto the road. She told him where to turn, sat silent for a minute, and then looked at him.

"I really do have a painting of you, but if you don't want to see it, I'll just —

"I do want to see it. I didn't know you're an artist."

"I'm not. I bought it."

He jerked his head around. "Where?"

"I'll make you a great cup of espresso, and tell you about it."

Roxanne held Marty's hand again across the hotel parking lot. In the elevator, she kissed him and pressed her body tight against his, all the way up to her suite.

Marty sipped espresso. Roxanne disappeared into a dark bedroom and brought back the painting. Surprised, Marty glanced from her to the painting and back again.

"You weren't kidding, Roxanne. Where'd you get this?"

She sat beside him and nodded at the painting. "The day after I met you on the plane, I had a three-hour layover in Albuquerque. I'd heard a lot about Old Town and wanted to see it. I hadn't been there twenty minutes when I found this on the wall in a small shop." She shrugged. "I'm always drawn to cowboys." She rolled her eyes and looked back at the painting. "I noticed the bull, and then the rider's face. I knew right away it was you"

Marty studied the painting. "Yeah, it's me. The bull is Rough Rider, and this is at the rodeo grounds in Albuquerque. It's painted from a photo." He studied the signature. "Nice work. Ever heard of the artist?"

She shook her head. "But I had to have the painting." Her eyes scanned him from head to toe and back again. "You must be quite a bull jockey."

Marty laughed. "Bull jockey? Call it what you like, I've worked hard at my career."

She set the painting aside, and stood. "Now, I have one more thing to show you. Give me a couple minutes." She disappeared again into the dark bedroom.

Marty drained his espresso cup, and a sudden thought hit him like a smack in the face. He set his phone on vibrate a few hours ago, and forgot about it. He snatched it from the holster, and stabbed it to hear a message from Elly.

Marty, something's happening with me. I don't know what it is, but please call me. That message was two hours old. She'd left another one ten minutes later. *Marty, I think I'm having labor pains. Please call me.*

Marty stepped outside the room and called. No answer. While he left a voice message for Elly, a text message arrived from Ken Kelly, Elly's father. *I took Elly to the hospital. She's in the labor room. I'll call back when I have more news.* Marty called the man, got no answer, and left a voicemail message.

He stepped back into the room just as Roxanne stopped in the bedroom doorway. She stared at him, a bottle of wine in one hand, two glasses in the other. But Marty's attention focused on the red-and-black negligee. His mouth went dry. His knees wanted to buckle. "Oh ... my ... God."

She stepped toward him. He held up his phone.

"Sorry, Roxanne. I uh … I really am, but I gotta go." He waved the phone. "This is urgent. Sorry." He scanned her up and down, backed toward the door, jerked it open and went out.

"You lousy bastard." She screamed as the door closed. He was ten steps toward the elevator when glasses shattered against the inside of her door.

Marty snaked around the cars and tour buses in the parking lot and went screaming toward the airport. He loaded his luggage into the car this morning, just in case. He would check out of his room with his phone. He gave himself an imaginary pat on the back for being that smart, yet felt really stupid about what happened with Roxanne. At least the airport was a short drive away.

Returning his rental car took far too long. Lines for the airport ticket counter creeped along at a maddening pace. Marty stood in line, shuffled his feet, glanced at his watch every five minutes, sighed, and checked his return ticket a dozen times. But the ticket did not change. He was booked on a flight three days from now, and a sudden curiosity caught him by surprise. Would Roxanne be working that flight? Oh well. Life was full of surprises.

That distraction from his troubles had a short life. He called Elly again. No answer. He called Ken Kelly again. No answer. Marty left no message for either.

The frustration fermented for another twenty minutes before Marty reached the ticket counter. He slapped down his ticket and forced a smile at the woman on the other side.

"I gotta get to Taos, New Mexico, and I want to trade this for the first flight going that way." He watched the middle-age woman click the keyboard and check the monitor at a pace that would make a sloth look like a gazelle.

"One-fifteen tomorrow afternoon, sir," she drawled. "It'll cost you ninety-seven dollars more. I need to see a photo I.D. please." She did not look up at him.

Marty did not use the people skills he'd always been proud of. The woman's appearance said she was exhausted and short on patience from dealing with rude customers. Marty ignored her looks.

"Don't give me that crap about flying out tomorrow. I'll pay whatever it takes, but I need to get out of here *now*."

Her chin sagged. Her eyes drooped. A strand of hair dangled on her cheek as she looked up.

"Yes, sir. You do." She shut off the monitor, switched off the light over the counter, turned and disappeared through a door marked Employees Only.

Marty snatched up his ticket and suitcase, and walked toward the exit. The woman who waited in line behind him shouted, "Thanks a lot, you jerk." He mumbled an apology on his way out and then shrugged. He'd been called worse by a woman only an hour ago.

Outside the terminal, he called Elly and then her father. Neither answered. He did not leave a message but told himself he'd try again later while he looked around the airport.

The light inside an open hangar reflected on a small, red and silver plane that drew Marty closer. From the doorway, the gleaming, private aircraft and bright red letters on the tail made Marty's jaw drop. He'd never seen one this close. "Wow" was all he could say, and he said it aloud.

A man with a large towel and a surprised look stepped from behind the tail.

"This is a private hangar, sir. Sorry, no visitors."

Marty dipped his head toward the letters on the tail. "A Learjet seventy-five? Beautiful. What most men only dream of. This yours?"

"It is."

"You do charter flights?"

The man stared at Marty as if he knew him. Then he looked at Marty's suitcase and nodded. "I do … for people who can afford it."

Marty dropped his suitcase and offered his hand. "I'm Marty Redman. I ride bulls for a living."

The pilot's face brightened as he shook Marty's hand. "Now I know why you look familiar. Good to meet you. I'm Hank." He motioned toward the plane. "Where you headed, and when do you want to leave?"

"Taos, New Mexico." Marty's head dipped toward the suitcase. "Right now."

"Taos. Nice little town. Another rodeo?"

Marty shook his head. "My first child is ready to enter this world, and I want to be there when it happens."

Marty laughed when he heard the cost for the flight, He stopped laughing, and swallowed hard when he realized Hank wasn't joking. But he told himself the birth of his first child could happen only once in a lifetime. Forty minutes later, Hank had a copilot, a flight plan, and eighteen thousand dollars from a champion bull rider.

The plane was not designed for tall people. Marty had to bend over to enter, but he found the seat just behind the copilot to be comfortable while the Learjet, at forty-five thousand feet above planet earth, streaked across the night sky at five hundred and seventy-five miles per hour toward Taos.

Marty watched the speed indicator and shook his head. "I've been on crotch rockets, fast horses, and a lot of fast bulls, but never on anything close to this."

Hank smiled. "And a lot of fast women, too, I'll bet."

Marty smiled and nodded. "Met a few of those." He looked at other gauges and meters, but most meant nothing to him. "How far is it from Cody to Taos?"

Copilot Roger finally spoke. "Highway miles? Just under eight hundred. Air miles? Five hundred, eighty-nine as the crow flies." Marty asked more questions about the plane and about flying. The men in charge didn't seem to mind.

Marty called Elly's number, but got a *no service* message. Two minutes later, he tried again. "No service," he said aloud.

The copilot looked back at him and grinned. "You won't find a cell tower up here."

Marty shrugged as his face turned pink. 'Uh, yeah … okay." He laughed. "Duh." Roxanne flashed through his mind again. He felt bad about the way things turned out but figured it was best. In spite of how likeable she was and how great she looked, he'd had no plans to spend the night with her. But she made it tough to say *no*. What would have happened if he'd found no messages on his phone? Would he be in her bed right now? Marty couldn't answer his own question, and told himself he was, after all, just a man.

One hour and nine minutes after it left the runway in Cody, Wyoming, the Learjet 75 touched down in Taos, New Mexico. Marty's phone clock said 2:47 AM when he said goodbye to Hank and Roger. He left the plane and headed toward the parking lot. His chest swelled. He'd conquered father time. Now, he'd surprise Elly and her father.

He called Elly. No answer. What the hell was wrong? He'd been calling her all night and got nothing. Did she have bad news she didn't want to share? He ran across the parking lot, happy he left his truck here instead of letting Elly drop him off. He jumped in the truck and called Ken Kelly.

"Mister Kelly, I'm so glad you answered. This is Marty. I'm in Taos. You still at the hospital?"

"I'm on my way home."

"Back to Santa Fe? Is everything okay?"

"Elly gave birth about an hour ago. Mother and baby are doing fine, and I'm a proud grandfather."

Marty couldn't speak. He'd wanted an update, but that was the last news he expected. All he could say was, "Oh."

"Marty, did you hear me?" Elly gave birth about—"

Marty's voice returned. "Yes, Mister Kelly, I heard you. Do I have a son? Or a daughter?"

"Sorry, Marty. My daughter made me promise not to tell. She wants you to find out when you get to the hospital."

Marty's gut flip-flopped. All along, Elly told the doctor she did not want to know the sex of her child until it was born. Marty respected her wish, but that meant he too had to wait. Since the day Elly told him she was pregnant, a private wish hid in the back of Marty's heart—he wanted a son. But he told everyone, including himself, it didn't matter. He just wanted a child of his own creation. He was, after all, a man. He'd waited, and now he needed to know.

His breath caught, and he glanced at his speedometer when a blue light flashed behind him. He was doing sixty in a zone marked forty.

The lady officer listened to the story about the Learjet and the baby and let the speeder off with a warning. She congratulated him and told him to slow down. Ten miles and ten minutes after she drove away, Marty entered the hospital and stopped inside the lobby door.

"Mister Kelly?"

The man smiled as he left his chair and reached for Marty's hand. "I turned around so I could be here when you see the baby."

Three minutes later, father and grandfather looked through the glass that separated the nursery from visitors. The father's heart pounded with pride. His mouth hung open. A small tear formed in the corner of his eye while he gazed at the tiny and beautiful pink face in a bundle under the nametag, *Kasey Redman*.

Five minutes later, the father said goodbye to the grandfather. The father shook with excitement as he eased into the mother's room, not wanting to wake her. Bright green eyes looked up at him.

"Hello, Cowboy."

Chapter Twelve

As he had promised, Marty moved to Elly's house after Kasey was born but made sure Elly knew it was temporary. Now, he sat in her bedroom, held his daughter, and watched Elly sort through her wardrobe of show costumes. *Costume* was Marty's word. She'd correct him. They were *outfits*.

She threw out a few things, stripped down to her underwear, and tried on everything she had left. Rodeo outfits filled most of the oversize closet. Hats, boots, gloves, belts, and accessories filled another closet. Every item in each outfit had to work together for the show.

Elly mumbled to herself as she sorted through show clothes but said nothing Marty wanted to hear. She looked good in her underwear while she held items against her body in front of the mirrors, but he was not here for entertainment. He waited for her to take a breather and suggest a new wedding date.

Within a week after Elly told Marty she was pregnant, they set a wedding date for the following month. But a major haircare products company sent a contract offer. They would pay her well to plug their products, and they needed her right away for a series of meetings and photo shoots. Elly and Marty set a new wedding date. Before the new date arrived, Elly was showing, so they postponed the wedding until after she gave birth.

Today, Kasey was a month old, but the subject did not come up. The career Elly built for herself had top priority.

*****

Marty hung up the house phone and shook his head. He hated lying to the schedule clerk in Fort Worth, telling her he had the flu and couldn't compete in the upcoming rodeo. Even more, he hated to miss the chance to defend his title. From the nursery came a reminder of why he had to make that call. Kasey was hungry … again.

Marty took a bottle of formula from the fridge, set it in a pan of water on the stove, and went to console his daughter while the bottle warmed. She turned six weeks old yesterday, and knew how to get attention. As soon as he entered her room, he knew she needed changing. She sucked her fist, and kicked and wailed through the changing battle, and her cries got louder while he washed his hands.

"Okay, Daddy's going fast as I can." He scooped her up and walked back to the kitchen. "Oh damn." The bottle had overheated. He put her back in the crib, and she screamed as if she couldn't live another three minutes without food. Marty grabbed another bottle of formula, mixed the cold bottle with the hot, and sprinkled a drop on his wrist. Just right. Finally, he could feed the monster, and told himself, the next time a salesperson calls to speak to the head of the household, he'd give the phone to Kasey.

Right now, Marty resented Elly. She left Kasey here with him, promising Annabella would be here. She'd have the guest bedroom, and would assume total care of Kasey. "I already paid her for two weeks," Elly told him. "I've known her a long time. She'll be here on Monday."

Marty knew nothing about the woman—no address, no phone number, not even a last name. But Monday was two days ago, and Annabella didn't show. He left a message on Elly's phone, but she had not returned his call. No surprise. She did not like to be bothered at work.

A child Kasey's age should have her mother in the house. A woman has natural instincts for child care. A man does not. He was a champion bull rider, not a babysitter.

Marty tried to convince Elly to take a few more days off work, to wait till February, for La Fiesta de los Vaqueros in Tucson, Arizona. The annual rodeo events and parade had been around since 1925, pulled more than two hundred thousand people each year, and attracted worldwide attention, the year's biggest attraction for Tucson. Elly had been a key part of that event for the past four years. She was a star. The people there loved her, and Marty understood why she felt she had to be there every year. It was good for business.

But Elly didn't wait for Tucson. She left last Thursday for the October rodeo in Fort Worth, booked for six days of work. Fort Worth was also a big event. Marty loved their Cowtown Coliseum, and understood why Elly felt she needed to be there. But she also needed to be here, and he needed to talk to her.

Marty left another message on her mobile phone but didn't know if she got either one. He didn't even know if she made a safe trip. With a horse trailer behind her pickup, that trip could take fourteen hours, maybe more. She was the mother of his baby. He had a right to worry. For now, he would care for Kasey as well as he could.

Before Kasey was born, Marty and Elly bought the rocking chair now in her living room, the first item the two bought together. The chair came as a kit that took Marty and Elly two hours to assemble, two hours that became a good memory of working together.

Marty now rocked the chair in slow motion while he sat with the precious bundle in his arms. He stared at his child as he fed her. Kasey's world was now serene. He took a slow and easy breath, let it go, and did it again. The stress left, and Marty's own world became a peaceful place. He'd always heard parents affect how their children feel. Now, he knew it was a two-way street.

"I'm sorry, Baby. It's not your fault. Daddy loves you very much." Milk spilled down the side of her face, made a track around her tiny ear, and left a damp spot on Marty's pants. And for the second time in her tender life, Marty's baby girl smiled and looked up at him. He cleared his throat, wiped a tear from his cheek, and wished Elly could be here too.

His phone rang.

He took the call. But before he could talk, a woman with a heavy accent yelled, "I'm Annabella. You Marty?"

"Yes, this is—

"I come Monday. Elisa say *Monday*."

"But Elly said you'd—

"Okay, I see you Monday. At seven." The call ended.

Marty closed his eyes and shook his head. Then he stared at the last number left on his phone. Annabella didn't say which Monday. And did she mean seven o'clock in the morning? Or evening? He called the number but ended the call when he heard an outgoing message in rapid Spanish.

****

When the grandfather clock bonged five times on Monday morning, it did not wake Marty. He'd been up more than an hour, fed Kasey, bathed her, changed her, and rocked her back to sleep. Now, he threw her dirty clothes into the washer. Next, he would wash bottles and nipples and mix more formula to store in the fridge. She'd be hungry again by seven. Then, maybe—just maybe—he'd find time to dress and feed himself.

Marty glanced at his watch at ten minutes before seven as Kasey finished her meal. Still no word from Annabella since ... *When did she call? Last Wednesday.* A lot had happened since then. Most of it involved caring for Kasey. Almost none of it involved sleep for Marty.

If Annabella didn't show, he'd take the baby on her first vacation. He'd pack her bags and his, and drive to Fort Worth. He'd find Elly, leave the baby with Mama, take a ten-hour nap, and ride a few bulls to keep his championship title and earn some money.

The clock bonged seven times. Marty picked up his phone. He'd try once more to reach Elly before taking off to Texas with Kasey in the car seat. But first, he had to get dressed.

He buttoned his shirt and leaped into his pants. The doorbell and an instant knock at the back door got his attention. Still barefoot, he yelled, "Just a minute," but the doorbell and the loud knock came again as he yelled. He stuck his head out the bedroom door, but before he could yell again, a woman peered through the glass.

"I'm Annabella. You Marty?" He started for the door in his socks, and the woman yelled again.

She carried in a suitcase as Marty opened the door. He stuck out his hand. "Nice to meet you, Annabella, Thanks for your patience. I'm—

"Just call me *Anna.*" She walked past, stopped and shrugged. "My room?"

Marty pointed to the guest room. Annabella went in, left her suitcase by the dresser, and threw her jacket on the bed. She turned toward him and shrugged again. "The baby?"

Marty pointed at the room next to hers. "Her name is Kasey."

Annabella hurried in and found Kasey asleep. A minute later, standing in the doorway of Kasey's room, Anna lowered her head. Her bottom lip stuck out and her eyes drooped. She looked up at Marty.

Marty shrugged. "Something wrong?"

She nodded. "Katy is too beautiful, Señor."

"Oh, uh, thank you, Annabella. Her name is *Kasey*. I'll—"

"Just call me Anna."

"Right. I'll show you around the house so you'll know—"

She shook her head. "I go to many homes. I find everything. Excuse me, por favor." She walked down the hall and disappeared into the bathroom. Three minutes later, she walked to the kitchen. Marty followed and opened the dishwasher.

"If you need to wash—"

Annabelle rolled her eyes. "I have a dishwasher."

"Sorry. When you need—"

She opened the cabinet door under the sink and pointed at the dishwasher soap. "Everyone keeps it there." She smiled. "If I need a vacuum for the floor, I will look in the hallway closet." She cocked her head. "No?"

Marty nodded. "Baby formula?"

She opened the refrigerator and angled her head toward the bottles. She shut the door and looked at him. "I have seven babies, Señor Marty. They all grow up big and strong, handsome and beautiful. Now I have *cinco nietos*." She held up her hand with her fingers spread. "Five grandchildren."

Marty's eyes widened. She looked forty. Could be sixty-five, but he didn't dare ask. "How long have you known Elly?"

Annabelle laughed. "Longer than you. I cared for Elisa when she was no bigger than a Chihuahua. Smaller than Katy."

Marty wanted to correct her again about Kasey's name, but didn't.

****

He eased the pickup into the parking lot at Johnson's Market in Taos, and glanced at Kasey, not sure if it was legal to have a child safety seat in the front seat of a vehicle. But his truck had no back seat. She'd been an angel all the way here, her feet pumping while Marty talked to her, and her wide eyes danced as she looked around.

Marty unstrapped her, and chuckled to himself. Annabella, or *Anna*, pouted when he told her he was taking the baby to the market.

"You don't trust me, Señor Marty?"

"Of course, I do. You have seven children." He extended his open hand toward Kasey. "But every girl likes to go shopping." Besides, he figured Kasey needed a couple of days to get to know Anna before he left his daughter alone with her.

Now, Kasey lay on her back in the basket of the shopping cart, a pacifier in her mouth, while Marty cruised the aisles to buy formula, jars of baby food, diapers, and a few things for Kasey's daddy.

But every three minutes, a woman customer would stop him to say what a darling little girl she was. They all had to ask her age and brag on the frilly pink dress and cap Elly bought for her.

84

Kasey needed changing again as soon as Marty got back to the truck. While he pulled off the dirty diaper, his phone rang.

The ringtone told him it was Elly. Bad timing. He'd have to call her back.

Chapter Thirteen

On the flight to Cheyenne, Marty wanted to sleep. Getting enough rest played a big part in riding a bull. But disturbing thoughts about his chosen career would not let go of his mind. He was strong, skilled, disciplined, and driven, and he'd always worked hard to be the best. No one could succeed in this business any other way. But riding bulls played hell on the human body. Though he tried to block it from his mind, age played a part also. And Marty was older than most other athletes in this business.

Kyle Kross was tough and determined, a great athlete. He and Marty competed often in Texas, New Mexico, Arizona, Wyoming, and dozens of other states. Marty always rode well against his friend, and Kyle rode better when he competed against Marty than at any other time. The good-natured rivalry inspired both.

For most rides, Marty took first place, and Kyle took second. Often, it was the other way around. But between the two, they ruled the event and soon became the crowd's favorite matchup.

Marty and Kyle often stayed at the same motel, and enjoyed meals together, before and after rodeos. Kyle would ask Marty about his background, and Kyle shared much of his own life.

His mother was a big woman, tall, strong, broad shoulders, big hands and big feet. Kyle's father was a small man and short. In spite of his size, his hands and feet were large though not as big as Kyle's.

"I get my body size from my dad, and my feet and hands from Mom *and* Dad." He shrugged, and showed a huge grin. "The boys at school made fun of me, till I punched them in the face." He made a fist, and shook it. "They'd never been hit with a fist this big."

Marty laughed. "How many did you punch?"

"All three."

Marty frowned. "All three?"

Kyle nodded. "There was three other boys and me in the school. And there was eight girls, all different ages. That's it. They used to call us the dirty dozen."

Marty's face puzzled. "Twelve kids in the whole school? Where you from?"

"Impact. Smallest town in Texas. When I left, about a year ago, the population dropped to forty-six. But people there fool around a lot, so it might be higher now."

Marty shook his head again, not sure he should trust everything Kyle said. "How'd you get into bull riding? Your parents ever in rodeo?"

"Ha, you gotta be kidding. Only thing my parents have in common … they're both scared stupid of big animals." Kyle's eyes grew large as he nodded. "I didn't want to be like either of them. From the time I was twelve, I hitchhiked to Abilene …" he wiggled his huge thumb, and grinned, "to go to the rodeos. Next thing you know, I talked a guy into teaching me to ride a bull."

"But you started with a horse, I'm sure."

Kyle frowned and shook his head. "Never been on a horse." He grinned. "Unless you count the ones on the merry-go-round in Abilene."

"How often do your parents get to watch you ride?"

Kyle pointed his big thumb at his own chest. "Me? Watch *me* ride? Never. They said they don't want to watch their son die. So … they won't see me when I get that big check and the world title." With the back of his hand, he tapped Marty's shoulder and snickered.

Marty liked Kyle. Although sometimes, the funny little man was a bit hard to take. They would meet again in Cheyenne. They would compete for the title of world champion, the big gold buckle. Marty kept ahead in total earnings for the year. But Kyle was close. Kyle was young. And the winner's check in Wyoming would be the biggest ever in the sport of bull riding.

If neither Marty nor Kyle stayed on a bull for eight seconds in Cheyenne, another rider may have a chance to win. If that happened, Marty would wish them the best of luck, and a safe ride, though every rider knew the risks of the world's roughest sport.

****

Every seat appeared to be filled, and the Cheyenne crowd sounded its impatience for the bull riding event. As always, it would be the last event of the night, but the crowd had waited, and now it was time. The spectators knew the riders with the best record would be the last to ride. That meant Marty and Kyle.

The weather couldn't be better, dry with a light breeze that swept through the grounds. But many in the crowd would have waited in pouring rain, strong winds, and maybe a hailstorm to see Marty Redman and Kyle Kross compete for the world title.

Their fans came just for the bull riding event and waited on hard seats until backs ached and butts were numb.

In spite of backs and butts, the crowd seemed excited. Many came to see if anyone could ride the famous bull called Cyclone. To date, no one had. He was huge, rumored to be more than 2000 pounds of mean meat, muscle, and madness. No rider had stayed on his back for the full eight seconds, and many in the crowd would place out-of-sight bets on the bull, no matter who tried to ride him.

The bull's owners and marketing team touted Cyclone as *beyond rideable*. But everyone knew that Marty or Kyle would be on that animal's back before this night was over. And if that rider stayed on for eight seconds, he would be the world champion when this rodeo ended. No other bull here tonight could match the performance of Cyclone.

To build excitement for the show, the manager waited until all eight of the other bull riders finished. Then, Marty and Kyle stood next to the announcer while he pumped up the crowd with tense moments about which rider would ride the monster. Marty and Kyle would draw from the last two bull names left in the bag.

Marty drew first. Dead silence from the crowd. He unfolded the paper and knew his expression would tell everyone the name before he leaned and spoke into the mic. "Lightning Bolt."

The crowd booed. The bull had earned a reputation as a tough ride and good performer. But no bull could match Cyclone. Marty took a deep breath, shook hands with Kyle and wished him a great ride.

Kyle reached into the bag, and pulled out the only name left, while the crowd went nuts. He grabbed the mic and screamed, *"Cyclone."* Crowd noise rose again while Kyle enjoyed the moment. Marty laughed and clapped.

Before the event began, the manager decided Cyclone would be the last bull to perform, no matter who drew his name. Marty headed for chute 5 to straddle Lightning Bolt.

Marty's bull charged out of the chute, executed a fast leap-and-twist move, and then showed his rider a tough ride, with fierce bucks, high jumps, and more twists. Lightning Bolt showed he was a well-trained animal, eager and motivated to win. He moved fast and did his best to dislodge the rider from his back.

The well-trained rider was also eager, ready, prepared, determined, and focused. At the eight-second buzzer, Marty left the bull and landed upright on the soft earth. He'd made a good ride, and his face lit up when he saw a score of 89.

****

On the plane ride home, Marty could not eat. He would not talk to anyone. He took a blanket from the overhead bin, wrapped up, closed his eyes, and shivered. But he could not sleep.

After Kyle's eight-second buzzer, the young man leaped off the bull, and landed on his feet. The momentum pulled him forward, but his big hands cushioned the fall. Kyle laughed aloud as he turned face-up. Barrelmen scrambled, ran in front of the bull, and slapped his ears to distract him. The bull spun and refused to be distracted.

Before the rider got to his feet, Cyclone took revenge. The animal dipped his head, and gored the hero of the night. Ripped him open like a sack of feed. Spilled his blood and guts in the dirt and manure while rodeo fans watched in shock and horror. Some covered their faces but then spread their fingers, shook their heads, and saw what no one wanted to see.

Men, women and children screamed, cried, and moaned. Some vomited while they witnessed the ghastly death of a young champion.

Kyle Kross, Kross with a *K*, not a *C*, won the big, gold buckle that night. He would never win again. The little man with big hands and big feet died on his birthday, at twenty-two.

Chapter Fourteen

Lefty led the giant Brahma into chute 3 for the final ride of the night's final event. The animal's shoulders pushed against the chute's front gate, and the rear gate slapped the bull's backside when Lefty slammed it shut. Only chute 3 could hold an animal this large, and only because the maintenance crew enlarged and reinforced the chute the day before.

Like every well-bred and well-trained rodeo bull for this sport, this spirited, young stud understood the game he was about to play. Yet this bull appeared more eager than any other, as if he had it all figured out.

The wide eyes and the shivers along his back showed his excitement. He knew what was coming. And he fidgeted, snorted, and pawed the dirt floor while he waited for the next victim to climb aboard. He knew this game better than the riders. He shook their confidence, exposed their fear, humiliated them in front of their fans. He'd thrown them all into the mud and manure or against the fence in four seconds or less. He knew he could do it again.

But he could not know what was about to happen before the next would-be rider arrived.

Emilio slipped through the shadows and into the chute area with his head down, and picked up a long-handle shovel. He opened his other hand behind him as he passed Lefty. Lefty took the hundred-dollar bill and disappeared into a storage room.

Most professional bull riders formed a tight circle of friends. A man who had never climbed on the back of a huge animal that wanted to kill him could not appreciate the thrill that came with the risk. Could not understand the excitement or the dangerous world of those who dared. Could not fully respect the skills, training, discipline, dedication, and raw courage, of men who belonged to that exclusive fraternity.

Emilio, known around the rodeo circuit as NLS, for Nasty Little Shit, did not belong to that select group. He was a cocky little rider with an oversize ego who wanted to win at all costs. He seldom did. His scores were low.

The scores for each ride depended on the bull as much as on the rider. The harder and faster a bull bucked, twisted, turned, and kicked to give the rider a greater challenge, the better the score. If ... the rider stayed on long enough.

At a time when all riders drew from the same stable of bulls, a low-rank rider on a high-rank bull had little chance of staying on. Yet a top rider on a low-rank bull seldom got the ride he needed for a good score.

PBR, the organization of professional bull riders, helped improve the sport, so that riders with the best record now drew from top-rank bulls. Bull riding events had long been the favorite rodeo sport, and cowboys and fans welcomed the change.

Nasty Little Shit drew from the supply of low-rank bulls. Often, before he climbed aboard his bull, he climbed the slats of the chute, and back-handed the caged animal across the nose again and again. A pissed-off bull would buck harder and faster, and improve the score ... if NLS stayed on.

Emilio would not be riding the bull in chute 3, but he knew who would be on the monster's back when the gate opened. Nasty needed only a minute to do what he had in mind. He hunkered down by the chute, shovel in hand, and reminded himself how much he despised the five-time world champion who would use every trick he knew to stay aboard this bull for eight seconds.

Two minutes later, Marty Redman straddled the big animal's back, and heard the rodeo announcer introducing bull and rider. But the man's words were only noise, like a radio broadcast that echoed off the walls of an empty room. Words didn't matter now. Nothing mattered except the rival beneath him in chute 3. Redman was a champion. He'd earned his way to the top. Paid his dues. This gargantuan bull was also a champion, and he'd paid his own dues.

After his divorce from Luna, Marty rode high-speed motorcycles, crotch rockets that gave a man a sense of power, an adrenaline rush. He added rock-climbing and bungee jumping, anything for a thrill. While in high school, he rode barnyard bulls just for fun, and they bucked and kicked, and gave him a rough ride. But he'd learned the difference between barnyard bulls and rodeo bulls was like the difference between sandlot baseball and the major leagues.

To train as a professional bull rider, Marty straddled mechanical bulls hundreds of times. They bucked, twisted, and spun, threw him in every direction, and taught him how to sit, where to place his knees, and how to grip the rope. They taught him how to let his body bend and move and flap like a wet rag in rhythm with the machine. He learned how to dismount at the sound of the eight-second buzzer.

For all the times he left the mechanical bull ahead of the buzzer, he learned how to fall, to keep his chin against his chest, and his head turned so his eyes could find the ground before it found him.

At full speed, a manmade beast could be a real challenge, a great trainer. But mankind had never built a machine that could give a man the chilling rush of adrenaline that came from straddling a trained rodeo bull. Nothing manmade could rival the beast below him now.

This deadly, 2200-pound mountain of muscle had earned his reputation, and Marty knew the animal would explode from the chute the instant the gate opened, when the rider nodded at the gatekeeper, or said, "Let her go."

Marty had been on some tough bulls. Bodacious and Sledge Hammer gave him the biggest challenges he'd ever known. He had never been on this bull, but he had seen videos where nine of the top ten competitors had tried. Nine failed. The lucky ones limped out of sight after the ride. The others were carried out on stretchers.

He tightened his butt and felt the monster's muscles ripple beneath him. What kind of madness possesses a man to risk a brutal death for money or glory? How could anyone justify this kind of insanity? What driving need, what level of ego, what distorted craving for fame or praise, or gold buckles could make a man straddle a killer ten times his size?

Today, for the first time, Marty knew it didn't make sense. He also knew that no mechanical bull could teach a man how to keep a real bull from killing him after the ride. And he knew this beast beneath him had only one desire greater than plunging his enormous bullhood into every hot, young heifer he could find. That greater desire was to kill the irritating, two-legged little pest that sat on his back. Slam him to the ground. Crush his skull. Break his back. Or rip open his belly with a deadly horn, spill his blood in the dirt, and leave his lifeless body in a pile of manure while others of his kind watch in horror. And gasp. And scream.

Marty's best friend, Zane, lost his life because of a bucking bronco. Yet horses did not have the killer instinct of bucking bulls. Kyle Kross proved that horror to the world.

Too many times, Marty watched the video of that night in Cheyenne, Wyoming, though he'd been there and watched the tragedy as it happened only a few feet away.

That killer bull would never carry another rider. The owners retired Cyclone. But they kept him as a breeder bull. Now, Marty sat on Son of Cyclone, a bull even larger than his sire. Larger. Stronger. Faster. Tougher. Meanest bull in the history of professional rodeo.

Marty reminded himself that this time, like every other time, he knew the risk, the danger. It was a game of skill, yet always a game of chance. No two bulls acted the same, but this one fidgeted, pawed, snorted, and bobbed his head more than any other, testing Marty's confidence.

His confidence would not be shaken. The animal below him did not know Marty's record, did not know the hundreds of bulls Marty rode for a full eight seconds, did not know how determined he was to win the world title once again. Son of Cyclone could not know Marty taught himself the art of focus and isolation. When he rode, only two things existed in the universe—Marty's butt, and the bull he straddled.

He loved the fame, popularity, and money. He loved being an idol for children and a magnet for good-looking women. But none of it compared to the day Elly told him she was pregnant. His chest swelled. He was going to be a father. On that day, at that moment, he knew he was a real man.

On this day, Marty did not know what happened moments before, when Nasty Little Shit peered between the slats of the chute and found just what he was looking for. He slid the shovel handle between the slats until it touched the bull's testicles. The big beast uttered a low, short moan, and shivered. Nasty eased back the handle, sighted down the length of it, and worked it back and forth in his hand like a pool cue.

"My turn to *break*," he whispered, and laughed from his gut while he rammed the handle forward as fast and hard as he could punch. He jabbed the young bull again and again while the animal danced and shook from the pain and torment, while he pleaded, pawed, and bawled, and drowned out Nasty's wicked snicker.

Marty knew none of that as he tightened his grip on the rope, as he scrunched his butt once more, as the muscles on the bull's back rippled again. Now, Marty did not see Lefty open the door of the dark storage room, stare at chute 3 and make the sign of the cross while the giant, restless brute shook his head, leaned against the front gate, and snorted. Son of Cyclone was ready for a fight.

Marty drew a deep breath and nodded to the gatekeeper.

"Let 'er go."

Chapter Fifteen

The behemoth shot out of chute 3 like a cannonball, and slammed the gate with a force that knocked the attendant flat on his back. Marty heard nothing but muffled noise. From day one, his trainers taught him to focus only on the hump, to see only his hand on the rope. "If you look to one side," they said, "that's when and where you fall."

Now, Marty found only blurred images of red, blue, and purple. He rode some rough and tough bulls in the past few years, bulls that few riders could stay on for a full eight seconds. But three seconds on this bull's back, told him he had never been on anything that twisted, spun, jumped, kicked, and bucked, as hard or fast, or as unpredictable as Son of Cyclone.

Grip and wrist exercises were part of Marty's workout routine since the day he began training as a professional athlete. The extra strength and flexibility made him a winner. He spent long hours teaching his body to focus on each split second he sat on a bull's back, to anticipate the animal's next move. There was no time to think. No time for decisions. It had to be intuitive, an automatic response.

Like fine-tuning a machine, every muscle in his body had to know when and how to react and, with precise timing, control every joint, every move of his feet, calves, abs, knees, thighs, butt, back, neck, hands, arms, and eyes to forecast the next twist, rise, dip, or spin. He had turned bull riding into a science and turned his body into a machine that served him well.

Until tonight.

This bull did not move with a force or direction any rider could calculate. Every move was random, as if it came not from training, not from breeding, not from any rational thought or animal instinct. Marty sensed that someone or something had messed with the bull's mind. This overgrown monster was psychotic.

Heat radiated from Marty's toes to his scalp. Sweat poured off his hands, off his face, and into his eyes. His feet felt wet inside his boots. Crowd noise now sounded far away, and a sudden chill made him shiver. He gripped the flank rope tighter than ever. Every dip, spin, and kick shot a lightning bolt of searing pain, and tore at muscles from his fingers through the arm and shoulder and across his back. His body could not adjust to the bull's rhythm or pattern because none existed.

Another stab of pain separated Marty's hand from the rope, and he no longer felt the bull beneath him. His blurred universe wobbled and spun like a bad dream as the bull rider's body collided with planet Earth. Marty heard nothing except the eight-second buzzer one second after his crash landing.

***

Marty's eyes opened. A woman sat beside the gurney that rocked and shifted while she talked. She shined a small light in his eye, and then the other, while she spoke. He heard the woman, but her words seemed disconnected from anything real. Although right now, nothing seemed real.

Blood from Marty's forehead trickled down to his nose and made him itch. He reached to scratch.

The woman caught his hand. "Don't do that. Your nose may be broken."

Marty's eyes grew wide. "Where am I?"

"In an ambulance. You're on your way to the hospital."

"What happened?"

"Just try to rest."

The blood now ran down Marty's cheek. When he reached to wipe it off, the woman shook her head. "Don't do that. Your arm could be broken."

"Why? What the hell happened?"

"Don't talk. Your jaw may be broken. Just try to rest."

Marty let out a heavy sigh. "What the hell happened? I hate hospitals." He knew that was true but he could not remember why. A speaker drowned out his words while the ambulance driver talked to someone at the hospital emergency room. The speaker was much too loud and echoed as if the person at the other end was in a barrel. He tried to sit up, but could not.

"Am I under arrest? Did I do something wrong? Why am I tied to the bed?" No one talked to him. Marty took another heavy breath and went back to sleep.

***

Marty's eyes opened in a different bed, in a room with a hint of disinfectant. A woman stood beside him, but not the same one. His eyes scanned up from her waist. This one was smaller and ... a tear slid down her cheek as he glanced up. Big green eyes looked down at him. Familiar and beautiful green eyes. But they looked sad, and her words were soft and slow.

"Hello, Cowboy." She wiped her tear but another appeared. "You scared the hell out of me and a lot of other people. You know that?"

"What did I do? What happened?"

Elly took a long breath and let it go. She caught his hand, leaned over him and kissed his forehead. She straightened again and shook her head. "You really don't remember, do you?"

He looked away from her and back. "I was on a bull in the chute, and …" His eyes met hers. "I don't remember anything after that." He looked down at the sling. "I broke my arm? What the hell happened?"

"Your arm is a little banged up. It's not broken, but your scapula is. That's your shoulder blade. The sling helps hold everything in place until it heals."

He looked away, and then snapped his head back toward her. "How's Kasey? Is she all right?"

Elly smiled and nodded. "She's at home with Anna, but she wants to see you."

Marty's eyes grew misty. "Tell her I love her, please, and I'll come to see her as soon as I get out of here."

He gazed across the unfamiliar room and felt out of place. His gaze shifted back to Elly, her arms now across her chest. He frowned.

"How come nobody told me about this before?"

"You have a mild concussion, so you don't remember. But I told you all of this yesterday, and so did the doctor."

Marty's eyes lost focus as they shifted toward the window. "Yesterday?" His eyes now jerked toward her and he sat up. Pain shot across his back, and he lay down again. "Oh, God, Elly. What the hell happened?"

"I know you're hurting, Marty, but you have a lot to be thankful for."

"Like what?"

"The barrelmen. When you fell off, that bull came back after you. It took both men to keep him away." Elly wiped a tear, turned her head away and raised her voice. "I hate to think what might've happened if they hadn't been there." She took a deep breath and looked back. "Oh, Marty, I was so afraid that—"

A short knock at the door interrupted her, and the doctor entered. He glanced at his patient and asked the usual questions. *Does this hurt? Does that hurt? How does that feel?* The doctor took a quick look at the chart and scribbled on it. "I'll come back in the morning. If everything still looks good, you can go home … if you have someone to stay with you for a few days." He paused and looked at Elly.

She nodded and smiled. "I'll be there."

Marty looked at the sling and back at the doc. "What the hell happened?"

***

After breakfast next morning, Marty went back to sleep. When his eyes opened again, a silver and turquoise Navajo bracelet told him instantly who now stood next to his bed. She had told him it was a gift from her mother, and Marty never saw this lovely young lady without the bracelet. His eyes widened as they found her face.

"Hello, Yan. What are you doing here?"

She smirked and nodded toward his sling. "Looks like you survived, cowboy."

Marty sat up and nodded at the sling. "Yeah, I'll be okay. But I'm surprised to see you."

Yan chuckled. "After I watched what happened, I figured I'd better come and have a look at you."

He looked up at her, his face serious. "I didn't know you were at the rodeo. Don't tell me you worried about me."

She rolled her eyes. "Hell no. The way you ride? I was more worried about the bull getting hurt. I've never seen any animal that crazy."

Yan's genuine smile and pretty face often made her appear soft and delicate. Marty knew better. She was no pushover, and behind those dark, dancing eyes and short, straight hair lived a sharp mind and quick wit. She was not a big woman, but strong and sure, and nobody pushed her around.

He looked down, shook his head, and looked back at her. "I don't remember much about the ride."

"Yeah, the newspaper said you have a concussion." She held up a small, wrapped box. "But hey, I brought you something." She looked again at the sling. "You'd never open it with one hand." She unwrapped the box, took out a small object, and held it out. "This will help your memory come back."

Marty laughed. "It's a bull. Where'd you get this?"

"I found it a few years ago, last time I was in Mexico, at a little shop down in Nogales. Ever been to Nogales?"

"A long time ago. When my dad was alive."

Yan's face turned serious. "Marty … I don't know how much you remember about your ride, but the barrelmen saved your ass."

"Yeah, somebody told me." His eyes lost focus and stared at the ceiling. Then he looked back at her. "I think it was Elly."

Yan and Marty talked for ten minutes before a nurse came into the room. She looked at Yan.

"Sorry. The doctor needs to check the patient. Would you wait outside, please?"

Yan turned to Marty. "I'll check on you later. Gotta git."

The nurse walked out behind Yan, and Marty was alone. He rolled the figure around in his hand, a bull no bigger than a mouse. He'd seen many figures of bulls over the years, most made of plastic, glass, clay, or carved wood. This one was pewter, very detailed. He liked it. It would remind him of Yan, and she was definitely a friend worth remembering.

She knew more about rodeos than anyone Marty had met. A former barrel racer, and a damn good one, Yan grew up in rodeos and around cowboys, *a tough bunch of hombres*, she called them. Now she worked at rodeos all over New Mexico, keeping events organized and keeping cocky cowboys in line.

Over the years, Marty got to know her. Her full name was Yanaha Yazzie. Yanaha, the Navajo word for *brave*, was too long for young schoolmates who shortened it to Yan. It stuck.

Yan's parents had been proud members of the Navajo nation. Yet they moved off the reservation when Yan was only two, convinced their daughter would have a chance for a better life *off the rez*.

As Yan grew, she had a love for horses, riding, and rodeos, and she participated in amateur barrel racing. She graduated high school with honors and enrolled in New Mexico University in Albuquerque. When her mother died two years later, Yan lost interest in school and dropped out to pursue barrel racing.

Marty trusted her and talked with her about his career and his girlfriends. Since Elly came along, most discussions between Marty and Yan had been about Elly. At one point, Marty said, "I asked Elly to marry me. She agreed, but every time we set a date, she finds a reason to put it off."

Yan nodded. "So, *she* should get married because *you* want to?"

"Why wouldn't she want to? Don't most women want to get married?"

Yan shrugged. "Elly's not like most women. I talked to her a few times. Personal stuff, but not private. She's happy with her life and doesn't need anybody else's money or opinions. She can manage her own career." Yan leaned her head and looked at Marty. "Maybe she figures she's already got it all." She wagged her head and slowed her speech while she looked at him. "There's nothing wrong with a woman wanting to be independent."

"Well, maybe." Marty shook his head, grimaced at the pain, and took a deep breath. "I guess I've got it all too ... except for one thing. I love her, Yan. I really do."

Yan took a long breath and shook her head. "She never talked to me about that, Marty. But I'm guessing that stint with Charlie Harmon left Elly with a big callus."

Marty's face wrinkled. "Callus?"

"A callus on her emotions. It'll likely wear off, but in the meantime, it could stop her from taking that big step ... getting married. It's a serious commitment."

Yan caught his arm and looked at him. "She's a beautiful woman, Marty, and she puts on one hell of a show in those costumes. Everything sparkles including that show-biz personality. But I know you've heard that old saying: *All that glitters is not gold*. When Elly finally understands that, she'll come around. Maybe instead of a *romance* on the rocks, she'll see that show-biz life as *glitter* on the rocks."

Marty's eyes lost focus, and he smiled as Yan's words soaked in. She was a good listener and offered a woman's perspective. Marty always felt better after their talk. He knew he could trust her, and Yan knew she could trust Marty when she shared a part of her life that few other people knew.

At twenty-two, Yan gave birth to a daughter, fathered by a man known as Butch Pershing, a married man who left town as soon as Yan told him she was pregnant. That darling little girl became Yan's whole world, her reason for living. But at two years old, Mandy died of meningitis. Yan's father helped her deal with the tragedy better than anyone else. Now, he was gone too, from liver disease.

After Yan's father died, the man who got her pregnant came back to see her. "I wanted nothing to do with that sleaze ball," she said. "And I told him so. He pushed his way through the back door into my kitchen, and backhanded me in the face. I kicked him in the crotch, grabbed a big knife, and told him if he ever touched me again, I'd change him from a bull to a steer." Marty had no doubt she meant what she said.

Talking with Yan helped Marty deal with rough spots in his own life. His troubles seemed small compared to hers. Yet, she always had a positive outlook.

She was a good friend. Marty appreciated her visit and the gift she brought. But before she left today, she told him about a bet she made at the rodeo. She lost a lot of money when Marty left Son of Cyclone ahead of the buzzer. When he pressed her, she told him how much. Marty could not shake it from his mind.

A quick knock at the door brought in the doctor, followed by a nurse, followed by Elly.

***

Elly lifted her hand from the steering wheel and glanced at her watch. "It's almost noon. You hungry?"

Marty grinned big as he reached across the car seat and touched her shoulder. "I need some health food. So how about a big, juicy cheeseburger?"

Elly grinned back. "Yeah? You buying?"

"You betcha, sweetheart."

"You're on, Cowboy."

An hour later, Sweetheart and Cowboy waddled out of Ben's Burger Buzz, stuffed with burgers, onion rings, and fries, and got back on the road. Country-Western music from satellite radio blasted from the sound system in Elly's Mustang as she drove Marty home. She and Marty sang along while Garth Brooks belted out his song about *that damned old rodeo*, and again when George Strait delivered his own rodeo song, *Amarillo by Morning*. When George finished, Elly turned off the music and glanced at Marty.

"We need to talk about something."

Marty cleared his throat. For the past hour, everything seemed easy, light-hearted, and fun. He sensed that was about to change. When a woman says *we need to talk*, she was about to suggest something a man would not, *could not* like. Often, something ridiculous.

"Oka-ay." He shuffled in the seat. He'd been through this a couple times before.

With her eyes on the road, Elly dragged out her words. "I don't want you ... to get back ... on a bull." She shot him another glance and again fixed her gaze on the road.

Marty stared. His face distorted. "Whaddaya mean?"

Her eyes did not leave the road. "Just what I said. Is it confusing?"

Marty shook his head. "You mean like ... never? You're not serious?"

"Never. And I *am* serious."

"So, you want me to pretend I can compete without riding. Yes, that's confusing. You want to explain?" A nervous laugh escaped as Marty shook his head again. Pain shot through his shoulder. He groaned.

Elly looked at him. "You see? That's what I mean. You're hurting, but you're too stubborn to quit. Does that pain confuse you?"

"Oh, come on, Elly. Quit riding? Give up everything I've worked for? I get hurt all the time. Pain is part of the price for being a champion."

Marty waited. Elly did not look at him and did not speak. He glanced at the sling. "I'm not dead. This'll heal in a few weeks and I'll be just fine."

Elly kept her eyes on the road. She did not respond, and her expression did not change. Marty leaned forward in the seat and turned toward her. His words came slow and measured.

"I'm glad you're concerned, Elly. I really am ... but I have to make my own choices about my career ... the same as you do about yours. I can't keep my title if I don't compete."

Elly clenched her teeth and shook her head. Marty watched her for a full minute. Silence made the car uncomfortable. Then she looked at him.

"I'm not trying to run your life, Marty. But another fall could leave you crippled or paralyzed. What kind of career would that be? Do you really want to spend the rest of your life in a wheelchair?"

With her eyes again focused on the road, Elly sat silent for another minute. Then she turned back to him. "You have enough money. If you use it right, you won't need to work."

"Money? I don't do this for money. I'm a professional athlete. And I *love* what I do."

"You're also thirty-one years old."

Marty laughed. "Yes, thirty-one, not eighty-one." He waited for her to reply. She did not. He took a deep breath and let it go. "Hmmmm. If you're really that concerned, I'll make a deal. "I'll retire if … *you* will." She jerked her face toward him, her eyes huge. He smiled and nodded. "And, if you marry me."

Her head swung back and forth from watching the road to watching Marty. Now, he grinned big. "You retire. We get married. I'll announce my retirement as soon as I'm all healed."

She watched the road, frowned and wagged her head, but would not look at him. "Well, Marty, I should have known you'd come up with something ridiculous."

Marty smiled and stared at her. She waited. He waited, too and did not speak. She turned off the road and stopped in a convenience store parking lot. Her face lost the frown while she stared at him.

"So, what happens now, Cowboy?"

Marty's voice was slow and easy. "Whatever you *make* happen. If you want me to stay home, then you have to retire and marry me, and we'll stay home together. Or we can travel, have fun together, maybe make some more babies. Whaddaya say?"

Elly's eyes grew wet as she shook her head. She pulled a tissue from her purse, wiped her eyes, and looked at him. "About marriage … I said yes to that a long time ago."

Marty nodded. "Yeah, a *hell* of a long time ago." He shook his head. "I took that as a promise." He leaned toward her. "But it never happened."

She dipped her head. Then she eased it back up and placed her hand on his. "Maybe it's not fair, but I'm just not quite at that point. And … I'm not ready to retire."

"Me, neither." Marty smiled, and angled his head toward the highway. "May as well get back on the road."

Silence in the car now seemed comfortable while Elly drove them toward Taos. She looked at Marty when he brought something from his pocket and held it near the steering wheel. She squinted.

"Is that a bull?"

He nodded. "Yan brought it to me."

"I saw her on her way out. How come she gave you that?"

"She read about my concussion in the newspaper. She said this would help me remember stuff. And ... she said it will help me get even with someone when I need to." He chuckled. "Who knows? Maybe it'll work."

Marty watched Elly drive the car, concentrating on the road and checking signs. She really was a beautiful woman, poised, graceful, strong, and comfortable with her own decisions. After another silent minute, Marty leaned toward her.

"She really likes you, you know. She admires how independent you are and thinks more women should be like you."

Elly's puzzled face turned toward him. "Who?"

"Yan."

Elly cocked her head toward him, her face wrinkled. "Yan?"

Marty nodded. "She's told me more than once, and said it again today. Does that surprise you?"

Elly watched the road, and her face seemed to change with her thoughts. She nodded but did not look at him. "It does. Truthfully … I always thought she had the hots for you." She turned and stared at him.

Marty laughed. "Not a chance, Elly. She's a great friend, and I could trust her with anything. But it's never been anything other than that."

Marty returned the gift to his pocket, and cleared his throat. "She was at the rodeo, and she also told me that, before the ride, she bet that I'd stay on Son of Cyclone for the full eight seconds."

Elly shrugged. "I guess she lost the bet."

"Big time. Five hundred bucks."

Elly jerked her head toward him. "Five hundred dollars? How many bets did she make?"

"One."

"One? Are you serious?"

Marty nodded. "That's what she said. A guy told her he really wanted to see me lose and would put up five hundred on an even bet. So she went for it."

Elly wrinkled her face. "Don't tell me it was Emilio. Sounds like something he would do."

Marty shook his head. "My ex father-in-law."

Elly's eyes grew large as her face snapped toward Marty. "Syd Long?"

Chapter Sixteen

Maybe the applause from the crowd was not louder or longer than Marty had ever known. But that's the way he heard it now, and he had missed it more than he'd ever dreamed. The amount of work to get back here had been brutal, and it took longer than Marty or anyone else predicted. The scapula took longer to mend, and his muscle damage was more severe than first appeared. So physical therapy, when it finally began, took ten weeks instead of the usual six. But Marty counted his blessings.

He stayed with Elly in Taos while he healed. Though not a big city, Taos was home to the US Olympic Ski Team. The team's doctor, a topnotch orthopedic surgeon, also treated Marty.

Marty liked the doctor. But during the last visit, the doc turned to his computer monitor and nodded as he mumbled. "Six feet, two inches. Two hundred and twelve pounds." The doc glanced at more detail and turned to face his patient.

"Except for the fractured scapula, you're in excellent condition."

Marty smiled and nodded. "Thanks, Doc."

The doctor's face turned serious. "Can I assume you're retiring?"

Marty drew back. "I don't get it. You tell me I'm in great shape, and then you ask if I'm retiring?"

The doctor shook his head. "I go to rodeos as often as I can. I'm not looking for business. I just enjoy the entertainment. But bull riding is the toughest sport out there, and the taller you are the tougher it is. And … it's been a while since you were nineteen." He spread his hands and leaned toward Marty. "I'm not telling you anything you don't know. I've treated a few bull riders before. You're in a dangerous business, and your chance of injuries increases with age. Maybe you should quit while you're ahead."

Marty stood. "I don't see how a broken shoulder makes me ahead of *anything*. Have you been talking to Elly Kelly?"

A shade of pink covered the doctor's face.

****

If his injury had a positive side, Marty knew it was Kasey. Now, at six years old, she was a ball of energy. Anna cared for her most of the time but needed an occasional day off. Marty and Kasey drew closer, and he could not imagine a parent loving a child more than he loved her. She was smart, quick-witted, and a fast learner, a joy to have around … most of the time.

She could also be a challenge when she didn't get her way. Strong-willed and stubborn. *Like her mother*. When he punished her, she would be still and quiet for a short time. Then a small tear would show up, and she would say, "I love you so much, Daddy. Please don't be mad." It left Marty helpless.

With therapy completed, Marty rode mechanical bulls eight or ten times every day, and retrained the muscles to respond by instinct. Conditioning took longer than he'd hoped, but he had a debt to pay to his fans and something to prove to himself.

Marty also hired a personal trainer who tailored a workout routine to condition muscles and joints for bull riding. The man demanded tougher workouts than Marty could imagine, six days a week. His muscles cried for relief, his body wanted more rest, and his lungs often begged for more oxygen. But Marty never missed a minute of the routine. He would not skimp on training.

On the road back to competing, Marty worked harder than he ever had. Three days a week, he drove to a ranch that bred and trained rodeo bulls. The job paid a hundred per ride, and he rode four or five bulls each day. He'd earned much bigger paychecks at rodeos over the years, but he'd been out of competition too long, and he welcomed the income. And he had no travel expenses, or entry fees at the ranch. The rides sharpened his skills and helped to train the bulls. He missed the crowds, the action, the attention, the adrenaline rush. He had to get back in the game.

PBR friends gave him moral support all through his retraining. Other friends encouraged him, believed in him. Reporters called and often came to the house without an invitation. They all wanted to know if Marty Redman would be back, considering his injuries. And they *always* considered his age. Most of all, they wanted to know ... could he win again?

Fans sent letters to the rodeo headquarters, urging him to ride. For months, Elly pleaded with him to retire but finally gave up. She was the last one to come around. But she respected his determination, how hard he worked, how driven he became to regain his title. She gave him her full support, and it meant more to Marty than all the rest. He told himself he was better than he'd ever been, though he knew he'd have to prove it.

That proof would start now, because now in Dallas, Texas, he sat on Dyno Myte, a tough bull with a reputation.

Marty's feet and knees were in place. His butt felt exactly right on the bull's back. And best of all, the crowd screamed for him to ride. He wanted to enjoy the crowd's excitement for a minute longer, but most bull-rider injuries happen in a closed chute, not out in the arena. He always tried to limit time in the chute to no more than thirty seconds. He tightened his grip on the rope and nodded at the gate man.

"Let 'er go."

His muscles tensed and then relaxed, pushed and pulled, anticipated the next kick, buck, jump, twist and turn. They responded the way he taught them. Every minute invested in training had been worthwhile. Every extra pushup, every step on the treadmill, every rep with the barbell, every skip with the jump rope, every squeeze on the grip trainer … all of it brought him here to this night in his career, this moment, this ride.

On TV, Marty had watched other riders on this bull. Dyno Myte was no Son of Cyclone, but he was big, quick, strong, and well trained. He knew how to perform, how to do the unexpected, how to challenge his rider. Marty liked him.

Maybe the timer flashed a 6 or 7. Marty didn't know. Every successful bull rider learned from *day one* that watching the clock or looking into the crowd brought an instant exit from the bull, no matter how much time was left on the clock. He must keep his focus on the bull beneath him, keep his eyes on the hump.

During interviews, Marty often tried to explain how the seconds creep by when you're on the back of a bull. "It seems more like eight minutes," he'd tell them, "like watching a movie in super-slow motion."

A couple of years ago, a reporter in Denver asked, "How long does it take for time to return to normal."

Marty's answer got a big laugh from the crowd. "The instant you part ways with the bull. That's when gravity grabs your ass and slams you to the ground at full speed."

This was a great ride, a high-scoring ride, but Marty's mind did not stay in the moment. It flashed ahead. His mind heard the cheering crowd after the ride. But it was not real, only anticipation.

When anticipation occupies the mind, the rider cannot trust his muscles to forecast the bull's next move. A kick instead of a twist sent Marty airborne. Gravity grabbed his ass, and his breath gushed from his lungs as his back smacked the ground at full speed. The ride was over when the timer displayed 7.3 seconds.

The word *scapula* raced through the rider's mind.

****

Marty felt overdue for good news. He got it. X-rays showed no broken bones. But his left hand, the one he used to grip the rope, could be a problem. He shrugged when the doctor told him about the pulled muscle.

"I can handle that. But I can't quit now. I gotta get in shape for the Cimarron rodeo coming up July fourth, next year. Can't let down the hometown crowd now, can I?"

The doctor shook his head as he wrote a prescription for pain pills. But Marty's mind had left the scene. For the first time, he felt glad Elly was at a rodeo in Oklahoma and had not been here to see him fall. He was not ready to retire.

A week later, Marty sat on a bull in San Antonio. He'd exercised and conditioned his arm three times every day, and rode a mechanical bull eighteen times since his fall in Dallas. Now, with a stretchable bandage around his left wrist, he straddled a real bull called Big Red.

Bull riding was more than a sport. For Marty, it was his business and, like any successful business, the owner had to know his competition. Marty studied other bull riders, watched them perform, and he paid attention to a rider's attitude, confidence, and determination.

Marty also studied bulls. Yesterday, he read two articles about Big Red, and knew this animal's age, his trainers, and how long he'd been on the rodeo circuit. His performance record did not match Dyno Myte. But this bull was a tough ride, the kind that could bring a high score for a good rider.

Big Red sprang from the chute as the man outside yanked the gate rope. Bull and rider became airborne together as the beast made a high jump and twisted his body. Marty's body also twisted. His muscles, his pulse, his autonomic reactions worked just the way he trained them. Big Red had real power, speed, and agility. Marty, too, was strong, quick, agile, and ready. His left hand felt the pain from the pulled muscle, and it made the ride much longer. But Marty kept his mind on the bull instead of the pain until the eight-second buzzer let him know it was time to leave Big Red. Marty landed on his feet and doffed his hat while the crowd cheered.

After a short interview, the announcer nodded at Marty and pointed behind him. Marty turned. A lady beckoned. Then she gave him the hand signal at her ear. He had a phone call.

Marty frowned, and felt a slight twist in his stomach while he walked toward her. His cellphone was in his truck. He hoped Elly and Kasey were okay. And Mom, and …

"Mister Redman, you have a call in my office." She pointed at a door.

He thanked her, stepped into the office, and picked up the handset on the desk. "Hello, this is Marty."

"Marty Redman, great to talk to you. I'm Joe Walker. I watched your ride tonight on TV. Congratulations."

Marty sighed with relief. "Thanks, Joe. Not many people call to tell me that."

He had never met Joe Walker, but Marty had done his homework. He knew the man's reputation for the quality rodeo bulls he owned. He was aggressive, and Marty could guess the man's reason for calling.

"I wanted to talk to you, Marty, because I own Dyno Myte, the bull you were on last week in Dallas. I assume you remember him?"

Marty chuckled. "He'd be a hard bull to forget."

"Yes, he would. So, I'd like you to try again."

"I'd like that, Joe, but I'm scheduled here in San Antonio tomorrow night and Sunday afternoon. And then I'll be headed to—

"I'll bring him to you for the Sunday ride, and I'll square it with the schedulers."

"Okay, Joe. See you Sunday."

Marty's research had told him Dyno Myte was the 'new kid in town,' with potential to be a star. To gain that stardom, he needed to throw the best riders in the business. Joe Walker needed his bull to throw Marty again. Marty needed that bull to *ride* again, so he could win on Sunday.

Mud Buster offered little challenge for Saturday night's ride. Marty, the only rider who kept his seat on a bull for the full eight seconds, scored a 72. The low score didn't matter. It was not Marty's favorite way to win, but he would take it. The rider who earned the most money for the year would capture the first-place title. Marty's check was more important than the score.

****

Sunday afternoon brought one of the biggest crowds Marty had seen in San Antonio. Bigger crowds gave him more

119

confidence, more purpose for his performance, more determination to win. But another reason boosted his determination even more. Just before Marty mounted the bull, Joe Walker waved and shouted "Good luck." Marty didn't know if Joe meant it for him or the bull.

As soon as Dyno Myte sprang out of the chute, Marty knew he was in for a battle. But he kept his focus on the bull, not on the bull's owner, or the crowd, or the timer, or on his championship title or gold buckles, not on Cimarron, not on yesterday, or even today. Not on this minute, but on this split second and on his fist curled around the rope, his lifeline to victory.

Dyno Myte jumped and kicked. Marty absorbed the moves. The bull twisted spun and bucked, Marty reacted and kept his seat. The animal ran, skidded to a stop, jerked forward, and bucked again. Marty tightened his jaw, along with his butt muscles, and stayed with Joe Walker's prize performer, though the ride seemed much longer than most. Dyno Myte's rear feet kicked high. Marty leaned back in response. When the rear feet came down, the front feet came up. Marty leaned forward to stay in sync, but the back of Dyno Myte's head slammed into Marty's nose. A lightning bolt of pain shot from his nose to his feet as the eight-second buzzer sounded. Marty released his grip on the rope and flew off the bull, twisting his body to land on his feet instead of his face. Both feet hit the ground together for a solid landing, but the landing shot pain through his body again. While the crowd stood, clapped and cheered, Marty yanked off his hat and held it over his face to hide the blood that dripped from his nose.

An hour later in the emergency room, a doctor said, "Well, they tell me you won first place. Congratulations. But your nose is broken. If you're done riding bulls, I'll reset it. If you're not, there's no reason to do that. Just let it heal the way it is."

Marty shook his head. "I can't quit now."

The doctor handed him a prescription for pain pills, along with a calling card. "Call my office for an appointment to see me in a week."

Marty nodded. His nose hurt when he smiled, but he had ridden Dyno Myte, another milestone in his career. And, with his prize check, he could buy a new hat, and have a few dollars left over.

Chapter Seventeen

Since 1923, the Maverick Club hosted an all-day event in Cimarron for the Independence Day celebration. Activities would begin with a morning parade and conclude in the evening with a championship rodeo. The event always pulled a large crowd and became the biggest event of the year for Cimarron.

This year, it could become the biggest, maybe *last,* event of Marty's career. For the past month, newspapers and rodeo magazines made sure everyone knew the name of the bull Marty Redman would be riding tonight, and many speculated on whether he'd retire after this competition, win or lose.

A TV crew from Albuquerque interviewed Marty when he arrived for the morning parade. They shoved a microphone in his face before he could get his horse out of the trailer, and began with the usual, pointless questions. "So how does it feel to be named grand marshal for the annual parade today?"

On his horse, he would lead the parade just behind the Boy Scouts who carried the American flag. Yes, it would be a real honor. The *hometown hero* they called him. Good for the ego but that only increased the pressure for him to win tonight's bull-riding competition. The stakes were huge.

The next question was worse. "Do you think you're the reason for the record crowd forecasted for today's event?"

Marty wanted to say, *Do you think you're responsible for the idiots in TV sportscasting?* But he kept his composure and said something socially acceptable while he saddled his horse.

As Marty expected, questions that mattered did not begin until he strapped the big gold buckle on his belt.

"Well, Champ, do you see tonight's ride as a turning point in your career, one way or the other? And do you feel ready for tonight's competition?"

Yes, he was ready. And no, he'd made no decision about retiring.

Interviewers mentioned the bull's name more often than the rider's. Marty didn't care. If he failed to win tonight, he would likely announce his retirement within a month and go out as just another has-been, with no celebration. He did not say that to the reporters, but told them losing to the best bull in the business would be no disgrace. No rider had ever kept his seat for a full eight seconds on the monster that now waited for him.

The TV crew would air Marty's interview in late afternoon, along with highlights of the parade. They would broadcast live coverage of the rodeo from the first competition.

Marty knew the crew considered him to be the focal point of today's event. He felt at once humbled, yet proud. He also knew the crew wanted something more, a focal point for the interview, a rack they could hang their questions on.

He took a microphone, stood tall, and faced the camera. He spoke loud and clear.

"I have never been more determined. I have never been more psyched-up, more ready for a contest, never more confident. And I, Marty Redman, will be the first to ride that proud animal, and the world title will be mine once again."

It sounded cocky, but that's what they wanted to hear. *That* was newsworthy.

A small crowd of fans had gathered to watch the interview. They cheered Marty's confidence and applauded his words. They cheered again when he mounted his horse and tipped his hat.

"Excuse me, ladies and gentlemen. I've got a parade to lead."

Though still morning, today's crowd was the largest ever, and it would swell by late afternoon. Marty liked to believe he was part of the reason for the giant crowd, but he didn't dare say that to the TV crew.

He and his father came to this rodeo when Marty was thirteen, when his family moved to Cimarron. He had not missed the hometown rodeo since that day but wished his father could be here with him today, to watch him ride a bull.

Marty liked most parades but never enjoyed being part of one. Waving at everyone, wearing a constant grin, pretending to recognize many people in the crowd, and acting as if he loved the attention. Maybe today would be different. He'd never been a grand marshal.

Today, fans cheered and clapped all along the route while Marty rode by on his horse. When fans yelled his name, he would stare big-eyed, with a grin of surprise, and point at them. Young girls screamed, "I love you, Marty." He would slap his chest and cock his head.

His mother yelled, "I love you, son."

He shouted, "I love you, too, Mom." Everyone in the crowd applauded or whistled.

Elly and Kasey waved and shouted from the sidelines, and he threw Kasey a big kiss when she yelled, "I love you, Daddy." His heart seemed to double in size. At seven years old, she was the highlight of his life.

Marty was the big star of the parade, and he ate it up. But he knew how crowds would react, how once-loyal fans could lose interest if they lost confidence in your ability. And they would lose confidence when their champion no longer won. The hometown crowd supported him better than any other. But local fans, too, would lose interest if their hometown champion let them down.

After the parade, Marty talked with fans, and_signed autographs. Then he took his horse home, had a sandwich and a beer, took a two-hour nap, and headed back to the rodeo grounds.

Tonight's rodeo promoters asked Marty to stay out front until the announcer tells him it's his time to ride. They wanted to excite the crowd, to hear the fans cheer their champion when he walked back to the chute to mount the bull.

Tension and excitement ran high. Tonight, the other bull riders had performed well. The high score would be tough to beat. Marty knew it, and the crowd knew it. But now, the crowd cheered while Marty walked toward the chute. Everyone knew his ride would be the grand finale. His fans were excited and impatient. He felt the same and now knew for certain what he'd only suspected before. Win or lose, this would be the biggest night of his career. This was the moment his fans had all waited for, the moment *he* had waited for.

Weeks ago, he signed his approval to ride this prize bull, and the owners brought him a long way to be here for this night. Everyone here knew the animal's name, and they knew the best bull in the business would give the best rider his biggest challenge. The outcome would make national sports news.

Marty approached the chutes. Lefty stepped out to shake Marty's hand and wish him luck. Marty remembered Lefty from many other rodeos, including the one in Albuquerque the first time Marty tried to ride the giant bull he now headed toward. The crowd grew impatient during the few seconds Lefty whispered to Marty. But they cheered again when the camera showed Marty stepping over the top rail of the chute.

Marty told himself the last thing he needed tonight was a distraction. Instead of a distraction, Lefty's words gave him more motivation, another powerful reason to win, and a tingle of nervous excitement trotted up his spine as his butt once again touched the back of Son of Cyclone.

A memory sprang to mind. Early in his career, a trainer told him, "No matter how many times you ride, or how often, it never gets easy. And every ride is unique." Now, Marty knew that was as true as anything he'd ever heard.

He fitted the rope into place and snugged his gloved hand under the rope. The giant bull uttered a low moan. His head moved up and down in a slow nod. A powerful shiver erupted at the animal's shoulders and crept along his back. Marty's butt tickled as the shiver crawled beneath him. The huge head of the beast tilted back, and nostrils flared as he sniffed. Was it possible this animal remembered Marty? Did the bull know who now sat on his back? And did he know the reputation for this rider's whole career would now ride with him? Marty could not believe Son of Cyclone was just another dumb animal.

With that just-right grip on the rope, his knees and legs slid into place. His back muscles relaxed, and the muscles in his butt knew he had the perfect spot on the bull. Marty would nod at the gateman, and say, *Let 'er go*, and that would begin the last ride of the night for the last competitor of the rodeo, the final event of this Independence Day celebration in Cimarron.

Marty understood that this ride, if it went well, would be the longest eight seconds of his career as a bull rider. If it did not go well, his time on this bull would be the *shortest* eight seconds of his career.

No matter what happened last year or year before, no matter how many gold buckles he had won, no matter how much money he earned in the sport, or how many people knew his name, he would leave here tonight as a world champion, with his head held high, with a sense of true satisfaction, a celebrated hero known as the man who rode Son of Cyclone.

Or he would walk out of this arena with his head down, with a lump in his throat, a twist in his gut, and a pain in his heart. He may leave here as a disappointment to his family, to this crowd and all his fans who came tonight to watch him ride.

But tonight's results would reach far beyond Cimarron, to those who watched this ride on television, or read about it in a newspaper or rodeo magazine, or heard it around a campfire, or on radio, in a coffee shop, tack shop, fishing boat, bunkhouse, or tavern, or at the local Saint James hotel and restaurant.

Marty could put all that out of his thoughts. But another matter plagued him. Throughout this year, fairly or unfairly, one rider rose fast in the ranks, and now had the number two slot in the nation. Marty had never seen him at this rodeo before tonight. But he was here, and he had earned tonight's highest score so far.

Only a few times in his career had Marty scored higher than that man scored tonight. To beat him again, Marty would have to ride better than ever before and stay a full eight seconds on the back of a bull no one else could ride. If anything went wrong, Marty would lose to Emilio, the Nasty Little Shit of rodeo who earned a score of 88. And that corrupt little weasel would be tonight's champion.

Hundreds of times, Marty stood in the arena before he rode. He wanted to be a part of all that a rodeo could be. He wanted to experience the sights, sounds, and smells that seemed to belong together for the spectacle. He wanted to feel the excitement of the event, and appreciate the skill and courage of the riders, and of the barrelmen who protect the riders.

He would breathe deep when he looked out into the stands at the bobbing sea of cowboy hats on people of all ages, sizes, and backgrounds. He could feel the energy from the crowd, hear cheering and clapping, or someone yelling to encourage a rider, and sometimes rooting for a calf, a bull, or bucking horse. And always a series of groans when a rider took a hard fall, or fell off his mount a half-second before the sound of the buzzer.

Arenas were unique, yet all served a common purpose. Each was a field of dirt surrounded by a fence that exhibited signs and banners for sponsors like Wrangler Western Wear, Resistol or Stetson hats, Tecovas Handcrafted Boots, and for saddles and tack. Colorful displays of streamers and flags decorated the grounds.

The dirt would soon be soft, and mixed with piles left behind by the animal stars of the show, and a crazy clown would get laughs and yuks from the crowd when he suggested the brown and green droppings were guacamole. Urine from cattle and horses contributed nothing of value. It made more mud, and the rank smell brought wrinkled faces and covered noses to those seated downwind. Everything worked together to create the atmosphere of American rodeo, and Marty took it all in before he climbed on the back of a bull.

When he slung his leg over the bull's back, everything else disappeared. He would hear nothing but sounds made by the animal beneath him. He would see only the hump at the base of the bull's neck. He would feel nothing more than the rope in his hand, and the movement of the beast he sat on.

Marty would smell only his own sweat and the odor of the bull. His mind blocked all senses of anything other than bull and rider. To win at this insane sport, the mind must be focused only on what matters. Marty's mind was now as focused as it had ever been.

Once again, the cocky, overgrown monster showed he was no amateur. He stood crouched and poised, waiting for the rider to speak. Marty nodded at the gateman and yelled. The big gray bull shot through the gate on the word *Let*. Marty swallowed '*er go*.

Son of Cyclone rocketed past the gate, launched a high jump, and hooked a wicked right twist, as if he wanted to slam his rider down on top of the fence, to humiliate him within the first two seconds,

But the rider did not slam.

With a full buck, the bull's butt pointed at the sky, leaving his rider looking straight down at a set of deadly horns. If the rider slipped now, he'd slide over the horns that could rip him open, and he would crash face-first in the guacamole.

But the rider did not slip.

The rider pressed his knees tighter against the bull. *Don't think* flashed through Marty's mind. He must rely on instinct, on auto-response from every muscle, every nerve ending, on thousands of hours of training and conditioning. The rider's body must anticipate, and react. *If the bull gets ahead of the rider, the bull wins.* Marty had heard that and said that, countless times. And this bull had always won.

Son of Cyclone leaped higher than any bull this rider had ever straddled. At the top of the leap, the animal twisted his body to the right, and back to the left, like a water moccasin in a stream. The bull landed on all four feet with a jolting thud. Marty groaned. is knees slid down, and the bull lunged forward again. If the rider lost his grip, he could land on his head, and leave the arena on a stretcher.

But the rider did not lose his grip.

Marty clenched his jaw, gripped the rope tighter, kept his mind on this instant, and moved his knees back into place. Sweat burned his eyes, dripped off his chin, and splattered on the glove of his gripping hand.

Don't think. React. Marty's reflexes sensed that this crazy beast knew that its last move almost worked. *He'll try the same trick again.*

But at the top of the next leap, the bull twisted first left and then right, opposite his last jump.

If the rider falls now, he'll cry out in pain as he makes a loud splat in the mud. But Marty tightened his knees for the bull's crash landing.

The rider slipped, and almost lost his grip on the rope. Almost.

Marty had anticipated this would be the longest ride of his life. It already seemed twenty minutes long when the bull stood up on his hind legs, his head now pointing at the sky, threatening to throw the rider off backwards. Marty hung on to the rope. He would not slide down the bull's back. But when the giant head bent down, Marty knew this demon would slam down on its front feet. It would use any move, even one dangerous to itself, to win this battle. Marty had no moves to counter an insane stunt that would likely cripple this animal when it landed. Halfway down, Marty let go of the rope, brought up his knees, and prepared to bail.

The eight-second buzzer sounded loud and clear a half-second before Marty's butt cleared the bull's back. Marty's feet struck the ground, and he turned to watch Son of Cyclone stagger out of the arena while everyone in the crowd stood and screamed, and clapped, and whistled, and laughed.

Marty wore a giant smile, removed his hat and waved it at the crowd, a crowd that would not stop cheering. He felt numb, trying to absorb what had just happened. This was the biggest victory of his lifetime, a lifetime filled with many accomplishments.

Emilio came out of the dark when the announcer called his name. He walked by Marty without speaking, without looking at him. NLS got his praise from the announcer, got his check for second place, and walked back toward the chutes without talking to anyone. The crowd booed him as a sore loser while he disappeared into the dark.

The announcer began his praise for Marty's lifetime record, his gold buckles, his courage and determination, and for his victory tonight that restored his title as world champion. Marty bowed and waved.

"Thanks for all your support. It means more to me than I can express. But you know, a score of 96 cannot happen without a great bull doing everything he can to kill the rider. I mean, uh … to throw the rider."

When the crowd laughed and clapped, and pointed to Marty's left, he turned. A man led Son of Cyclone out to get his just praise. While the fans clapped their appreciation for the bull, Marty turned back to check on something that caught his eye earlier. It was still there. Emilio stood in the shadows behind him with his middle finger extended.

Marty raised his fist high above his head to keep the crowd on its feet while he stepped back into the shadows and grabbed a handful of Emilio's collar. He pulled NLS close.

"Lefty told me about your little stunt in Albuquerque last year, you low-life little prick."

"I … I don't know what you mean, sir."

Marty leaned toward him. "You know exactly what I mean, you lying piece of crap. He told me what you did with the shovel, how you tortured the bull before I got on."

The little man's eyes grew wide as he wagged his head. "He's lying, Mister Redman, I didn't do—"

Marty opened his fist and stuffed a gift into Emilio's shirt pocket. "Lefty wanted me to give that back to you."

NLS looked down and pulled the hundred-dollar bill from the pocket, his mouth hanging open. When he looked up again, an oversize fist slammed into his face and sent him crashing back into a soft pillow left behind by a thoughtful bull.

Noise from the crowd drowned out all other sounds as fans stood and yelled, "Marty the Champ, Marty the Champ."

The champ reached for a long-handle shovel that leaned against a nearby chute, turned toward Emilio, and looked down at him. "Your little stunt could've got me killed." He jabbed the handle. A loud moan escaped as Nasty Little Shit's eyes bulged. He yanked his hands from his bloody face and grabbed his crotch.

Marty grinned and leaned over him. "That's from Son of Cyclone. He wanted to return the favor."

Marty walked back to the microphone. The crowd cheered and clapped while he held up the big, gold buckle he'd just won. Tiny tears wet his eyelashes.

"Thanks to all of you for your loyal support, for sticking with me through tough times, for believing in me even when it was hard for me to believe in myself. I've had a great career because of you."

He laughed. "I hope none of you saw me the first time I rode in competition. It was ugly. I did not win. But since then, I've been fortunate enough to win five gold buckles before this one." He waved the buckle back and forth to more applause, and the applause grew louder while he hooked the buckle to his belt.

"But tonight, you have seen my very last ride. I … am … retired."

While thousands of people stood and yelled, "No, no, no," Marty waved goodbye and backed out of the arena.

"Hey, Champ, how 'bout a big hug?"

Marty spun around. "Yan, I didn't know you were here." He grabbed her, hugged her and stepped back. "Why didn't you come and find me before I rode?"

Yan's bright eyes were almost as big as her grin. "I didn't want to distract you."

"You could've just wished me luck. Nothing wrong with that."

"You didn't need luck. You just had to give it your best. I knew you'd win." She pulled an envelope from her pocket and waved it in front of his face. "And I won a thousand bucks."

Marty's face paled as he shook his head. "A thousand dollars? How many bets did you make this time?"

"Only one. Your ex father-in-law was here. He wanted to bet five hundred. I doubled the bet, and he went for it."

Marty laughed aloud while she waved and walked away. He walked toward his truck, where he'd planned to meet Elly and Kasey and felt a sudden loss. At thirty-two years old, he'd just ended his career.

For months, he had tried to convince himself he was ready for this day. Now, he knew he was not. He stopped, wagged his head, looked up at a brilliant night sky, and spread his hands.

"What am I going to do now?"

Chapter Eighteen

The first horse Marty owned was one he broke to ride, and it became his favorite. He never understood why that horse always bucked a lot more without a saddle than with one. But he accepted the horse's odd behavior and named him Buck Naked.

Within ninety days after he retired from bull riding, Marty set up his own business, buying and selling horses and breaking them to ride. He named his new business in honor of his first horse. But he soon tired of the jokes and snickers on the phone. Too many people assumed the *Buck Naked Ranch* was a nudist resort. He renamed his ranch.

He soon established regular customers, and the Long Family Guest Ranch was one of the best. Syd Long suffered a stroke, and Luna now ran the guest ranch. Once or twice each year, she would need to buy horses or bring some for Marty to break and train. And she would stop by often just to discuss business.

When Marty told Elly about his new customer, she didn't like the idea of his ex-wife hanging around when his wife-to-be was away, especially when Kasey was not there. Marty laughed and told Elly she had no reason for concern. *But, let her worry. Maybe, just maybe, it would make her set a new wedding date, and keep it.*

After horse business, Luna often stayed a bit longer, just to talk. Once, she'd looked in his eyes and touched his hand.

"You're a good man, Marty Redman. I wish I still had your last name."

Marty stared at her, his mouth open, searching for words.

She squeezed his hand. "Letting you go was the dumbest thing I've ever done."

Marty shrugged and found his voice. "We can't change the past."

He refused to say more, and the subject never came up again. But in a town the size of Cimarron, people often knew too much about their neighbors. Everyone knew that within two years after she divorced Marty, Luna married a politician campaigning for a state office. Marty didn't care who she married but pegged most politicians as too lazy or too crooked to find a real job.

A couple of years after the wedding, Luna gave birth to Precious, a daughter with Down's syndrome. Her husband lost the election and, like a true politician, skipped out before the baby was six months old. He moved to Oregon, and never showed up again. Now, Luna's daughter often came with her to the ranch Marty had renamed the *M R Bar*.

The woman who always wanted a houseful of kids divorced Marty because he couldn't father her child. Now, Luna and Marty each had one child, daughters near the same age who became friends. Life often came with ironic surprises. Sometimes funny. Other times not.

Elly still lived in Taos, but lived on the road even more. Since Marty retired, he and Kasey were together three or four days every week when she was not in school. Kasey had always been a daddy's girl and, at the end of the school year when Kasey was eight years old, she begged to spend the summer at Marty's house. Elly did not object, and caretaker Anna seemed happy to have a vacation.

With many things in common, Kasey and Marty enjoyed a summer of true memories. Fish tacos, ice cream, camping, hiking, fishing, and lots of rodeos, where most announcers asked Marty for an interview. Marty and Kasey traveled to Albuquerque to see Grandma, spent a day at Old Town and another day at the zoo. They went for leisure horseback rides two or three times a week, and grew closer than they'd ever been, closer than Marty ever realized a parent and child could be. Only then did he know the love his parents had felt for him, and often thought of how close he had been with his own father.

****

A big lump grew in Marty's throat when he got the notice. Taos schools would re-open in a week. While Kasey finished her lunch, he left the notice next to her on the kitchen table, walked out the back door and headed for the barn, where he could think without distractions. Somehow, the barn made it easier to pluck the splinters of life, to scratch the mind where it itches.

He did not make it to the barn. Kasey ran after him, screaming and sobbing.

"No, no, no. I'm not going back. If they make me, I'll run away. I want to stay with my daddy."

Marty turned to face her. He knew his darling daughter was as broken-hearted as he was.

"Please, Daddy, please. I'm almost nine and I can make up my own mind." She took a deep breath and shook her head. "I want to stay with *you*, Daddy. I love you so much."

He gathered her up in his arms. She cried from a broken heart. He cried from sheer joy.

"Kasey, dear, I'll never let them take you away from me. You can stay right here forever."

Marty enrolled his daughter in the Cimarron school, and he and Kasey went to share the news. Anna was relieved. She wanted to retire. Elly was furious, and planned to hire another sitter. She stood with her hands on her hips and faced him. "No way, Marty. You're not taking my daughter away from me."

"Your career already did that, Elly. Kasey needs a parent, not a fulltime babysitter."

"Kasey loves Anna, and Anna loves Kasey. Without Anna, my daughter will learn to love a new sitter."

Marty removed his hat and wiped a tear. "Maybe. But your daughter still won't have a mother. Do you know what it's like to wake up at night and hear that precious child calling for you? Too many times, I've heard her sobbing herself to sleep, saying *Mommy, please come home.* That tiny heart of hers is breaking because she wants to live with a parent, and she can't live with you because you're never home. Is that too much for a child to ask, Elly?"

Elly stood silent, breathed hard, but did not respond.

Marty wiped another tear. "I'm taking her back with me, back home, where she wants to live." He rested his hands on his hips and leaned toward her. "I'll file for custody if you try to stop me, and Kasey can tell a judge who she wants to live with, her father, or a new babysitter."

When Kasey wouldn't budge, Elly gave in. Marty hoped she would consider moving to his house to be with Kasey and him, like a real family, at least when she was not working. Maybe now, he thought, would be the right time for them to marry, though many right times went by over the years.

They got a marriage license long ago. A small ceremony would take little of her time for planning. She could wear one of her show outfits for all he cared. He mentioned it, and Elly gave her standard answer.

"I'll think about it."

****

Two weeks after Kasey turned ten, she walked through the barn, and peered out the back door into the corral where Marty groomed horses. He smiled big. "Hey, girl, what are you up to?"

She didn't smile. Her face seemed a puzzle of fear and shame as she hung her head. Marty walked to her and lifted her chin. "Kasey, talk to me, please. What's wrong?"

Marty followed her into the barn. She looked up, wiped a tear with the back of her hand, and shrugged. "I don't know, Daddy. I don't know." She pressed her knees together while she hung her head and cried.

"Then tell me what you *do* know, Kasey. Are you sick? Does something hurt? I can't help you if you won't talk to me." He took a deep breath, blew it out hard, and grabbed her arm. "You're scaring me, girl. If you don't tell me what's wrong, we're going to the hospital." He lifted her and sat her on the whiskey barrel. "Now talk to me, please."

She crossed her arms over her lap. "I'm sorry, Daddy. Something happened when I … when I went to the bathroom."

Marty shrugged. "Something? Like what? Help me out here."

"There was blood and I … I didn't know what to do."

Marty's face paled. He took another deep breath as he shook his head. "Oh, God. Uh, sorry, dear. I have to ask this. Which place … I mean, uh, tell me exactly where it came from."

139

A puffy red face looked up at him. "When I peed."

"When you …? Oh, uh. O-o-oh, Kasey. You must've …." Marty cleared his throat. *She seems too young, but it must be his little girl wasn't so little anymore.* He wanted to laugh with relief but didn't know whether to be happy or sad. He didn't want to embarrass her. He lifted her from the barrel and held her hand as they walked to the house.

Just last week, Marty signed a consent form from the school. Fifth-grade girls would learn about menstruation next semester. It seemed soon enough at the time. After all, Kasey had just turned ten.

Marty found the discussion to be the most awkward he'd ever had when he tried to explain the basics to his daughter. He could tell her *what*, but not *why*. Or *how*. It was not easy for her, either.

He learned Elly had never discussed this with Kasey. That was a mother's job, not a father's. But father couldn't reach mother on the phone. Marty's message told Elly why she had to call her daughter.

Chapter Nineteen

At four years old, Kasey began riding horses, loved it and learned fast, like everything she tried. At twelve, she began helping Marty break horses. Three days ago, Kasey turned fourteen. Daddy gave her a small party and her own horse, a three-year-old filly she broke a month ago and learned to love.

Marty's chest swelled as he hugged her and handed her the reins. She jumped into the saddle, dug her boot heels into the horse, and took off across the field behind the barn, her long hair flying behind her beneath the hat brim. When she rode back, her huge grin looked permanent.

Minutes later, Kasey and Marty sat in the swing on the deck, sipped lemonade, laughed, and joked. Her eyes grew big and bright, and she jerked her head toward him. "You'll never guess what I named my horse."

Marty shrugged and shook his head. She squeezed his arm. "Well Dressed."

He laughed. "Well Dressed? Where'd you come up with that?"

She cocked her head and spread her hands. "Don't you have a stallion you call Buck Naked?"

Marty laughed harder and longer. "Oh, come on. You're not serious?"

Kasey nodded. "I'm just as serious as you. I'm your daughter, and my horse is your horse's daughter."

"Yeah, but my horse doesn't count. He's little more than a pet. Too old for long trails."

Kasey rolled her eyes. "He's had that name all along. But, okay, fine. When my horse gets that old, maybe I'll change her name."

When the conversation stalled, Kasey planted her feet to keep the swing from moving, and turned to face her father.

"Daddy, when you gave me my horse, you said, *Like father, like daughter*. But you're a man and I'm a girl."

Marty nodded. "We're so much alike. We're good with horses. Both good riders and love to ride fast. In high school, I was the best hitter on the baseball team. You're the best hitter on the girls' softball team. We have fun hiking, fishing, camping. Think about it."

Kasey left the swing, turned, and stared into the distance. Her head made a slow nod. Then she turned back with a jerk. Her eyes flashed bright, and she slapped Marty's arm.

"We should get our DNA checked."

Marty drew back and stared. "What? Where the heck did that come from?"

"We've been learning that in school. You just send a little spit to a lab, and they can tell you a lot of stuff about you and your family, stuff you'd never know otherwise."

"Yeah? So what's that got to do with you and me? We already know you're my daughter."

"We'll have them do a paternity test. I bet it will show all the connections, and the reasons we're so much alike."

Marty grinned. "Wanna hear something crazy?"

Kasey grinned too. "Always."

"My father didn't talk about it much, but he was interested in that DNA stuff, too. He died when I was in high school. I picked up his personal things at the hospital after he died, and a nurse gave me a vial of frozen blood. She said my father wanted me to have it."

"Oh, God." Kasey covered her mouth and shook her head. Her face paled. She crossed her arms in front of her and shivered. She pushed her face toward him. "Is that what's in the back of the freezer? I looked at it once and put it back."

Marty laughed and nodded. "I didn't want to keep it, but how could I say *no* to my dad?"

Kasey leaned toward him, hands on her hips. "So how do you say *no* to your daughter?"

Marty wrinkled his face and shrugged. "Okay, I'll think about it."

She folded her arms and wagged her head. "That's what Mom always says, *I'll think about it*. That means you're never gonna do it."

Marty stood and hugged her. "Okay, baby. I'll do it, but not right now. Okay? Remind me later."

Kasey gave him a bear hug. "I love you, Daddy."

Marty knew she appreciated all he did for her and how much he loved her. And on her birthday, she had pretended to be happy, but something was eating at her, and he knew what it was. Her mother missed a few of Kasey's birthdays, working out of town. But Mom always called, sometimes twice, during the day. This time, Mom was in Texas, and the birthday girl had not heard from her.

With a foot injury and an overnight stay at a hospital, Marty missed Kasey's fourth birthday, but they were together for all others. As he grew up, Marty's parents made his birthdays a big deal for him. He learned that every birthday is a milestone for a child, and every parent should make it special.

When his rodeo schedule prevented Marty from being home on Kasey's birthday, Marty took her with him. They always enjoyed the day. Yet Kasey often wondered aloud why that day did not seem special to her own mother.

Still, Kasey tried to be tough. In spite of that, today she went to her room early and busied herself with cleaning and rearranging. In the living room, Marty watched rodeos on TV, but he could hear her, and he knew what it all meant. When he heard something moving across the floor, he stepped to her room. She'd moved her desk to the other side of her bed, and now carried her desktop computer to its new location.

"Kasey, dear, I'll help you if you want."

She did not look at him. "Thanks, but I'm almost done."

Minutes later, Marty heard her shut off the water in the shower, and her room was quiet. He settled back with a bag of popcorn, a drink, and the latest edition of Rodeo World magazine. But a large lump swelled in his throat when he heard his daughter crying. He walked to her door and tapped.

"No, Daddy. Don't come in, please."

Marty hoped she would come out, so they could talk. He would tell her some jokes or funny stories. Make her laugh. But Kasey didn't come out. Later, Marty heard her crying herself to sleep.

After school the following day, Kasey acted as if nothing bothered her. Elly finally called after nine PM.

Kasey's phone lay on the nightstand across the room. After three rings, Marty yelled from the kitchen, "Kasey, that's your mom. I know the ring." He walked to her bedroom door and leaned in.

She looked at the ceiling. "Yes. Daddy, I know who it is." She stepped to her phone and tapped the speaker button. "Hello, this is Kasey Redman." She folded her arms and stood back.

"Happy birthday, Kasey. My little girl is growing up so fast."

Kasey looked up at the wall and talked loudly. "Oh, I'm sorry, Ma'am. You must have the wrong number. Today is not my birthday."

"I know, Baby. I'm so sorry. Yesterday was ... well, it doesn't matter, but I apologize." After a few seconds, Elly sighed. "Kasey? Kasey, are you there? Kasey, this is Mom."

Kasey leaned back and looked up at the ceiling. "Oh ... sorry, you caught me by surprise."

"By surprise? You knew I'd call."

Kasey wagged her head. "Well ... no, actually I didn't."

Marty ducked out of the room, went to the kitchen and grabbed a beer. He could still hear the conversation but did not want to be in the same room. He knew what was about to happen. He didn't want to hear it, yet he couldn't stand to miss it.

"It's after nine, my dear mother, and I figured you were just too busy. So, I said to myself, *Well, what the hell, maybe that soft-hearted old broad will call next year.*"

Elly's voice pitched. "Kasey, don't swear ... and don't talk to me that way. I'm your mother."

"Oh, how noble of you to admit that."

"That's enough, Kasey. Show some respect."

"Respect for what? People don't deserve respect just because of their name or title. They earn it by how they treat other people, or they don't get it."

Marty jerked and sat up straight in his chair. He and Kasey talked about respect maybe a month ago. Just now, it sounded as if she repeated his exact words.

Silence hung in Kasey's room like the aftermath of a tornado until Mother sniffed, "I'm sorry, Kasey. I uh, I won't miss your next birthday. No matter what I have to give up, I'll be there. I promise."

Kasey took a heavy breath and blew it out. "Why? So, you can pretend you love me?"

Minutes later, Kasey sat in the chair by her bed, her face in her hands, and sobbed. Marty heard her leave the chair to blow her nose, and he went back to her room. He kissed her forehead. They stood and hugged. Marty's eyes filled with tears and his heart broke while his daughter suffered.

When the tears were gone, Kasey stepped back and squeezed Marty's hand.

"Daddy, I know you heard me talking to Mom. Are you mad at me for what I said?"

Marty squeezed her hand and shrugged. "Kasey, you'll always be my baby girl, the best thing that ever happened to me, and I love you so much." He stepped back and smiled. "And I'm not mad."

Three days later, Kasey wanted driving lessons more than anything else, so she could drive her own car the day she turned sixteen. Marty wasn't nuts about the idea, but he wanted the same thing when he was her age. And, during a casual daddy-daughter discussion, he made the mistake of telling her that his father began teaching him to drive at fourteen. He didn't tell Kasey he sat behind the wheel of his father's truck and found it easy to drive.

Today, daughter drove daddy's truck up and down the dirt road on the back of his property. Marty laughed. She drove like she'd been doing it for years.

They just grow up too darn fast. And, if she grows up too fast when she starts dating ... Was there any way to prepare for that?

Chapter Twenty

Elly removed her makeup, and stared at her bare face in the mirror, looking for a distraction from nagging thoughts and pain in her heart. Three days ago, she called her daughter to wish her a happy birthday. She was sorry she called a day late, but Kasey had no right to be rude and disrespectful.

She finished her wine cooler, left the bathroom, and threw her phone on the dresser. Then she grabbed the phone, switched it to silent, threw it in the drawer, and slammed it shut. If the phone rang, she did not want to hear it, no buzzes, no vibrations, no flashing lights, nothing. If anyone called, she did not want to know, especially if it was Kasey calling back to be rude again.

Nothing on TV got her attention. *That's the way it goes when you're in a motel room alone. Nobody to talk to, can't find your favorite shows, and can't fight boredom with boring TV.*

What will I say when Kasey calls? If she calls? What if she calls to apologize? Elly shrugged. *Let her cry for a while? Give her time to feel sorry for how she treated me. I never talked to my mother the way Kasey talked to me. I should have. My mother deserved it. She didn't care about me. She didn't hug me. She left Daddy and me alone. Moved to California, and didn't even call me on my birth ...*

Oh, God. What have I done?

She snatched open the drawer, and grabbed her phone. *Oh, no. Can't call Kasey now. She'll be asleep. It's almost eleven o'clock. School tomorrow.*

Elly crashed on the bed, and cried herself to sleep.

After a fitful night with little sleep in her Houston motel room, Elly spent an hour on her laptop, and found information she'd wanted for many years. She called the ranch where she boarded her horse and trailer between rodeos. She extended the boarding and storage time, and caught a plane for Costa Mesa.

****

John Wayne airport in Orange County was always busy. That was true of every airport near Los Angeles. This one became Elly's favorite, though she'd flown here only twice. Maybe she liked it because of the name, though she told herself it was because this airport was well organized and efficient.

For area rodeo performances, she drove her truck with the horse trailer. But she was not here to perform. This trip was unique.

Elly's hand shook as she sat in the rental car and entered the information on the GPS. When she came to Costa Mesa years ago trying, but failing, to find her mother, Elly had only a post office box number. Now, she had an address, and she would do anything necessary to talk to the woman who wanted no contact with her own daughter.

Elly moved to her forty-acre ranchette in Taos before she turned nineteen, though she grew up in Santa Fe. Many neighborhoods around Santa Fe became pricy, where most middle-income families could not afford to live. But Elly's father, through hard work, long hours, and diligence, established a successful art gallery there, and other kids sometimes called her *rich girl*.

On a day when Elly's father shopped for artwork in Albuquerque, her mother tended the gallery. A man from out of town came to the gallery and bought an expensive painting. He and Mom talked for a long time. The next day, the man came back and bought more. Elly never knew the details of what happened between Mom and that man and did not want to know. But Elly did know that, two months later, Mom filed for divorce. Elly was thirteen.

But New Mexico was not like California, and Santa Fe was not like Costa Mesa. This California town had a reputation as an expensive place to live, play, and die. Elly didn't know if it was true, but she had heard cemetery plots in Costa Mesa often cost more than homes in some other areas of the nation. It didn't matter. Her mother had married a wealthy man.

The drive took Elly from the too-busy, downtown plazas to an exclusive community where she found a maze of winding streets with tiny yards and an endless variety of houses with barely enough room to walk between them.

Her mouth felt dry, yet her hands perspired, as she turned onto the street where her mother lived. For a few seconds, Elly almost hoped she had the wrong address. But before she reached the third home on the street, the GPS startled her.

"You have arrived. The destination is on your left."

Elly turned into the drive and stopped, almost hoping she was at the wrong house, or that nobody would be home. *What the hell am I doing? I show up without letting anyone know, and I don't know what to expect.* But … she'd invested a lot of time and money to get here. Elly took a deep breath, and put on her cowboy hat. She opened the door, and planted her boot on the designer driveway.

The doorbell played a classical tune. When the tune ended, a man opened the door, stuck out his head, and shook it. "Sorry, Miss, we don't—"

"Harold, I'm Elly … remember? Elly Kelly … your wife's daughter?"

His eyes grew large. His chin dropped as he opened the door. With a slow nod, he stepped back and made room for her to enter. He nodded again, this time toward her hat, and held out his hands. She ignored him. He clutched the door again and waited.

Elly laced her hands in front of her. Her vision shifted from wall to wall in a room too quiet for comfort, too crowded with dark, antique furniture, and a too-strong scent of jasmine. Or whatever it was.

Sunshine through a round, overhead window, created a circle of light on the floor across the room in front of her. Elly glanced at Harold, still standing with his hand on the door. She ignored the hint, and opened her mouth to speak, but turned her head again at the sound of soft footsteps.

From a hallway, a woman eased into the room and stopped in the circle. Light reflected from a perfect pixie of bleached hair and showed her age in spite of an obvious, extensive facelift. She looked much older than the last time Elly saw her. Elly knew that she, too, looked much older than she had at thirteen. Still, Elly saw the unmistakable sign of recognition in the older woman's eyes as they stared.

Again, Elly started to speak, but waited to see if the other woman would speak first to her uninvited guest or intruder.

"Elisa?"

Elly drew back her head. No one other than Anna had called her that in a long time, not even her own father. The door closed behind her with a soft click as she rested her hands on her hips, and leaned forward.

"It's been twenty-one years, Mother."

Mother's expression did not change. "Since what?"

Elly scowled. "Since *what*? Since you left. Since you deserted me. Twenty-one years since you've seen me, dear mother. That's what."

Mother's stare grew hard as she shook her head. "If you came here to ask for money, I won't—"

"Money?" Elly stepped closer and shouted, "You think I came here looking for money?" She leaned forward. "I came here because I have a fourteen-year-old daughter, your granddaughter you've never seen, who is the most precious thing on earth. But I've been an awful mother to her because of you." Elly pointed. "Yes, you."

The woman wagged her head. Elly sneered. "Don't try to lie your way out of it. You know I'm right. The worst thing I've ever done is follow your example. But that's over. I'm going back and tell my daughter I love her, something you never said to me."

Elly's mother glared, still wagging her head. Elly took a deep breath and then another, and spat out her words.

"I don't need your damn money, old woman. I make all the money I need and more. I came here because I blamed myself all those years, wondering what awful thing I did to make you stop loving me. I came to see if there was an ounce of love for me still hiding somewhere in the back of your heart. Now I know it wasn't my fault. You *never* loved me. You didn't want children, and I just got in your way. There is no hiding place because you don't *have* a heart."

Elly turned and stepped toward the door. Her mother moved up behind her, and stopped. "You come here talking about love. You don't know anything about it. You don't even show respect for your own mother."

Elly whirled and pointed at her mother's face. "Respect? Let me tell you something I learned from my daughter. You don't deserve respect just because of your name or title. You earn it by the way you treat other people, or you don't get it."

Elly cocked her head and offered a mock smile. "You've never done a damn thing to deserve respect from anybody." She grinned big. "And I'll bet Daddy would agree with me."

Harold eased open the door, and angled his head toward the doorway. Elly turned, stared, and grinned at him. "Nice talking to you, too, old chap. I hope your butler job pays well." She stepped out, grabbed the handle, and yanked the door closed with a loud bang.

Elly laughed aloud while the tires of her rental car left ugly black marks on the designer driveway, knowing Harold and Mother would be watching through the window.

Sometimes, life was just plain fun.

Chapter Twenty-One

Elly took a week off work and stayed with Marty and Kasey the week of Kasey's sixteenth birthday. Marty bought steaks for the grill and set up a big tent in his yard. He'd told Kasey to invite all the friends she wanted.

Her friends were near her age and had their own tastes in music. That taste was not what they heard from the local cowboy dance band Marty hired. The band left early. Kasey's friends stayed and brought out their latest high-tech music downloads. No one danced. Marty shrugged. At least the September weather was perfect, so the kids wouldn't have to fix it.

Elly went into the house. Marty followed three minutes later. He had to talk to her, and guessed it would be awkward. After his first words, Elly stood straight, her hands on her hips, and frowned as she stared at Marty across the bedroom.

"You think *I'm* uptight? You're the one who's been distant all day … like you're lost in a cloud."

He took a deep breath. *Marty, you dumbass. Will you never learn how to start a conversation with a woman? Say something positive about her first.*

"Sorry, Elly. I was just saying that Kasey is—"

"You don't have to tell me how old my daughter is. Sixteen is a big deal, with driver's license and all that. She's growing up. Why can't you just be happy about that, Marty?"

He held his hand over his mouth as he sighed, then dropped his hand and looked at her. "I *am*, Elly. I am happy about it. I'm not concerned as much about her driving as I am about what may happen in the back seat, whether it's her car or someone else's."

"Okay, fine. I'll talk to her, okay?"

"You'll talk to her? It's not about a parent talking to their kids. You won't be there to talk when she's making out with her boyfriend." He opened his hand toward Elly. "You're a single woman with a teenage daughter. Why would she take advice from you?"

"Oh, and who made me that single mother, Marty? And it didn't happen in the backseat of a car." Three times, she stabbed a finger at the bed. "It was right here in your room." She extended her open hand toward him and smirked. "Kasey's father is an unmarried man who has probably banged more women than any man I ever met. So why the hell would she listen to you?"

"Okay. Sorry. I guess I deserved that."

Elly shrugged. "Besides, I don't think she has much interest in boys."

Marty lowered his voice. "I didn't think so either until today."

Elly's face grew puzzled. "What's that supposed to mean?"

"I started into the tent today. I thought nobody was in there, but Kasey and Woody stood near the back. There was some heavy kissing going on and he had one hand on her ... on her hip."

A tear popped into Elly's eye. "Oh, God. Really?"

Marty nodded. "They had their eyes closed, so I don't think they saw me. I backed out and called her. They both walked out with red faces." Marty walked around the bed and caught Elly's hand. "After the party, I'll tell her I want to make an appointment and get her on birth control. But I want her to know we're together on this."

Elly nodded. "I wasn't sixteen, I was twenty. I was on birth control then, and still am. It doesn't always work. But I guess it's the smartest thing we can do for her."

Marty smiled. "There's something else we should do before the kids start leaving."

Elly grinned. "Give her the gift?"

They headed for the storage building hand in hand. Marty opened the overhead door as Elly turned and called Kasey. Kasey glanced side to side, a look of suspicion on her face as she made a slow walk toward her mother. Her friends followed at a distance. Mother handed her a key and motioned toward the car inside.

"Happy Birthday, Kasey. Surprise!"

Kasey seldom cried. Today, she broke down, and her hands shook while she approached a new, red Mustang.

"Oh, Mom, is this really mine?"

Elly nodded. "Your dad and I are so proud of you, dear. You deserve it."

Marty stared as the two hugged. A lump grew in his throat and his eyes turned misty. He'd not seen the two of them do that in years.

Marty rose early the next morning, and said goodbye to Elly. She left without breakfast. Wanted to get home, care for the horses, and clean house. The next day, she'd be leaving for Tulsa.

Marty waited a half-hour, and made breakfast for Kasey and himself. After a few minutes of silence at the table, Kasey dropped her fork on the plate.

"Okay, Daddy, what's bothering you?"

Marty looked up. "What?"

"You're so obvious. You sit there picking at your food, nodding your head or shaking it, and you keep clearing your throat. So just say what you've got to say. Please."

Marty laughed. "You figure out people better than anyone I know. How the hell did you get that smart, girl? Don't you know you're only sixteen?"

"You're stalling. You want to talk more about last night's big pow-wow with you and Mom, about birth control. I told you I would take it."

"No, it's not that." He wiped a napkin across his face and looked at her. "Yesterday when you got your new car, you and your mom stood out there hugging and talking like close friends. If I'd known a new car could do that, I would've bought one for you when you turned two years old. But … I don't believe it was the car." He shrugged as he looked at her.

With a hint of a smile on her lips, her head wagged in slow motion. Her eyes aimed at the tablecloth.

Marty looked down, too. "I heard her say, *I love you, Kasey.*" He retrieved his napkin, wiped it across his eyes, and looked up at her. "That was the highlight of my day." He held his hands wide apart. "Oh, hell, who am I kidding? … of my whole *year*. I can't remember the last time I heard that, and I hope it's a sign of things about to change between you and her."

Kasey's eyes sparkled. "Me, too, Daddy. Me, too." She glanced at the wall clock and jumped up. "I gotta get to school." She grabbed her new car key off the counter. "After all, I'm driving myself. And I don't want to *speed*." She made a goofy face, and danced her way to her room.

Marty looked at the clock. She had lots of time. He went to the barn, fed the horses, and then stood in the driveway whispering, *Please, be careful, Kasey.* He waved goodbye as she drove off. His stomach twisted as he watched her drive away alone—her first time.

He went inside and kept busy with housework. Making the bed would be his last chore before going to work at the barn. On the bed, he found an envelope with a sticky note from Kasey. *Dad, please read this letter.*

He peeled off the note, exposing the postmark. Elly mailed the letter to Kasey more than a month ago. He stuck the envelope in his pocket. He would read the letter in the barn in case it revealed something to deal with. First, he'd make the bed. And he made the bed faster than ever before.

Horses munched hay and oats. The barn cat stalked a mouse, Marty sat on the Jack Daniels barrel and read.

Dear Kasey,

I'd like to tell you about a grandmother you've never met. Truth is, I barely met her myself, even though she's my mother. She left my father, and me, for another man and moved to California when I was thirteen. She never called, but we exchanged birthday cards for a few years. Then that stopped too.

Twice, when I was doing shows in California, I tried to find her, but the only address I ever had was a post office box. I even hung out at the post office one day for a couple of hours, hoping she'd show up. She never did.

The last time she replied to one of my messages was when I let her know I was pregnant, with you. About two weeks later, she sent back a note that said, "We all make mistakes." Something else happened between my mother and me just after your fourteenth birthday. I'll tell you about that when the time is right.

Kasey, I'm not asking for sympathy, and I'm not blaming my mother for the way I treated you. In fact, when I was your age, I told myself if I ever had a daughter, I would never treat her the way my mother treated me. My mom and I were never close, and if she ever hugged me, I can't remember it. It seems so crazy now thinking back on things. I've made a lot of the same mistakes she made.

I wanted us to be close, you and me, but I didn't know how, and I was afraid of being hurt. Now I know you're the one who hurts, and it's my fault, Baby, not yours. I am so sorry. Maybe I can't make it up to you, but I promise I'll be more like a real mother from now on. Even if I don't deserve it, I hope you can forgive me. I'll do everything I can to earn it.

I really do love you, Kasey.

Mom

Chapter Twenty-Two

On a perfect spring morning, Marty relaxed and drove home with his window down, his arm resting on the window frame of his new pickup as he hummed an easy tune. For six months, maybe longer, he'd been meeting a bunch of guys for Saturday morning breakfast at Saint James in Cimarron.

Located on the Santa Fe Trail, the old hotel, bar, and restaurant served as a holdover from the 1800's Wild West, and had a colorful history that rivaled hotels, saloons, and gambling halls in towns like Dodge City, Kansas and Tombstone, Arizona.

Cimarron's famous landmark once attracted celebrities like Buffalo Bill and Annie Oakley, along with well-known lawmen like Bat Masterson and Wyatt Earp. Wyatt and Morgan Earp rented rooms there with their wives as they made their move from Dodge City to Tombstone. The hotel also appealed to famous outlaws. According to legend, Jesse James stayed many times, always in room 14.

Now a peaceful hotel and popular restaurant, Saint James still offers customers a glimpse of the past while they stare at more than twenty bullet holes in the tin ceiling. The building is home to twenty-six murders.

Marty appreciated the building's history. The place fascinated lots of people, but he didn't go to see bullet holes. He went for a great breakfast and to spend time with friends, local ranchers, elk hunters, and out-of-town guests.

Those get-togethers relaxed him, and they also proved good for his business. Saint James customers, whether they were part of his group or not, often asked questions about horses. His knowledge and experience brought new customers to the M-R Bar. Life was good.

Now, he stopped at the mailbox before turning into his driveway, found one envelope and stuck it in his shirt pocket.

His phone rang.

"Mister Redman? Is this Marty Redman?"

"Yes. Who's calling please?"

"Mister Redman, this is Deputy Sean Vincent with the Taos County Sheriff's Department. Do you have a daughter named Kasey Redman?"

"Kasey? Yes. Yes, I do." His voice cracked. "Is she okay?"

"Mister Redman, your daughter was involved in a car accident. I don't know the extent of her injuries, but she is being transported to the hospital in Taos."

Marty wheezed. "Oh, God. Oh my God. What happened? Is she —"

I'm sorry, Mister Redman. I have no information about her condition. You'll have to check at the Taos hospital. Are you okay, sir? Do you need help? Do you need transportation to the hospital?"

"No, I'm on my way there."

Marty knew he should call Elly. He also knew he couldn't handle a phone call while taking forty-mile-per-hour curves at seventy. He'd wait until he could tell her about Kasey's condition. He shook his head to keep out the nagging thought of not knowing whether his darling daughter was still ...

An hour later, he left his truck at *Doctors Only* parking, raced into the hospital, and stopped at the first help-window. Marty paused and caught his breath. Tired eyes looked up from behind the glass. A woman slid the window open.

"May I help you?"

"I'm Marty Redman. My daughter, Kasey is here and I need to find out how she is. Right now, please."

She drawled, "I need to see a photo ID, please."

Marty gritted his teeth while he pulled his driver's license from his wallet and passed it to her. She closed the window, turned her chair, ambled to the back of the office, and placed the license on a copy machine. The copier buzzed when she pressed a button. She dug a handful of paper from a cabinet, and reloaded the machine.

Marty stuck his face down and spoke through a small hole in the window. "Ma'am, please hurry. My daughter's been in a car accident, and I need to know how she is."

His plea did not make the woman move faster. She made a copy of his license and slow-walked back to her chair. She sat, faced him, opened the window, and returned his license.

"What was the patient's name again?"

"Kasey Redman, Ma'am." He spelled her name. Seconds seemed like hours while the woman tapped a keyboard. She looked up from the monitor and nodded.

"Yes sir, we have a Kasey Redman in E-R."

Marty swung his head side to side, searching for a sign. He stuck his face back down to the window.

"The sign outside said Emergency Room. Where is it? How do I get there, please?"

"Sir, only doctors, nurses, and patients are allowed in E-R."

Heat rushed to Marty's face. He glanced at the woman's nametag. "Come on, Rosita. Tell me at least one thing about my daughter. The doctors have to know *something* by now."

Rosita's eyes moved back to the monitor, and she shook her head. "I'm sorry, Mister Redman. I can't tell you anything I don't know. I have no report at this time on your daughter from anyone in E-R."

"Don't you understand? I have to know something. If you can't help me, I'll find it on my own. I'm going in there, and I don't give a damn about your policies."

Rosita jerked the window closed and pressed a button on her desk phone. Five seconds later, a voice came through the speaker.

"Security."

"This is Rosita at the E-R desk. I need an officer here right away, please."

Marty glared at her. She shook her head, looked up, and spoke through the hole. "You left me no choice, Mister Redman."

Marty turned when he heard someone approaching fast behind him. A security guard stopped beside him. A police officer stopped on the other side of him. Rosita opened the window, and the officer bent down.

"What's the trouble, Rosita?"

She nodded at Marty. "Mister Redman threatened to bust into E-R after I told him he couldn't go in there."

Wearing a half-smile, the officer turned. "You're Marty Redman, the bull rider."

Marty nodded. "Retired." He shrugged and spread his hands. "Look, officer, I just want to get some information about my daughter. She was —"

The officer held up his hand. "I know. I'm officer Vincent, the one who notified you about your daughter's accident."

A lump swelled in Marty's throat and his eyes misted as he struggled to talk. "Look, I uh, I don't want trouble. But for God's sake, *someone* has to tell me something about her. Please. I don't even know if she's still, uh . . ." Tears rolled down his cheeks. He shook his head and looked away.

The officer placed a hand on Marty's shoulder. "I know it's tough, but if you'll wait here, I'll go see what I can find out. It may take a few minutes, but I'll come back as soon as I can." He leaned toward Rosita. "Would you buzz me in please?" He went around the corner and down a hallway. A buzzer sounded as Rosita pressed a button.

Marty paced, wiped his eyes, and checked his watch again and again. He made three trips to the drinking fountain, and said silent prayers nonstop. Ten minutes dragged by.

"Mister Redman?"

Marty whirled. Officer Vincent came down the hall toward him. A woman with a white jacket and stethoscope walked beside him. They stopped as Marty sprinted toward them. She nodded.

"I'm Doctor Shaw. Are you Kasey Redman's father?"

"Yes, Doctor. How's my daughter?"

"She has a concussion and a few cuts and bruises that appear to be minor. It may be —"

"Oh, thank God." A deep laugh escaped on its own as Marty held his palms together and looked up.

The doctor smiled and nodded. "We want to run some more tests just to be sure. But I'll tell her you're here."

"Oh, thank you so much. When can I see her?"

"We want to keep her overnight. You can see her as soon as she's moved to her room. Forty-five minutes to an hour."

Marty laughed again as the unbearable pain left his chest. He sat on a cushioned, bench-for-two in the empty waiting room, and pulled out his phone. Elly was out of town, and his cloudy mind could not recall where.

Her phone rang. He glanced at his watch. Almost noon. He left a message, struggling to sound calm and confident, even matter-of-fact, but was sure he failed.

"Mister Redman?" Rosita beckoned him back to the window as he looked up. When he reached her, she asked for Kasey's age.

Marty wasn't sure he liked the woman, but knew he had to get along with her. "She's seventeen."

"So, she's under eighteen?"

Marty wanted to make a smartass remark about seventeen being less than eighteen, but fought it off, and nodded. "She's seventeen."

Rosita pushed a clipboard through the window. "If you're Kasey Redman's father or legal guardian, I need you to fill out these papers, please, so we can get her admitted."

Marty carried the clipboard to the waiting room and took a deep breath as he sat on the bench. After twenty minutes of repetitious forms, aggravating questions, two signatures, initials and dates on every page, he took his autobiography to Rosita and pushed it through the window.

"Thank you, Mister Redman. How is your daughter?"

"Oh, uh … she's okay. A few bumps and bruises, but she's okay."

"I'm sorry about what I had to do earlier, but I had to follow procedure."

"You have children, Miss …?" He looked at the long last name on her badge.

She smiled. "Just call me *Rosy*. And yes, I have four children."

"Okay, just call me Marty. Now tell me what you would do if one of your young children … well … if you were in my spot a short while ago."

"I'da likely been worse than you. And probably in jail by now." Her eyes grew big and she shook her head.

****

Marty stood by Kasey's bed and talked to her. He wanted to hug her, but she had an I-V in the back of her hand, an oxygen tube fastened at her nose, and a concussion somewhere on her head. A hug would have to wait. When he first came in, she smiled and her eyes were wide, but she did not talk. As he turned to go, Elly called.

He found a chair in the empty Family Waiting Room down the hall, and tried to convince Elly that Kasey was okay and would likely be home tomorrow. But Elly would leave her truck, trailer, and horse at a nearby ranch, and catch the first flight home. He smiled at the end of the call. What a drastic change he'd seen in Elly in the past two years.

Marty went back to Kasey's room. Doctor Shaw came in behind him. She reviewed the information on her I-pad, and looked at Marty.

"Kasey needs additional tests and another scan. We should know a lot more within twenty-four hours."

Marty's face wrinkled. His mouth hung open. He wiped a small tear.

The doctor cupped his shoulder. "It's routine. We want to make sure we don't miss anything." She handed him her card and Marty gave her a card from the M-R Bar. She glanced at it, smiled, and left.

Kasey said, "Hi, Daddy," but she did not look at him. Marty's heart raced. "Hello, Kasey. I love you, dear." His eyes teared again as he watched her. Minutes passed. She stayed awake but did not respond.

Marty walked to Paco's Tacos across the street, wolfed down three tacos and a drink, and went back to the hospital. A minute in Kasey's room told him nothing had changed. He went back to his chair in the Family Waiting Room, looked around for something to read, and remembered the envelope in his pocket. He took a deep breath and began to relax. The envelope came from the DNA test lab.

On her fourteenth birthday, more than three years ago, Marty promised Kasey he would get the paternity test she asked for. She was proud of being so much like Marty, and excited to see how science could show the reason for that.

About six weeks ago, Marty kept his promise, and sent samples for Kasey and him to a testing facility. Without telling Kasey, he also sent the vial of blood that came from his father. Though it seemed impossible to Marty that so much time had flown by, he had kept the blood in his freezer for twenty-five years.

Before he returned the test kit sent to him by the lab, Marty sent the lab an email message to explain the situation about the blood. The experts there were quite confident the blood would be a good sample, but asked him to ship it in dry ice. He had, and now he looked forward to surprising Kasey, though he may have to wait a day or two because of her condition. Maybe the report would make her feel better.

****

Along with his twelve-year career as a professional bull rider, Marty knew he had many other things to be happy about and proud of. Kasey meant more to him than all other things combined. But today's news left him dumbfounded. Today, Marty walked out of the hospital in a daze, trying to find his truck.

Sidewalks, trees, cars, clouds, buildings ... everything around seemed pretentious, surreal, without purpose. He found his truck, stopped beside it, and lost his lunch on the parking lot.

Minutes ago, in the hospital, Marty pulled the envelope from his pocket, glanced over the top DNA report and shook his head. His name appeared under Child, and his father's name under Alleged Father. An alphanumeric list under those headings told him nothing. But below that stack of letters and numbers, the lab offered a conclusion.

The alleged father <u>is not excluded</u> as the biological father of the tested child. Based on tested analyses of the DNA loci listed the probability of paternity is 99.9998%

Marty read the conclusion, nodded, smiled, and read it again. Chances were extremely high that Walter J. Redman was Marty's true father. No surprise.

The next report showed the test results between Child, *Kasey Redman*, and Alleged Father, *Martin J. Redman.* Marty ignored the letters and numbers, and read the conclusion.

The alleged father <u>is excluded</u> as the biological father of the tested child. Based on tested analyses of the DNA loci listed the probability of paternity is 00.0002%

Marty talked aloud to himself. "What? Wait a minute." He read the conclusion again and then again. "That's crazy. What the hell is this?" He read the words once more, aloud. His breath grew ragged. His chest tightened. Tears clouded his vision.

With his eyes wide and tearing, Marty grabbed his chest, and read the report three times. But it refused to change. His heart hammered in his ears. His stomach knotted. His mouth hung open. He could not force his mind to focus on anything beyond the test results.

No, no, no. It just could not be. The child he loved before she was born, the infant who wore his last name when he first saw her. He missed her birth by an hour but never regretted spending eighteen thousand dollars for a one-hour flight trying to get here before she arrived.

The baby he fed and changed and rocked to sleep so many times, the darling girl who surprised him with her antics, the teenager he taught to drive, and tried so hard to discipline, the girl who disarmed him with a hug and a smile, who loved him and worshiped him as if he was the grandest person on earth.

The young lady he was so proud of, the precious child he loved more than life itself now needed him, depended on him more than ever as she lay in a hospital bed in the same building where he saw her on her first day of life more than seventeen years ago.

If any test could measure love, he knew every cell in his body would show how he felt about Kasey and how much she meant to him. She was his. Yet she was *not* his.

Conflict crammed his mind faster than Marty could think. He told himself the test must be wrong. Everybody makes mistakes. If I have it redone, will they want new samples? What do I tell Kasey? What if a new test shows the same result? What would Kasey think of her mother? Would it destroy that precious new bond between them? Cause lifelong heartaches?

Marty had never felt so confused, had never hurt as much as now.

Chapter Twenty-Three

Tires skidded on the gravel as Marty swerved his pickup to the side of the road and stomped the brake pedal. He gripped the top of the steering wheel, rested his forehead on his hands, and closed his eyes. His head wagged side to side while he tried to shake the nagging questions from his mind. He wanted to cry. Yet, he knew tears would not come. They may bring relief from the pain of sorrow, but not from the pain of anger. For too many years, he'd been played for a sucker. Marty's pain wanted revenge.

Minutes later, he walked out of the E-Z Pik with a bag of chips and a six-pack. He downed a beer in the parking lot, and stared at his phone while it rang. *What the hell could Elly want? A ride from the airport to the hospital?* He laughed. *Let her call Kasey's real father, whoever the hell that was.* His breath grew ragged. He sniffed, and felt a pain in his gut when he laughed.

He played her message. "Marty, I can't get a flight out till ten o'clock tonight. So, I'll take a cab from the airport to the hospital. Don't wait up for me. Get some rest. Call me if there's anything new about our daughter."

He glared at the phone. "*Our* daughter?" He opened another Corona and guzzled half of it before he brought the bottle down. His phone rang again, showing a number he didn't know.

"Hello."

"Mister Redman, this is Doctor Shaw. Are you still here at the hospital?"

"No, I left for a snack."

"I don't want to alarm you, but I think you should come back right away. Call me back at this number when you get here, and I'll tell you where to meet me."

"You're scaring me, Doctor. Is Kasey all right?"

"Yes, Mister Redman. Just get here as soon as you can, please, and I'll explain everything."

Marty threw all bottles, empty and full, into a dumpster, He kept the chips, and ate them as he drove onto the highway and headed for the hospital. Two minutes later, he left the road again and parked.

What the hell am I doing? The doctor calls, and I jump and run as if that girl was my own daughter. He choked on his thoughts as if he'd said the words aloud. He fought with the pain, anger, and confusion, and drove back onto the road.

At the hospital, Marty shook his head and stared at the doctor. "What? Obstetrician?" He shook his head again. "You've got the wrong patient. My daughter is Kasey Redman. She's seventeen. She just graduated from high school, and she's not—"

Doctor Shaw rested her hand on his shoulder. "We have the right patient, Mister Redman. Your daughter is in the delivery room. Did you not know she was pregnant?"

His unfocused eyes stared into nothing. "That's impossible. I thought she'd gained a few pounds lately, but she didn't look …" Now his eyes widened. Two or three months had passed since Kasey had been on a horse. Said she'd lost interest in riding.

"The sonogram didn't show anything abnormal, Mister Redman, but the baby is only about seven months along. Your daughter's car accident may have brought on the premature birth."

An hour later, Marty stood in the viewing area, his arms across his chest, and stared through the glass wall of the nursery. "Déjà vu," he muttered. The tiny creature in the bundle under the nametag, *Katy Redman,* looked just like the one here years ago under the nametag, *Kasey Redman.* But at little more than five pounds, this one was even smaller. His mind could not yet sort out the events of the day, did not yet think of the new arrival as part of the family.

After the delivery, Marty had walked beside the bed and talked to Kasey while the nurse wheeled her back to her room. His congratulations to the new mother felt awkward and out of place. Her shivers and radiant face showed her excitement. But when Marty asked for the father's name, she said only, "My baby's name is Katy."

***

Marty talked aloud to himself as he drove toward home. "Kasey's accident would've been enough to deal with for one day. But no. Then, I get the bombshell—she's not my daughter. Was that enough? No. Hell no. Next, I find out she's giving birth, and I didn't even know she was pregnant. How much more could a sane man take in a single day?" He shook his head and laughed. "And what makes me think I'm still sane?"

Before he left the hospital, he'd created a voice-text to send to Elly. "Uhm, Elly, something has happened that you need to know about. Kasey is okay, but she, uh, she was … I mean, uh. Oh, hell, Elly, you're a grandmother. If you want the details, call Doctor Shaw." He left the doctor's number, then said, "I'm dead in my tracks, and I'm going home."

An hour and twenty minutes on the road from Taos to Cimarron got Marty away from the hospital, but the trip could

173

not get his mind away from the day's events. He left the hospital without telling the doctor.

Why hadn't Elly called him? She must have read the text message by now. He glanced at his phone, and realized he forgot to hit the send button for the text. Marty felt bad, but only for a few seconds. *When she gets to the hospital, let her find out the same way I did.* For the first time, he wondered if Elly had known Kasey was pregnant. Not likely. If Kasey had told her, Kasey would have told him.

It didn't matter. Nothing mattered now except his home. He would tend to the horses, feed himself, shower, suck down a half-dozen beers … and crash. Tomorrow would have to be a better day.

Before Marty reached home, the setting sun highlighted a sign for the Cold Beer place in Dawson. What the hell. They make great pizza.

A half-hour later, Marty sat between two young women at his table, and they kept telling him how impressed they were he was a champion bull rider. Marty didn't know them, but he paid for the pizza and their drinks, and they became instant friends. He'd been through the routine a few dozen times in the past. And, as in the past, the more these ladies drank, the more friendly they became. The dark-haired one leaned against him.

"I'll bet you had a lot of dates in your career." She looked up at him and licked her lips. Marty smiled when she placed her hand on his thigh.

The red-haired friend leaned against him from the other side. "Ever had two dates at the same time?" She placed her hand on his other thigh.

Marty ordered more drinks.

****

Nearly awake, Marty grunted, dragged himself out of bed, and stumbled to the bathroom. After a deep breath and a groan, he held his eyelids open long enough to see the clock on the counter.

"Damn. Nine forty-five."

He brushed his teeth, washed his face, and stumbled out of the bedroom to make coffee, but stopped at the edge of the kitchen and covered his face. Two women sat at his kitchen table, and laughed when Marty came into view. His red face was the only part of him covered as he spun around.

While he grabbed his robe from the closet, the redhead stuck her face in the bedroom doorway and grinned.

"We're leaving."

Marty squinted. "What the hell happened?"

"Not a damn thing. We followed you home, and you conked out ten minutes after we walked in. You're one hell of a date, Marty. You didn't even wake up when we took off your clothes. *That* is why we're leaving."

Chapter Twenty-Four

Elly sat in Marty's living room trying to absorb all that had happened in the past month. Her daughter's car accident, and a new baby in the family. And the Sweetheart of the Rodeo was now a grandmother. It all seemed so unreal, too much to think about all at once.

Something else had happened, though she couldn't be sure what it was. Marty made a sudden change and took on a bad attitude. He stopped talking to her and seemed distant with Kasey and the baby. But that's how he was. He didn't talk much when something bothered him. Maybe he'd been overloaded with the horse business. She would wait till he wanted to talk.

Kasey brought the baby into the living room and sat in a chair across from her mother. The hospital released the tiny infant just yesterday. Elly stared at the baby and then at Kasey.

"I love the name *Katy*. Why did you pick that?"

"That's what Anna called me until I was old enough to correct her. But I liked the name. Besides, I wanted my baby's name to end with a *y* just like everybody in this family."

Elly grinned, and then grew serious. "I don't understand how you got pregnant, Kasey."

Kasey glared. "The same way every girl gets pregnant, Mother. The same way you did."

Elly's face grew warm as she leaned toward her. "You know what I mean, Kasey. You were on birth control. Or so I thought."

Kasey stared at the floor. "Sometimes I forgot to take my pill."

"I'm sorry, dear. I didn't mean to be critical." Elly looked at Katy and back up at Kasey. "You two look so much alike. You look just like your dad, and Katy looks just like you."

"She's only a month old, Mom. She could look a lot different in *another* month."

Elly shrugged. "Maybe a month from now, she'll look like *her* father instead of *yours*."

Kasey gave a loud sigh. Her head made a slow wag while she laid the baby on the sofa. Without looking at her mother, she went to her bedroom, and brought back a suitcase. A puzzle formed on Elly's face while her daughter sat in the chair and opened the suitcase on her lap. She searched through papers and pulled out an envelope. Kasey looked at the baby while she handed the envelope to her mother.

"What's this?" Elly looked at the envelope and then at Kasey.

Kasey took a deep breath. "It's what you've wanted to see since the day Katy was born."

Elly's face paled and her hand shook. "Her birth certificate?"

"What else?"

"Well, Kasey, she's my granddaughter. I just want to know who—"

"Just open it, Mom. Please." Kasey lowered her head and stared up at her mother.

Elly's wide eyes scanned the document. Tears formed, and she bit her bottom lip. She looked up and nodded. "Oh, Kasey, I'm so glad. Your dad and I both like Woody. Why didn't you tell us it was him right away?"

Kasey blew her nose, and then looked up, her own eyes now tearing. "It's because … he, uh … I mean, I wanted to tell him *first*. But it's too late *now*."

Elly's eyes widened as she stood and leaned toward her. "What? Kasey, are you serious? Woody doesn't know about the baby?"

Kasey turned away, stared at the floor and shook her head. Elly stepped closer, caught Kasey's arm and turned to face her. "How can that be, Kasey? When was the last time you saw him?"

Kasey shrugged. "A couple of months ago."

"A couple of months?" Elly backed away and folded her arms. "Didn't he know you were pregnant?"

"No, Mom, nobody knew. Katy was born almost two months early. I was only five months along the last time I saw him." She gave her mother a hard look. "It wasn't obvious, and it was nobody's business but mine."

Elly's forehead wrinkled. "Nobody's business? You don't think a father has the right to know about his own child?"

A noise on the deck drew their attention to the back door. Marty kicked off his boots and walked in. He looked at Elly and then at Kasey, but neither one spoke.

"Did I interrupt something?"

Elly glanced at Kasey. "You gonna tell him? Or should I?" Kasey gave a slight nod as she turned her palm toward her mother.

Her mother held up the birth certificate. "Kasey shared this a few minutes ago. Now we know who the baby's father is."

Marty spread his hands and looked at Kasey. "Well?"

Kasey did not look up. "Woody."

Elly stood with her hands on her hips. "But he doesn't know it yet."

Marty's head drew back as he stared at his daughter. "Kasey, are you sure about that? About Woody?"

Kasey's eyes teared as she turned toward him and spat out her words. "Oh Dad, how could you say that? Of course, I'm sure. He's the only one who *could* be." She sat again in the chair, covered her eyes and cried.

Marty rushed to the chair, knelt beside Kasey, and put his arm around her. "No, Kasey, no. That's not what I meant. Are you sure Woody doesn't *know*? That's what I—"

"He doesn't know because I didn't tell him." Kasey looked at her father, her face a mess of tears and smeared makeup. "I didn't tell anybody. How could I not be sure?"

Marty hugged her again and stood up, his voice now soft and slow. "Kasey, dear, did you see who left the barn right before I came in? Did you recognize that pickup?"

Kasey blew her nose again, and then looked at him and shook her head. "Sorry, I don't know what you mean. Mom and I were talking and—"

Marty held up his hand. "Kasey … it was Woody."

Her eyes grew big as she stood and stared. "Woody? Why did he come here?"

"He was here last week. I didn't have time to consider what he wanted. So, I told him to come back in a few days, and I'd let him know."

"Know what? What did he want?"

"He wants to work for me. Said he needs a job."

Kasey's tears were gone, her face still a fright. "He *was* working with the crew on the Cumbres and Toltec railroad. But it's not a year-round job."

Marty nodded. "Both times he was here, he asked about you. He heard about your accident. I told him you were fine, but … well, he seemed concerned. I think he really cares about you, Kasey."

Kasey shrugged but did not reply. After a minute of silence, Marty put his arm around her. "Isn't it time you and Woody talked about this?"

Kasey hugged Marty and stepped back. "I don't know what to do, Daddy. It seems everything happens at once."

Elly stood with her arms folded. "Are you saying Woody hasn't called you for two months?"

Kasey stared at the wall. "He called a few times, and left messages. But … I wasn't ready to talk to him."

"You have to talk to him, Kasey. You *have* to. You know that." She angled her head toward the baby and then back at Kasey. "And the sooner, the better."

Kasey looked at Marty. "Is he coming back?"

Marty smiled and nodded. "He starts his new job tomorrow."

Kasey looked at the baby, and back at Marty. "Everything seems so awkward I don't know what to say."

Elly took Kasey's arm, eased her around, and lifted her daughter's chin. "Want a suggestion?"

Kasey shrugged. "Okay."

"When Woody gets here tomorrow, just walk out to see him with the baby in your arms." Elly glanced at the baby and then back at Kasey. "Everything else will fall into place."

Chapter Twenty-Five

While the sun showed the first glimpse of its morning face, Marty opened the barn door. Before seven o'clock, he'd fed all horses and cleaned all water troughs, and figured he'd earned a break. He grabbed his Thermos bottle and heavy-duty Waffle House mug and parked himself on a bench outside the barn door in the shade. He'd have a cup or two, rest a bit, and wait for his new hire.

Today would be Woody's first day on the job, and he would be responsible for all the chores Marty had just completed. But Marty wanted him to see how everything should look when the job is done right.

He sipped his coffee and nodded, telling himself he made a good decision. He'd known Woody for a few years and trusted him. The young man was a year older than Kasey, and the two seemed drawn to each other from the day they met, during Kasey's first year in high school.

Marty had driven to the school that day to pick her up. He stood outside and leaned against the fender of his pickup to enjoy the weather. He thumbed through a copy of Rodeo World, and waited for the bell.

He glanced up as a middle-age couple left their car and walked toward the school. They slowed and looked at Marty, and then stopped. The gentleman touched the brim of his hat.

"Afternoon to you, sir." He stared at Marty. "You look familiar but I don't know where we met." He turned to the woman. "He look familiar to you, Rachel?" She grinned and nodded.

Marty held out his hand. "I don't know if we met before. If not, this is a good time. I'm Marty Redman."

The man laughed as they shook hands. "I'm Raymond Clark, and now I know why you look familiar. You're the bull rider." He nodded to the lady. "This is my wife, Rachel." He turned toward her. "Honey, this man's a world-champion bull rider."

Rachel stepped forward with her hand out. "We saw you ride bulls a few times. You're amazing."

"Nice to meet you. And thanks, but I retired from that a few years ago."

She peered over her glasses. "Do you still go to rodeos?"

The bell rang. Three seconds later, noisy students poured out of the school. Marty spoke louder. "I do. I'm here to pick up my daughter, and we're going to the rodeo in Taos to watch her mother perform."

Rachel's eyes bugged. "Does *she* ride bulls, too?"

Marty laughed as Kasey walked up beside him and hugged him. He introduced her to the Clarks, and then explained, "Kasey's mother rides a horse and carries a flag for the opening ceremony."

Kasey beamed. "She's the sweetheart of the rodeo. Her name is Elly Kelly."

The Clarks looked at each other, and Raymond squeezed Rachel's hand. Rachel looked at Marty. "Oh, my. We've seen her many times. She's a beautiful lady. And so is your daughter."

A dark-haired student came down the sidewalk, and stopped next to the Clarks. He looked at Marty. He looked at Kasey much longer. "Hi, I'm Woody Wagner." He angled his head at the Clarks, and offered a big smile. "This is my mom and dad."

Kasey gave him the *once over*. "I'm Kasey. I saw you in gym class, but I guess we never met."

Woody smiled. "Now we have."

Mister Clark looked at Marty, and clutched Woody's shoulder. "Every year, Rachel and I sponsor scouts from out of town for the big jamboree here in Cimarron. Woody was one of the boys we sponsored last year. He's so special to us, and … well, he didn't really have a home of his own. So … we adopted him."

Rachel jumped in. "And every year we have a party at our house for the three boys we sponsor. We're here to invite some of the students." She looked at Kasey. "It would be great if you could come."

Raymond held up his hand. "If it's okay with you, Mister Redman."

"My daughter is quite level-headed. I'll let her decide."

Kasey looked at Woody again. Her eyes grew large. "I'd like that."

Woody grinned. "Give me your number. I'll call you."

***

Marty drained his coffee mug, and nodded again. *That's how it all started between those two.*

A truck came up the barn driveway. Marty checked his watch. Woody was almost a half-hour early. The truck stopped, and the door slammed. Marty stood.

"Good morning, Mister Redman."

"Good morning, Mister Wagner." Woody stopped. His face went blank. Marty grinned. "Why don't we skip the formality, and just use first names?" Marty offered coffee. Woody refused and wanted to get started.

The two spent a half-hour in the barn while Marty insisted that a clean barn was a healthy barn, and explained the benefits of keeping saddles, tack, and tools organized, everything in its proper place.

With Woody behind him, Marty stepped toward the door, and then stopped. "Any more questions?"

"Uh, yeah." Woody looked down and then up at Marty. "How's Kasey?"

Marty stepped through the doorway and looked toward the house. "Why don't you ask *her*, Woody? She just stepped off the porch, and she's coming this way."

Marty waited by the barn, struck by the image of his daughter. She was only seventeen, yet she became the perfect picture of a mother whose radiant face said she loved what she held in her arms more than life itself.

Woody stepped toward Kasey but stopped and waited. As she came closer, he bent forward and stared at the bundle, his mouth open, his eyes huge. Kasey stopped, her eyes tearing while she unwrapped the blanket.

"Woody ... this is Katy. She's ... our baby."

Woody stared blank-faced. "Uh … our … She's … she's …" Woody shivered, placed his hand on Kasey's back, and escorted her to the bench by the barn door. He shook as he eased her down. He stood in front of her, and his eyes shifted from the baby to Kasey, and back again and again.

"Kasey, I … uh, I don't know what to say. I didn't know." He spun and looked at Marty. But Marty was walking away. Woody turned back to Kasey and spread his hands. "Why didn't you tell me?" He laid his hand on the blanket. "I love her. She's so sweet and beautiful." He moved his hand to Kasey's shoulder and looked in her eyes. "Just like you." He dug a bandanna from his pocket, wiped his eyes and his nose. Father, mother, and baby all cried together.

Grandpa Marty walked to the house, wiping tears from his cheeks. Elly left for home last night to get an early start for Tucson this morning. *She should have been here to see this, and to cry with everyone else.*

Chapter Twenty-Six

Near the end of the workday, Woody removed the bridle and saddle from the last horse he'd worked with. He brushed him down, and patted him on the neck. "You're one of my best students. I'm proud of you, Sam." Woody seemed unaware that anyone watched him. Marty watched from the back deck of the house.

The young man pulled an apple from his pocket and coaxed the horse into the barn. Marty walked to the barn, and took the saddle and bridle inside. He put them away and sat on the whiskey barrel in the corner.

Woody fed the horse. Then he sat on the floor, leaned against a post, and looked at Marty.

"What's up?"

Marty cleared his throat. "Well, Woody, you've been on the job for three months, and I put you on full-time after your first month, because I like your work. But now, there's something we need to talk about."

Woody sat up straight, and crossed his arms over his chest. His face paled. "Uh, is everything okay?"

Marty shook his head. "Not everything." He paused for a few seconds, and stared. "You work hard and learn fast. You're always pleasant. Easy to talk with, and you get along great with the horses. But there's one thing about your job I just don't like." He reached into his shirt pocket. and pulled out Woody's paycheck.

Woody's face paled, He lowered his head and looked up at Marty. "I like the job a lot, and I'm trying hard to learn everything. Am I doing something wrong?"

Marty nodded "Yeah. I don't know how to tell you this, but … you're working too cheap."

Woody cocked his head. "Too cheap, sir?"

"That's right. I hope you don't get mad, Woody, but I gotta give you a pay raise. I added it to this check."

Woody stared. His pale face wrinkled. "Uhmm, what?" He jumped up, turned up his palms, and spread his hands while he leaned forward. "What? You gotta … I mean, a pay raise?"

Marty scowled as he nodded. "Twenty percent."

"Really? I mean, uh, twenty percent?"

Marty's face became a giant grin. "You're not mad?"

Woody laughed. "Well, if I am, I'll get over it in a hurry." He wiped his hands on the front of his shirt, took the check, and stared at it.

"But … it comes with more responsibility, Woody. Sometimes, I need to be away for a couple of days. I'm gonna trust you to run the business while I'm gone."

"Thank you, Marty … sir. I'll do the best I can for you." Woody shook his head, looked at the check again, and laughed.

Marty rested his hands on the barrel rim and leaned forward. "Woody … I only know a bit about your background, but you impress me as someone who was brought up the right way. I know your parents adopted you a few years ago, so you must've made quite an impression."

Woody nodded. "They're terrific people. It's kind of crazy in a way. It all started with scouting."

"Scouting?"

"The Clarks only had one child, a son. He loved the Scouts, and he made Eagle Scout. But he died of some disease right after that." Woody shook his head. "I owe them so much."

Marty nodded.

Woody's head dropped. "My family lived in Denver, and my real father died in a motorcycle accident when I was two. Before I turned five, my mother was messed up on drugs, and couldn't take care of me. I lived in orphan homes after that."

"Sounds like you had a pretty rough life for a while. Do you still have contact with your birth mother?"

Woody's mouth tightened as he shook his head. "She died when I was nine." He shrugged. "I hadn't seen her for three years, so it didn't make much difference." His vision drifted across the barn, his eyes unfocused.

"What *did* make a difference was the Cub Scouts. A friend of mine from school got me interested, and I loved it. I never felt like I *belonged* to anything before that. My friend's parents had horses. They taught me to ride, and I've loved horses ever since."

Marty smiled and nodded. "And after Cub Scouts ... Boy Scouts?"

Woody sighed as he looked at Marty. "Yeah, and when I was fifteen, the Clarks sponsored three scouts for the summer program here in Cimarron. After that, I stayed at their home for three days. Before I left, they said they wanted to adopt me. By the next summer, it was all done."

Marty smiled big. "From Cub Scouts to Boy Scouts. From Boy Scouts to new parents."

Woody nodded. "One of the happiest days of my life was when I made Eagle Scout. Mom and Dad came when I got the award. Dad had a big grin for a half-hour, and Mom cried through the whole thing."

"Your parents are super people, Woody. I liked them the first time we met."

Woody leaned, and looked at Marty. "I guess you know Kasey and I took Katy to my house again last week, and my parents are nuts about her, too."

Marty made a slow nod. "Woody, I don't know how much Kasey told you, but Elly and I were really happy when we found out you're the baby's father."

The young man's face glowed. "Me, too, sir." He stared at the floor and fidgeted. "I really care about Kasey. She's so … uhm … she's just …" He lifted his head, and stood up straight. Tiny tears appeared. "I love her, Marty."

Marty stared at the floor, nodded and waited.

Woody took a deep breath and dabbed his eyes with his sleeve. Marty watched Woody's face grow intense while the young man poured out his heart.

"Sorry. I don't mean to get emotional, but I'm very much in love with your daughter. And I would do anything for her."

The rhythmic crunch of horses munching hay and oats created the only sound in the barn for a long minute while Marty waited. Woody seemed to be running his words through his mind before he spoke.

"Well, Kasey is … she's just the best girl I ever met. She's always kind and good to me. And she said she loves me, too. I was so happy when she told me about the baby. I love little Katy so much, I can't explain it." He shrugged. "Sorry."

"You never need to apologize for loving someone, Woody."

Woody nodded. "Truth is … I would've wanted Kasey and Katy even if I found out I was *not* the father."

Marty stared at Woody, and swallowed hard.

Chapter Twenty-Seven

Rodeo World sent Marty an offer, a total surprise. He jumped on it. Since he'd retired from bull riding, the leading rodeo magazine published a short story Marty sent about the ups and downs of his own career. They also bought his story about how rodeo barrelmen, sometimes dressed as clowns, are often the real heroes of the show.

Now, the publisher would pay expenses for Marty to visit various rodeo locations and interview the right people. He would write stories about rodeo athletes, their dreams, struggles, victories and heartaches.

That's what the editor said. Marty knew what he really meant. He wanted personal stories about how rodeo life often destroyed marriages, split up families, broke the hearts of girlfriends, and kept many athletes on the verge of bankruptcy. Marty also knew about the parade of women who chased rodeo athletes and often caused more headaches than they could relieve.

Marty considered that was reason enough to accept the offer, but the well-read mag would kick in another three grand for Marty's time and effort. He wanted to get away, and he'd waited long enough.

***

It seemed impossible. A year had gone by since Kasey's accident. Since Marty had learned she was not his own daughter, and since Elly's deceit ripped out his heart. He assumed the first year after that would be the toughest. But he'd been proving how tough he was for a long time. So, he'd made no life-changing decisions in the past year.

It also seemed impossible that he'd been a grandfather for a full year. Katy turned a year old yesterday. Kasey invited only a few guests to celebrate. Even fewer showed. Three babies, two mothers, and a babysitter. Elly was not one of those mothers. Her rodeo schedule did not allow her to attend the party. Woody took a break from his ranch duties and enjoyed cake and coffee, but didn't stay more than twenty minutes. Marty stuck around, yet felt out of place in his own home.

On that fateful Saturday a year ago, many things seemed to fall apart. But he had survived. He and Kasey were still close, and he felt a similar bond growing between baby Katy and him. His relationship with Elly was nothing more, or less, than confusing.

Marty also knew that sometimes things fall into place just the way they should. Almost a year ago, he hired Woody part-time to help with chores at the M-R Bar. The young man loved the job and learned fast. Now, Woody would take charge of the ranch while Marty was away. And now, Marty was away, on a plane headed toward Cody, Wyoming.

He'd been to rodeos in Wyoming many times since that night he walked out on the flight attendant who had a movie-star face and a body like the girls in a teenage boy's dream. Marty could still hear wine glasses shattering against the door of her room as she screamed at him. He humiliated that lady, and regretted it, but knew he had no choice at the time.

The events of that night happened more than eighteen years ago. He had not seen Roxanne since. But, like now, he remembered her every time he came here, when the last leg of his flight took off from Salt Lake City.

On that unforgettable flight years ago, Roxanne had been the only attendant on the Western Sky flight to Cody with only a dozen or so passengers aboard. Now he was on the same airline. But this plane was full, staffed with three flight attendants. He wanted to ask them if they knew Roxanne, but he wouldn't. If one of them knew her, what would he say? *Tell Roxanne that her favorite bull rider says hello*?

What would she be like now? Still gorgeous? Married? Three or four kids and a husband who takes her for granted? Marty smiled at his next thought. *Maybe she found a good husband but wore him out.*

He wondered how often she remembered *that night*, and would she know him if they met now? He'd changed too, probably more than he admitted to himself.

Marty needed a distraction, and thumbed through a rodeo magazine from the pocket in front of him. Yet, a bull rider on the back cover brought another memory to mind. Years ago, rodeo mags often featured Marty as the main attraction. That's how he met …

"Hello, Marty."

Marty jumped, and the magazine fell to the floor as he looked up. A woman stood in the aisle facing him, her arms across her chest, her eyes resting on Marty's face. They looked familiar but showed no emotion, no clue about her thoughts. Long dark hair hung down the sides of her face and covered the front of her shirt. She pushed back a long strand with her thumb, and Marty felt the blood drain from his face as he read the badge on her shirt. *Roxanne, Cabin Service Supervisor*

She smiled at the woman seated next to him. "Hello, I'm Roxanne. Are you Marty's wife?"

The lady shook her head. "Oh no. We just met on the plane."

Roxanne smiled. "Lucky girl." She dipped her head toward the lady's seat belt. "Better buckle up. It's time to land."

Roxanne caught up with Marty at baggage claim. He glanced down at her luggage cart. "I didn't expect to see you here."

Her eyes locked on his. "I like to surprise people." She looked away and then back. "And I'm good at it."

Marty jerked his head toward the luggage carousel and then back. "You are. First on the plane, and now here."

Her eyebrows arched. "Best I remember, you're pretty good at surprises, too."

He snatched his pull-cart suitcase off the carousel. His face grew warm as he turned back. "That was a long time ago." He unfolded the axle and wheels on his suitcase, extended the handle, and started away.

Roxanne pulled her cart alongside. "It *was* a long time ago, Marty. I forgive. But I can't forget."

Marty stopped, and she stopped beside him. "There's a story behind all that, Roxanne. If I had to do it over again, I'd have to do the same thing."

She dropped her head, grinned, and rolled her eyes up at him. "I'll buy you a drink if you'll tell me the story."

"You're on, but first I gotta get a car."

"I have two days off and a rent-a-car waiting in the parking lot."

Marty nodded. "I'll get mine later, Lead the way."

After a quick stop at the rental car counter, Roxanne and Marty rolled out of the parking lot in a new, red Jeep Cherokee.

****

Marty sipped his second margarita while he told Roxanne the story, all the way from Elly's eighth month of pregnancy, to his $18,000 trip in the Learjet. She sipped her drink between laughs.

"Oh my God. I had no idea a Learjet flight could cost that much." With a bright smile, she leaned toward him, her elbows on the small table, and took his hand as her penetrating eyes found his. "As for your question about me … yes, I've been married twice since I saw you last. I've been divorced now for almost three years." Her smile disappeared. "Truth is, I never learned how to stay true to just one man." She dropped her head and shrugged. "I guess that makes me a bad girl."

Marty grinned. "If you are, I must be a bad boy."

She looked up. "Why's that?"

"Stand up, and I'll tell you."

Her curious eyes never left his as she slid off the seat and stood with her hands on her hips.

His eyes scanned from her face to her knees and back up. "I've always liked bad girls."

With a cocked head and a half smile, she held her hand toward him. "Then what the hell are we doing here?"

Twenty minutes later, Roxanne turned into the motel parking lot. As soon as the car stopped, she pulled him toward her and gave him a long, open-mouth kiss. When she pulled her lips away from his, he breathed hard, smiled, and looked down at her lap.

196

"Got any of that sexy stuff like you wore before?"

She leaned her head toward the back of the car. "Maybe. I'll check my suitcase."

Marty sprang out, opened the hatch, and pulled out Roxanne's luggage cart. He stood it up beside him, picked up the bottle of wine he bought at the bar, and grabbed his own luggage.

Roxanne appeared beside him, clutched her luggage handle, and looked down at the phone hanging from his belt.

"This time, you have to turn that off or leave it in the car." She looked up at him again. "Otherwise, I'm not going in."

Marty smiled. "Fair enough." He threw the phone in the car, closed the hatch, and started for the check-in counter. Roxanne laughed and followed.

On the elevator, Marty stabbed button 4. With her back to the door, Roxanne wrapped her hands around his hips and pulled him tight against her. She caught his hand and rubbed it over her body. As the elevator slowed, she explored his body with her hands. The elevator stopped. As the door opened, she growled, "So, Cowboy, you ready for a wild ride?"

Marty's face turned a rosy red. Behind Roxanne, a wide-eyed young woman waited to get on the elevator. She stared at them, and shook her head as she held the door. Roxanne smirked, and grabbed a handful of Marty's backside as he walked out.

The young woman gasped and slapped her hand over her mouth.

With the wine in one hand and his luggage handle in the other, Marty headed down the hall. Roxanne grabbed her luggage, winked at the young woman, and laughed all the way to the room.

They drank wine, laughed, and talked, and Roxanne asked Marty if he'd ever been married. He told her his first marriage didn't last long. And, as for Elly, she'd put off the wedding for many years. Then, without meaning to, he told Roxanne about the DNA test. A tear came to his eye, and when he looked up, Roxanne, too, had tears. She caught his waist, pulled him to her, and smiled. "You still ride bulls?"

He shook his head. "I retired. Left the bull riding for the younger guys."

She squeezed his hand as she stepped back and looked at him. "I still have the painting."

Marty's eyes grew wide. "The painting?"

Her chin dropped. "You didn't forget the painting, did you?"

"No, but I haven't thought about it for years. I figured you would've burned it long ago."

"I almost did a couple of times, but that doesn't matter now. What matters is that you need something to make you feel a lot better." She closed the curtain, stepped to the door and slid the night latch into place. She turned to her suitcase on the bed, and lifted out lingerie. She used it to wipe the tear from his cheek, and shook the outfit in front of his face. He rubbed the garment between his fingers, and his breath grew heavy again as he gazed into her eyes.

"Put it on. Right now."

She reached into the suitcase, turned back with men's skimpy, see-through underwear, and held them out.

"These are for you." She nodded toward the bathroom. "Don't take too long. I'll be ready."

Two seconds later, Marty slammed the bathroom door behind him, threw off his hat and kicked off his boots. Getting out of his socks, shirt, pants, and briefs took far too long. But his heart beat in his throat while he watched himself in the mirror, and a strange, wicked sensuality crawled over him from his feet to his face as he pulled on the gift from Roxanne.

He gripped the doorknob and, with another quick look in the mirror, told himself all of this was justified. Elly had been unfaithful. He stood up straight and stuck out his chest, sensing his life was about to change as he stepped out of the bathroom.

Silence.

Marty shook his head while he stared at the bed. She'd moved her suitcase out of sight. "Roxanne?" A nervous laugh escaped his lungs as he glanced at the door. The night latch was open, and he heard someone in the hallway. He yanked open the door and yelled, "Roxanne."

Walking by, the young woman from the elevator snapped her head toward him. Her eyes bugged wide as she screamed and ran down the hall.

Marty ducked back and slammed the door. He turned and eased open the closet door. "Roxanne?"

He leaped back into the bathroom, jerked on his pants, and ran to the window. His face paled, his jaw dropped as he opened the curtain, and heard tires squealing. Marty watched a new, red Jeep Cherokee tear out of the parking lot.

Oh shit. I'll have to call a ...Oh damn, my phone's in that car.

Chapter Twenty-Eight

On the flight back to New Mexico, Marty sent text messages to Elly and then Kasey. *Hope all is well there. Everything is good here except I lost my phone. Got a new one, but don't have all my contact numbers. Guess I'll learn to cope. Stay well.*

Losing the numbers would be inconvenient for a while. What Roxanne could do with them, if she chose, could be more than inconvenient for a long time. But she got her revenge, so maybe he was safe. At the Albuquerque airport, he would rent a car, and go see Mom. He could always trust *her*.

***

On Yan's patio, Marty leaned in his chair beside her, squeezed her hand and told her about Kasey's accident and the new baby, now more than a year old.

Yan nodded as Marty talked. "I didn't know all the details," she said, "but I heard most of it right after it happened."

"I should have known. No such thing as a secret in the rodeo circuit."

Yan covered her mouth and belched. She drained the last drop from her bottle, took Marty's empty, and brought more beer from his cooler. She moved her chair to face him and sat down.

Marty knew she would soon bring up vacations or travel. Yan loved to travel but seldom had enough money. She left too much of it in the local casinos and gambled too much at racetracks and rodeos. Even so, she was a treasured friend. Later, he would take Yan out for a great dinner. She would say no. He would insist.

She interrupted his thoughts. "So, how's retirement?"

"Hah. I never worked so hard until I retired. But I love the horse business, and now I have help. So I can get away."

"So, you took a vacation."

"A working vacation." He told her about the offer from Rodeo World magazine, and how he spent six weeks traveling, interviewing, and writing.

"I'm jealous. I don't travel much now, but I always loved it because something unexpected happened on every trip. I'll bet you find the same thing." She snickered.

Marty's face glowed pink as he drew back his head, thinking he may have told her too much in the past. "Uh ... no. It's not like it used to be."

She laughed. "I've known you a long time, Marty, and I know how all the girls just wanted to jump in the sack with you. Some of them told me so. You don't have to tell me about it, but don't' tell me it never happens anymore."

He laughed. Color flooded his face again, and he shook his head while Yan nodded.

"You got hit-on this time, didn't you? While you were out traveling and doing interviews. I'd bet good money on it."

Marty took a long swallow and then a deep breath. "Well, maybe, but just once."

Yan didn't pry, but snickered again and stared at him. By the time Marty finished another beer, he'd told Yan about

Roxanne and how she ran out on him. He wagged his head. "I'm surprised you didn't hear about it already from somebody in rodeo."

Yan laughed, and then looked concerned. "Maybe you got lucky after all."

"Meaning?"

"You didn't cheat on Elly." She took his empty and brought more full bottles from the cooler. She stood in front of him, her face growing pink, and shook her head as she handed him his beer. "Sorry, Marty. I had no damn business saying that." She covered her face. "Just tell me to shut the hell up."

"Forget it, Yan. It's okay. We're still friends."

"That's what I want to be … your friend, not your mother."

Marty laughed. "I'll drink to that." They clinked bottles, and took a drink.

Yan leaned forward. "Speaking of *mothers*, how's your mom? You didn't come to Albuquerque without seeing her, did you?"

"I stayed at her place last night. At dinner, Mom said, *Did you know Yan lives here in Albuquerque now?* I don't know how she found out, but I pretended I didn't know. Truth is, I told Elly and Kasey I was coming down here to see Mom. But I really came to talk about something I can't discuss with anyone …" he looked into her eyes, "except you." He leaned his head. "Yeah, I know it's not fair. The only time I come around is when I need help."

She leaned toward him and took his hand. "That's what I'm here for. I love you, Marty ... as a friend."

"I know. You couldn't put up with me otherwise."

She grinned. "That's true. But you do the same for me. Besides, you brought the beer."

Marty nodded and tried to smile. Instead, he drew a long breath and let it go. His chest tightened as he told Yan about the paternity test.

Her face paled. She bit her bottom lip and her eyes grew misty as she leaned in her chair and hugged him.

"Oh, damn. That's a heartbreaker, Marty. A lot to handle." She stared at the patio floor and shook her head. "And I was giving *you* crap about messing around. I'm sorry."

"Let it go, Yan. It's all right."

A minute later, she looked up and stared at Marty. "Kasey's accident, a surprise baby, and the test results? All that happened in one day?"

Marty nodded. "In one afternoon. That Saturday started out great. But it sure went to hell in a hurry."

Yan rested her chin in her hand. "Kasey doesn't know about the test results?"

Marty shook his head. "I didn't bring it up, and she hasn't asked. Maybe her concussion blocked out everything in her memory about DNA tests."

"The test could be wrong, you know."

Marty nodded. "I thought of that. But if I get new samples and send them in, Kasey will be waiting for the results."

Yan leaned toward him. "So what? Maybe the new test will prove she's your daughter."

"Yeah, *maybe*. And if it doesn't?"

"Oh, my God, Marty. I didn't think about that. It would tell Kasey … well, she'd be --"

"I can't do that to her, Yan. It would break her heart. Maybe forever. And … she might never forgive her mother."

Yan stood, walked around the patio while she gazed into the sky. She came back, stopped, and leaned toward Marty. "What did *Elly* say about all this?"

"I didn't tell her. But since I got that report … it's like a solid brick wall between us."

"Yeah? Who built it?"

Marty's face wrinkled. "What?"

"The wall. Who built it?"

He glared at her. His voice rose. "It sure as hell wasn't me."

"You told me Kasey and Elly don't know about the test." Yan leaned toward him again and stared. "So, who laid the first brick in the wall?"

After a long swallow of beer, Marty took a deep breath and sighed. Yan copied him and said, "So what happens now?"

He shrugged. "Who knows?"

She turned, looked into the distance, and then turned back and looked in his eyes. "How do you *want* it to turn out?"

Marty stared blank-faced at her. "Honestly … I don't know."

"You two have been together a long time."

"Yeah … together, but … not always close."

She moved closer and leaned toward him again. "Do you love her, Marty?"

He shifted in his chair, took another long breath, and let it go while he shook his head.

"Yes, you do, Marty. Yes, you do. I can see it. Right now, you feel cheated. You're hurt and you want to strike back. But if you give in to that anger, you'll regret it for the rest of your life."

She stood with her arms across her chest and shook her head. "If there's anything I've learned in forty-two years of life, it's that the human brain cannot be trusted to make decisions about love. Never. It does not understand it. You have to let the heart be in charge of that." Yan waited in silence as if to let her last point sink in.

"Give it a while longer, Marty. When you look back at this a year from now, you'll see it all from a new angle. Then you can decide what's best."

"I have, Yan. It's already been a year."

"Then give it another. Some things take longer to work out." She sat again. Her eyes wandered into the distance as if the answers to life's mysteries waited in another dimension. Her next words came out an octave lower.

"Marty, what you shared with me could be damn hard to handle ... for anybody. But don't let it control your life. You are the same loving, caring father to Kasey you've always been, the same man today as you were before any of this happened. Everybody says Kasey's just like you, and they're right. If that's not caused by DNA, it must be for a much better reason. She loves you, worships you ... and everybody can see that, too. You, Marty Redman, are the best father she could hope to have, no matter what some scientific test tells you."

She leaned toward him. He nodded, but would not look into her eyes. She turned away, and again her eyes seemed to find answers from beyond.

"You told me how much Kasey always meant to you, how you took care of her when she was growing up. No father could love a child more than you love her. It's not about science, Marty. Love is not passed along in the genes. It grows and lives in the heart and soul. No test can steal it away. Only *you* can choose whether it lives or dies. You've lost nothing, because you're too good a man to ever let that love for Kasey disappear."

Yan's vision now seemed fixed on the cloudless sky just above the horizon. But she sat without talking, and breathed deeper, as if making room for deeper understanding.

Marty's own father had believed one could access a greater level of knowledge by opening the mind to sources beyond the physical world. Marty, too, believed. On his own, he'd had little success in making contact. But Yan was the best he'd ever seen.

"Excuse me. I'll be right back." She smiled and went into the house.

Marty rubbed his chin. Yan's words bothered him, and he searched for a way to disagree but did not find it.

She came out and stopped in front of him. "You hungry, Cowboy?"

"Yeah, I'll treat you to a big steak dinner, or anything you like. Whadaya say?"

"I say, I just stuck a giant frozen pizza in the oven. Will that work?"

Minutes later in the kitchen, Yan pulled scissors from a drawer to slice the pizza. Marty laughed and jumped back.

"Jeezo, I've never seen scissors that big. You could kill somebody with those."

A grin spread across Yan's face, and her eyes grew wide as she held up the scissors, snapped them closed, and growled, "Don't ever turn your back on me."

Marty laughed again. "I'll remember that."

They returned to the patio, and sat across from each other with the pizza on a small table between them. For twenty minutes, Yan and Marty laughed and talked while they ate and drank more beer. When a quiet moment crept in, Yan leaned forward and stared into Marty's eyes until he grew uncomfortable and shifted in his chair. She smiled.

"You know, Marty, I tell you things about me I'd *never* tell anyone else."

Marty nodded. "Same here, Yan. We have a rare trust in each other. I've never had a better friend."

"Me, neither. How did that happen?"

Marty shrugged. "Well, we got to know each other and—"

"So, it's not about DNA?" Yan showed a hint of a smile. Her eyes widened.

Marty frowned. "How *could* it be? You and I are not even …" He took a deep breath, turned away and stared up at slow-moving clouds.

Yan waited. When he turned back, she reached for his hand. "You should thank God for your daughter. That girl made you a better man than you would have ever been without her. And she should thank God for you." She waved her hand in front of his face. When he looked at her, she said, "DNA didn't cause any of that, and DNA can't take it away. Only *you* can." She leaned close and whispered. "If you did, she would lose the only daddy she's ever had. And you would lose the only darling daughter you've ever known." She looked away and then back, and raised her voice. "Is your pride worth that much? Will you sacrifice the best part of your life just to get even? C'mon, Champ, show me you're a better man than that."

Marty turned away again and looked up. Seconds later, with a slight smile and a blank face, he looked at her. "How the hell did you get so smart, Yan?"

She returned his light smile. "I don't know that I'm smart, but I read a lot and I pay attention to music that has real meaning. Good songwriters are the world's best authors. You remember, *Goodbye Ruby Tuesday*?"

"Rolling Stones?"

Yan nodded. Marty frowned. "I've heard that song a thousand times, but I don't remember anything that's—"

Yan waved her hand like a windshield wiper. "You've heard the song. You haven't *listened* to it." She took out her smartphone. "It's right here." She stabbed a few buttons, and the song began to play. She made the tune skip ahead. "The last verse is my favorite. Listen to the words."

Catch your dreams before they slip away.
Dying all the time.
Lose your dreams, and you will lose your mind.
Ain't life unkind?

Marty looked away, eyes unfocused, and nodded. "Heavy."

A minute of silence hung in the air as if the world had stopped turning. Marty looked at her.

"So, what now, Yan? Don't you know Kasey sees how awkward everything is between Elly and me? How can I pretend otherwise?"

"Don't pretend, Marty. Everyone will see right through it, especially Kasey."

Marty's shoulders dropped as his puzzled face lost color. He turned his head away. "So, there's nothing left. I can't fix it, can I?"

Yan left her chair and stood beside him. "Depends on what you're willing to give, my dear friend. That DNA report? Burn it, and don't tell anybody it ever existed."

"That won't fix anything between Elly and me."

She turned his chin toward her. "Look at me." His eyes drifted up and found hers. She leaned closer, her face almost touching his, and whispered. "Forgive her, Marty."

His eyes narrowed and his head drew back. Yan leaned closer. "Forgive Elly."

Now, Marty's eyes grew wide and turned away from her. In an easy side-to-side motion, his head said *no*.

Yan cupped Marty's shoulders and put her mouth to his ear. "Not for her, Marty," she whispered. "For you … and for Kasey. Let go of it before it destroys everything you love, everything you have, and everything you are." She pushed back, and looked into his eyes. "Look at me, Marty." His eyes found hers again. Her voice came soft and low.

"Bitterness comes with one hell of a price. That brick wall you were talking about? You don't have to knock it down with a bulldozer. Just take off one brick at a time, Marty. One brick at a time … and see how it feels."

Chapter Twenty-Nine

Marty watched the growing cloud of gray smoke while his truck neared Cimarron. A brush fire, he figured. But who would be dumb enough to burn brush on a day as dry and windy as this one? He had no time to get involved, and hoped someone had reported the fire.

Most of his own work would not get done today because Elly called last night.

It was unlike her to leave anything half done, but this time, she ordered hay and told the delivery man to stack it outside the barn. She'd move it inside after she cleaned the barn loft. But … something came up.

Like most days, she was out of town, but she said the fifty bales had to go in the barn before the deer, elk, and antelope ate it all. Marty doubted elk and antelope would venture into the barnyard to eat hay, but he didn't argue. Besides, Elly said *please*. So now, he headed toward Taos, knowing most of the day would be gone by the time he got back.

The cloud grew bigger and darker. Marty pulled off the road, called 911 and reported what he saw. Now he could get back on the highway to Taos. He *could* get back on the highway, but he took the first left turn and headed toward the smoke.

The air got heavier as he drove. He was getting closer to the fire. But Marty remembered only a few scattered homes along this road, each with a driveway that zig-zagged a quarter-mile or more through the woods before it reached the house. Finding the right driveway could be a challenge, and he hoped he would not find a burning home at the end of it. But by now, he could not imagine anything less.

When smoke seeped into the cab, he stopped and pulled his bandana, what cowboys often called a *wild rag*, up over his nose. Minutes later, he squinted to see the road while his truck creeped along. The heat became intense, and Marty knew the fire was close when the smoke began to clear at ground level.

He pulled down the wild rag, took the first driveway, and wound through the woods toward flames visible through scattered trees. But the drive made an abrupt left turn and took him in the wrong direction. Would it head back toward the fire? Or was he on the wrong driveway? Now convinced the fire was a burning home or barn, Marty knew the wrong decision could cost a life, but *not* deciding could cost more. He hit the brakes and turned around.

Back on the highway, he jerked his head side to side and stared back into another wooded tract where flames leaped high above the sparse forest. He searched for the next drive, and prayed he'd find the right one.

Another thought plagued him. This area had no fire hydrants, so the fire department would bring tank trucks that required a lot of room to turn around. Most driveways were narrow, with both sides lined by trees. If a driver brought one of those big tank trucks down the wrong driveway, he may have to go to the end of that driveway or drive in reverse all the way back to the highway.

Marty slapped himself to get rid of that worry. But his heart sank when he found the next drive. Mixed emotions clouded his mind at the sight of the familiar black mailbox with the large, white Z. He hoped this was another wrong turn. That box belonged to John and Jane Zachary, Zane's parents.

Marty whipped into the driveway and stomped the gas pedal, swinging the steering wheel back and forth to cope with the winding turns. The flames shot higher above the trees. The roar of the fire pained his ears. Sweat poured off his burning face and down the back of his neck while the heat grew more intense, and he said aloud, "Oh please, let it be only the barn."

At last, the driveway ran straight. The yard came into full view. Marty's gasp startled him, and he shivered. Horses screamed and ran back and forth in the corral, though the barn seemed unaffected by the fire. But the home Marty had visited so often, where he enjoyed laughs, good times, meals, and a true connection with real friends was now being swallowed by a monster of red and yellow flames. He knew nothing could now save that precious home, and he prayed again that no one got trapped inside.

A man carried a woman out the back door of the house. He eased her to the ground under a garden faucet, caught water in his hands and splashed it on her burning clothes. After a quick glance around, he turned and ran back into the house.

Marty's truck slid on the gravel as he stopped behind a black pickup truck parked a few hundred feet from the house. He jumped out, and ran toward the woman. But the heat sapped his energy, shortened his breath, and dragged him down like a hundred-pound weight on his back. He slowed to a hard walk, but his heart raced, sweat poured off his forehead into his eyes while the hot air burned his lungs. He pushed himself harder.

The man came through the back door again, carrying a man with burning clothes and hair. He lowered the victim to the ground next to the woman, and splashed water on the man while smoking pieces of the rescuer's own clothes fell around him. The rescuer turned back toward the house, took two steps, and collapsed.

Marty caught the stench of burning flesh and hair. He turned away, grabbed his stomach and took long breaths. But an image flashed through his mind and interrupted the nausea. Like many other local homes, the Zachary home had a fireplace fueled by a propane tank near the house. At the instant the image appeared, the ground shook beneath him.

The explosion shot flames into the sky above surrounding trees and blew a massive hole through the hovering cloud of smoke a thousand feet up, turning the cloud into a giant, ugly donut. And the deafening roar from that explosion drowned out the scream of sirens from the ambulance and firetrucks now approaching.

The sound of another boom made Marty gasp again, and a searing gush of heat blew his way when the barn became a giant flame. Horses darted back and forth at the opposite end of the corral, their ears flattened back, their eyes wide and wild as they screamed.

Three firemen jumped from a tank truck, unrolled hoses from the reel, and sped toward the house while the ambulance crew loaded the two fire victims into the ambulance. The crew went back for the rescuer, placed him on a gurney, and asked if anyone else was in the house.

"No." The man answered but did not move. Marty turned his head away while the crew carried the man past him. But he jerked back around when the man groaned, looked up from the stretcher and moaned, "Marty."

Shocked by the burned scalp and the puffy red and purple face with no eyebrows, Marty stared at the man but had no idea who it could be.

***

In Taos, Marty struggled again with hospital disinfectant. He stood near a hallway intersection where the busy hospital staff pushed beds and wheelchairs past him in all directions, with patients being admitted, or going to surgery, or exam rooms, or to their own rooms. The lucky ones were going home, and he guessed that some would never go home as he thought about burn victims.

He'd followed the ambulance here, hoping to get information about the Zacharys and the man who rescued them, whoever he might be. Marty shook his head and felt sick when the image of the man's face came back to mind. He wanted to find out who the man was but did not want to see him again.

A few steps away, a nurse glanced up at Marty again and again from her work station. He walked to the station and stopped in front of her.

"I need to get some information about patients, please."

She did not look up. "Try the front lobby, sir."

"The front lob—"

"Yes, sir. The front lobby." She did not look up, but pointed a pencil toward the hallway behind him. "Just give the clerk the patient's name."

He looked back as a bed rolled by behind him in the opposite direction of the pencil point, and heard the patient's loud whisper.

"Marty."

Marty turned, and sprang toward the bed. But the big man pushing it stepped between Marty and the patient, and pressed a switch on the wall. A set of doors opened. The man glanced back at Marty while he pushed the bed into the room.

"This is the burn unit. You are not allowed in."

The doors closed.

Marty turned back to the nurse at the work station. "Excuse me. I need to know that patient's name, the one who spoke to me just now. Can you—"

Without looking up, the woman stabbed her pencil at the hallway behind him. "See the clerk in the front lobby, sir. Just tell her the patient's name."

Marty gritted his teeth. "Thanks for listening." He hurried away to keep from telling that woman where she could put her pencil.

***

Marty spent two hours at Elly's to solve her hay problem. No elk or antelope when he arrived, but near her barn, his truck chased away seven deer feasting on the bales left outside. He regretted that he could not get there this morning like he planned.

He wagged his head at what remained of the hay. A large herd of something must have fed on it through the night. Of the fifty bales Elly bought, most were gone, or ripped apart and scattered. She would likely be home tomorrow, and would need to feed her horses.

In the barn, a card on the wall identified Elly's hay supplier. Marty ordered another fifty bales. Diego complained about having to deliver the hay within an hour, until Marty offered to pay extra. He and Diego stacked the fifty bales in the barn, and Marty tipped him an extra forty bucks.

Marty formed a habit of generous tipping a few years ago. He could afford it, and most people he tipped needed the money. Marty also found he often got better service. As Diego left the driveway, Marty saw the huge grin still on his face. He'd made a friend.

Before he left home this morning, Marty felt that driving to Elly's would be a big waste of time. But the small chore at her barn became a welcome relief that took his mind off other events, and this had been one hell of a long day. He climbed into his pickup to head home, and hoped he could relax.

Elly's barn made him think of the burning barn. Tomorrow he would contact the Colfax county sheriff and ask about taking the horses to the M-R Bar to care for them until everything was settled for the Zachary's. Now, instead of relaxing, Marty's mind would not let go of his afternoon at the hospital.

After his last bout with the pencil woman, Marty asked the clerk in the lobby about patients brought in from the fire in Cimarron. The clerk seemed kind and caring, but could find patients only by names.

The idea seemed crazy and risky. But Marty had to know, and he had few options. He found a local uniform shop, told the clerk he was on his way to a costume party. He needed a white smock, and whatever goes with it, to look like a doctor.

He changed clothes in the shop's restroom, drove back to the hospital, and parked in *Doctor's Only* parking. A flashback reminded him he parked here after Kasey's car accident a few years back. This time seemed more appropriate.

Marty walked through the hospital's back door, assuming his clothes would not attract attention. He remembered to leave his hat in the truck, but his first two steps told him what he forgot. In Taos, New Mexico, the sound of cowboy boots on a hospital's hard-surface floor may not draw attention to a cowboy. But a doctor …

He tried to tiptoe but found it impossible. The effort looked ridiculous, and captured the attention he tried to avoid. A man in a suit and tie walked toward him. Marty figured he was busted when the man spoke.

"Excuse me. Doctor?"

Marty stood tall and turned away, but the man came closer.

"Sir, are you a doctor?"

Marty kept walking as he tapped his left chest and turned his head toward the man. "I forgot my nametag. Just call me *Martin*."

The man nodded. "Okay … Doctor Martin, which way is the burn center, please?"

Doctor Martin smiled. "Come with me. I'm on my way there."

He had to get past the woman with the pencil. If she looked up and recognized him, he'd run for the nearest exit as fast as cowboy boots would allow.

As they approached the burn center, Marty moved to the other side of his visitor so he could put the man between him and the pencil woman. Doctor Marty whispered to the man. "Don't say anything to the woman at the nurse's station. She likes to give people a hard time." The man nodded, and did not look her way as they passed.

Marty pressed the wall switch. The doors opened. The man, who told Marty earlier he was not allowed in, was busy with a patient. The man glanced up but showed no concern. Marty turned away, and motioned for his visitor to follow him down a hallway. When they were out of sight of the man, Marty stopped.

"Okay, sir, who are you here to see?"

"John Zachary and his wife, Jane."

Marty's jaw dropped. "Are you family?"

As they shook hands, the man said, "I'm Albert Zachary. John's my brother. I just got here from Houston. I hope you can help me."

Doctor Martin glanced at his watch. "From Houston? That was a fast flight."

The man nodded. "Learjets are quick."

Doctor Martin understood. "Well … Mister Zachary, I believe your brother and his wife are here, but they are not my patients. I have another patient I need to see. Ask the man we saw when we first came in, and best of luck to you." Marty walked away, telling himself the man who rescued the Zachary's would be in surgery, or he'd be somewhere in here.

Minutes later, Marty spotted the same burned scalp and puffy red-and-purple face with no eyebrows, the sight that made him sick a few hours ago. He turned his head away. Though he sympathized with the patients, this whole burn center gave Marty the creeps, like a scene from a two-bit horror flick. Still, he had to talk to the man he came to see. He shivered and approached the bed.

Pings from across the room sounded like sonar signals from a submarine. Machines around him made weird noises like someone in pain breathing hard and slow. Marty stood in the cold, shivered, and waited. But the man's eyes did not open.

Marty took a deep breath. Maybe he could come back in a couple of days and find a way in here again, or ask the Cimarron fire department for victim ID's. He turned to go, but as he turned, John Zachary stopped beside him. After the greeting, Marty heard what he expected to hear. Zane's parents were in critical condition. Recovery, if it happened, could take a long time.

The man left, and Marty turned back to the bed. The patient's eyes opened.

"Marty."

Marty eyes widened. A feeling of dread and recognition coursed through him. He dropped his head, and shivered again while he stared at the floor. He could no longer look at the man.

The voice was clear but weak. "Marty … I saw the smoke … from the highway. I went there to … see if I could help." He breathed hard, looked away, and then back at Marty. "I know the Zachary's don't … like me, but …"

Marty forced himself to look up. "You did everything you could, my friend."

The patient's eyes turned away, and Marty spoke louder to force his voice over the growing lump in his throat.

"You saved their lives, Billy."

Chapter Thirty

Marty jerked the phone away from his ear and stared at the screen. The voicemail came just over an hour ago. His heart sank. *How did I miss it?* He tapped the speaker button and listened again. The message was slow and drawn out, and sounded more desperate than the first time he heard it.

"Marty ... help me ... please. Sorry ... I can't ..." A gasp followed the words.

"You can't *what*, Yan? Hear? Talk? Breathe?" He punched *Call Back* but heard only her outgoing message.

"Yan, this is Marty. Are you all right? Call me, please. Right now." Three minutes later, he called again. "Yan, this is Marty. Please call me. I'm worried, and I want to help you. Call me, please."

He dialed 911. "My name is Marty Redman. Can you connect me to 911 in Albuquerque? Hurry, please."

"Sorry, Sir. I have no way to connect you. Tell me your emergency, and I will try to contact Albuquerque."

"I got a call from a friend who needs help. Her name is Yanaha Yazzie, and—"

"Sorry, sir. Would you repeat that name and spell it for me, please?" Marty took a deep breath, said her name again and spelled it twice.

"Thank you, sir. Now I need her address and a contact number."

"Her phone number is on my contact list, but I don't know how to pull it up while I'm on the phone." Marty sighed. "Ma'am, my friend called more than an hour ago. She needs help right away, please."

"Shouldn't you have called me an hour ago, sir?"

"Oh, to hell with it." Marty disconnected, and called his mother. As her phone rang, he kept repeating, "Please, Mom, answer the phone." After four rings, the line switched to an answering machine. "Mom, this is Marty. Pick up, please."

"Hi, Son. Sorry, I'm making peach pies and—"

"Mom, please just listen. Yan needs help. Write this down, okay?" Seconds later, Mom uttered a nervous *okay*. Marty gave her Yan's phone number and a brief explanation. "She lives on Mountain Road near Old Town, but I don't know the house number. Call 911, please."

Mom promised to call Marty as soon as she talked to the 911 people. Marty breathed a bit easier, called Yan again but left no message. He changed his boots and hat, grabbed the travel bag he always kept ready to go, locked the house, and went. He had to find Yan.

Ten minutes after Marty jumped into his pickup, Mom called to say responders were on their way to Yan's house. Mom always kept her promises. Now he could call Kasey and Elly.

Kasey loved her part-time job at a local childcare center, and Katy was always with her. But she insisted on keeping up with everything around her. Marty called her first. The news upset Kasey, and she had lots of questions. But Marty kept it short to concentrate on his driving. Kasey and Yan met only once, when Yan came to the M-R Bar to see about horses for barrel racing.

The connection was instant. Yan and Kasey got along like old friends and talked nonstop for more than an hour. When Marty called Elly, she thanked him for calling, wished Yan the best, and told him to drive carefully.

Driving the speed limit from Cimarron to Albuquerque took three hours. At sunset, two hours and thirty-five minutes after Marty left his driveway, he turned his pickup onto Mountain Road near Old Town. Since emergency crews responded more than two hours ago, Marty doubted he would find Yan at home. But he had to know.

A minute after he turned onto her street, his heart caught in his throat. Trucks and squad cars with flashing white and blue lights blocked a traffic lane a half-mile ahead. Marty prayed it wasn't connected with Yan's house as he inched along in the traffic. Five long minutes later, flashing lights from vehicles scattered across Yan's front yard, turned night into day.

"Oh, damn." Marty's mouth went dry.

He left his truck on the side of the road, and ran toward the house. His heart pounded harder while he drew closer to a small crowd who stood behind the black-and-yellow tape that surrounded the yard. Small tears formed when he read the tape. CRIME SCENE. DO NOT CROSS.

He stood on his toes, and peered over the crowd. Officers and emergency personnel traveled in and out of the house with flashlights, measuring tapes, plastic bags, and cameras. As the sun sank below the horizon, camera flashes inside the home flickered on the windows like lightning bolts. Outside, police radios squawked from various vehicles, officers talked and pointed, and a man on the porch swept up glass from a broken window.

Marty spoke loudly. "The woman who lives here is a close friend of mine," People in the crowd turned to look at him. He spread his hands. "I gotta find out what happened." A few mumbles told him no one here knew more than he did, but they made room for him to move to the front.

Next to Marty, a tall man glanced at his watch. "I've been here almost two hours. They took one person to the hospital in an ambulance. Another ambulance came, and then *he* showed up." The tall man pointed at a bald man with glasses who held the door while two others brought out a gurney. The two began a slow walk toward the ambulance.

Marty's heart caught in his throat at the sight of the gurney with a human form covered from head to toe. He grabbed the black-and-yellow tape, and stepped over it. When his boots hit the ground in front of the tape, an officer near the door spun around.

Eyes glared from the officer's stone face. He shoved his open hand toward the intruder. "Stop right there."

Marty stopped. "Excuse me, sir, I—"

"Get back on the other side of the tape." Stone Face yanked a nightstick from his duty belt, pointed it at Marty, and jerked his head toward the ambulance. "Unless you wanna be the next one on the gurney."

The crowd groaned and mumbled. Marty's head wagged as he threw up his hands and backed away.

The man who had held the door, followed the gurney, but stopped at a black sedan in the driveway. A squad car's flashing lights reflected off the bald head as the man opened the car door, lettered *Bernalillo County Coroner*.

Back on the other side of the tape, Marty wiped a tear from his cheek, and his voice choked as he turned toward the officer. "I just want to know about my friend."

The man at the black sedan waved at Marty. "Who's your friend?"

"Yanaha Yazzie … the young lady who lives here." He wiped another tear as the man motioned him forward. Marty stepped over the tape again, stopped and looked at the officer. The officer put away his nightstick and nodded.

Marty brought out his ID to satisfy the coroner and then played the message on his phone while he told the man how worried he was about Yan. The man angled his head toward the phone.

"The police may need those messages. Can you stop at the local station, and share that?"

"I will. Now please tell me that body on the gurney was not her."

"We're investigating. I'm not allowed to identify anyone at this time. I *can* tell you …" he nodded toward the ambulance as it eased out of the driveway, "that's a male on the gurney."

Marty sucked in a deep breath and let it go. "Was my friend in the house?"

The man shrugged and motioned toward the officer Marty dealt with earlier. The officer shook his head. "According to the report I read, the first responders found only one female in the house, and the first ambulance took her to Albuquerque General Hospital." He glanced at his watch. "About two hours ago. That was before I arrived. Sorry, I don't know anything about her condition."

Marty thanked both men, and hurried toward his truck. At the street, a reporter with a camera hanging on his neck, snapped pictures, and then jumped in front of Marty with a microphone.

"Did the coroner tell you who's on that gurney? Can you share some—"

Marty closed his hand over the microphone. "Not now. Leave me alone." He'd dealt with dozens of reporters during his career. Most were courteous and professional. Some were pushy and demanding, like this one. He sidestepped the reporter, but the man grabbed Marty's shoulder.

"Can you give me just one minute, Mister?"

Marty spun, glared, and poked his finger at the man's nose. "In one minute, I can knock you flat on your ass. Maybe you can interview the ambulance driver on your way to the hospital." The reporter's eyes went wide, his mouth hung open. He backed away.

Marty reached his truck, and glanced back. The reporter was flipping him off.

Chapter Thirty-One

Living in Cimarron had made him forget the irritation of stop-and-go traffic. But Marty remembered how to get to Albuquerque General, where he spent a couple of days following a bull wreck several years back. Yan came to see him there and brought a gift. That pewter bull still occupied a prime spot on Marty's bedroom dresser, a reminder of how thoughtful and caring she could be. Now, Marty's stomach churned. She was in that same hospital and he had no clue about her condition.

An hour later, he tried to rest in a waiting room near the emergency entrance. But the room reminded him of the day at the hospital in Taos when he waited and prayed to hear that his daughter was alive. He barely escaped arrest before anyone told him anything about her. This time, patient information could be a bigger challenge. Marty was not family, and got nowhere with Yan's hard-nosed doctor until the man saw Yan's messages on Marty's phone.

Yan was in stable condition in ICU, after surgery to repair a stab wound. She could not have visitors before the doctor made his rounds the next morning. Somewhat relieved, Marty gave in to exhaustion, settled back on a cushioned chair, and closed his eyes. A sudden commotion near ER brought him awake.

A man on a gurney moaned and yelled as EMTs wheeled him in. A stout hospital worker entered information on a keypad as she approached and asked the patient's name.

An EMT nodded toward the gurney. "Arty Covic."

Marty sat up straight, covered his mouth, and tried to not laugh aloud. He failed.

The stout lady shook her head and frowned at Marty. "You know this man?"

Marty stood, shrugged, and tried to hide his grin. "We met."

Fists pressed to her sides, the woman leaned toward Marty. Her glare convinced him she could stare down a giant Rottweiler. Her bottom lip distorted.

"I see nothing amusing about this patient's injury. You will excuse us." She jerked her head toward the exit.

Marty nodded and backed toward the door. He resisted an urge to flip off the man on the gurney, just to even the score. But Marty could not avoid laughing again as he backed through the exit. People inside stared with their mouths open.

He was sure someone punched the reporter he encountered earlier. Bloody bandages hid the patient's face, but Marty remembered the nametag on the man's shirt from a short while ago. *Arty* was too much like *Marty* to forget.

***

Next morning, Marty enjoyed breakfast in the restaurant of the Best Western Hotel in Albuquerque where he'd spent the night. He called Mom last night after he checked in, knowing she would ask him why he didn't spend the night at her place.

"Well, Mom, that would be nice, but Yan is in critical condition, and I'm a lot closer here in case I get a call from the hospital."

It sounded phony, but it was the best he could do. At her house, Mom would fuss over him, and make his favorite breakfast every morning. She would try too hard and do too much. He would not be comfortable there, so he was here.

From the time he woke up this morning, Marty had been eager to see Yan. Yet, he fidgeted, and his stomach seemed to disagree about the visit. He stopped to fuel up his pickup, and stopped twice again to look around on the way to the hospital.

After two hours in a waiting room, an ICU tech allowed him in, but she said he could take nothing in with him. He shrugged and gave her the vase of flowers he bought for Yan on his way there. "These are for you."

She pointed to a bed, "You have five minutes." Marty frowned at her, checked his watch, and shook his head as he entered a room that appeared much larger from the inside.

He approached the bed, glimpsed at the patient, and looked around. No one in the room looked like Yan. He glanced back at the ICU tech. She pointed again at the bed, nodded, and mouthed, *That's her*.

After a deep breath Marty forced himself to look at the patient, at the long, black hair pulled up and tied above her head, a swollen black eye, bruised chin, and large scratch on the side of her face. His chest grew tight as her eyes opened, aimed at the ceiling, unfocused.

"Oh God, Yan, I'm so ..." He choked back the words. His knees grew weak while he stood by the bed and held back his tears. She might turn to look at him if he cried, though she seemed unaware of anything around. The eyes closed again without looking his way.

Seconds dragged by like long minutes while he shivered in the cold room and waited by the bed for her to open her eyes again. The tension exhausted him. Marty glanced at his watch once more and walked out. He'd been in the room only three minutes.

He spread his palms and smiled an apology at the tech as she looked up from her workstation. She held up her hand, stood, and took the flowers to him.

"These are beautiful. Take them home and bring them back tomorrow. She'll look better then, and maybe she'll be out of ICU."

Marty shook his head. His hands hung at his side until she pushed the vase against his chest and nodded. "Your friend in there needs these more than I do."

On the following morning, Marty sipped his coffee in the same restaurant and told himself he had to see Yan again today. He picked up his phone to find out if Yan was out of ICU and then changed his mind. He would go back regardless. He had to see her again, if only for another three minutes.

Marty offered a big smile, happy to see the same tech at the ICU desk. She stood and returned the smile.

"Good morning, sir."

He smiled back and held up the flowers. "Hi, I'm here to see—"

She shook her head. "You're in the wrong place."

"Wrong place? But I was here—"

She smiled big again and pointed at the ceiling. "Two floors up. Room 307."

Marty's mouth dropped open. He dipped his head toward her. "You mean she's out of …"

She nodded. "Six o'clock this morning."

He glanced at her nametag, then looked up. "Oh, God. I could kiss you, Elyse."

She covered her grin and shook her head. "Better not."

Five minutes later, Marty stood next to Yan's bed, glad to see much of the swelling had gone from her face, but troubled she looked pale and weak, until she opened her eyes, looked at him and smiled.

"Mister Bull Rider. What brings you here?"

Marty tried to be positive, but something he depended on was not there. Yan had always been a high-energy girl with a lilt in her voice like a happy, fun-filled song. In a crowd, she absorbed attention. Today that energy, that spark, was absent. The *real* Yan was missing. He leaned and kissed her forehead.

"You called a couple days ago and said you needed help." He smiled and gave her hand a gentle squeeze. "Sorry I'm late."

She sniffed the flowers when he held them near her face. When he set them on the table by her bed, her eyes grew puzzled. "What happened to me, Marty?"

Marty straightened and stared. His chin dropped. "The doctor said you, uh … you got stabbed."

She looked down. "Same story he told me." She looked up again. "But why would somebody do that? I don't remember anything about it."

Marty shrugged. "Maybe it's better that way." He dug a small package from his pocket, and held it out. "Hey, I brought you something."

When she struggled to close her hand around the crudely-wrapped gift, he unwrapped it, and held out a miniature, hand-carved wooden saddle. Her face lit up as she touched it.

"That's beautiful, Marty. Where did you find it?"

"An older man stops by my ranch every month or so. I think he just wants to talk, but he carves saddles, hats, horses, all kinds of western stuff to sell. Barrel racers spend a lot of time in a saddle, so I thought you'd like this."

He could not recall why the saddle carving had been in the glovebox of his pickup for weeks, but when he fumbled across it this morning, he knew it would make a good gift for Yan.

"You're right, Marty. I really do like it. Thanks. You're so sweet."

He placed the saddle on the table next to her and looked down at the bed, imagining the nasty stab wound in her side, or wherever it was.

"Yan, I'm so glad you're doing better." He closed his fist and tapped his chest. "There's a special place in my heart for you, and I worried about—"

A soft snore made him look at her face. Yan was asleep.

Chapter Thirty-Two

Feeling guilty, Marty spent last night at Mom's house. She did everything he expected, and more. In spite of it, he enjoyed her breakfast of pancakes, eggs, bacon, and hash browns. And coffee that would slap you awake, along with one of her homemade, fried peach pies. She knew they were his favorite.

Now, at the hospital for the third day in a row, he shook his head as he jabbed the elevator button. Maybe on his way to the third floor he could figure out how to tell Yan he has to get back home, and may not see her again for several days.

"How ya doin,' Yan?" Marty tapped on the open door and walked in. She did not reply, and her eyes closed as he approached. He sat in the guest chair near her bed, tempted to take a nap while he waited. Instead, he picked up the folded newspaper on her table and glanced at the front page.

Man Dies, Woman Wounded in Mountain Road Break-in

According to police reports, in a recent break-in that may have been an attempted robbery, an intruder forced open the back door of a home on Mountain Road while the owner was at home. An apparent knife attack followed.

Police say the homeowner, a 42-year-old woman, was admitted to the hospital with what appeared to be a stab wound. Investigators have not yet determined whether the incident was domestic violence, or if the woman had been sexually assaulted.

The report also shows that a 57-year-old man identified as James D. (Butch) Pershing was found at the scene of the crime. Authorities have not determined whether Pershing was the perpetrator or a guest in the home, but say the man's pants had been cut off with a sharp instrument. Bernalillo county coroner pronounced Pershing dead at the scene. An autopsy showed Pershing died from loss of blood caused by wounds to the groin area.

Marty's stomach churned. He stood and shivered, stared at tear stains on the newspaper, and assumed they belonged to Yan. He slapped the paper back on the table with a loud splat.

Yan looked up. "Well, now you know, Cowboy."

Marty's face wrinkled. "Damn, Yan, what a nightmare."

"Yes, it still is." She looked at the paper on the table. You recognize the name of the sleaze ball that attacked me?"

Color drained from Marty's face as he stared at her. "Oh hell, I read it but it didn't register. Pershing? Isn't that—"

"Yeah, the one I told you about. The useless father of my daughter." Her eyes stared at the ceiling. "I was at home, just doing stuff on my computer. The doorbell rang, and I went to the front door to see who was there. By then, he was at the back door, and he kicked it open. I froze, and by the time I turned around, he was running toward me. He grabbed my throat and started laughing and screaming, *I got you now, bitch.*" She stopped talking and inhaled heavy breaths while tiny tears appeared.

Marty leaned over the bed and shook his head. "Yan, you don't have to talk. You don't have to tell me anything."

Her gaze did not change. "Yes, I do, Marty. I have to tell *somebody*, and I don't want to say this to anybody else."

He pulled tissues from the box on her table, kept one for himself, and gave her the rest. He sat again in the chair.

She took another heavy breath. "I couldn't breathe, and I felt like I was gonna pass out. Then he threw me down on the living room floor and began ripping at my clothes. After he got what he wanted, he went into the bathroom. I stayed still for a minute. Then I got up and tiptoed to the kitchen. He must've heard me because he came out of the bathroom, running toward me with a knife. I grabbed my big scissors from the drawer and, when I turned around, he stabbed me."

Marty covered his face and groaned. "Oh, God, Yan, I—"

"It hurt really bad, Marty, a burning pain, and I thought I was gonna die right then. When he pulled the knife out of me, I figured he was gonna do it again. It was weird, and everything seemed to happen in slow motion. I had never been that scared or that mad in my entire life."

Marty wiped his eyes and looked at her again. She paused, and a slight smile formed on her lips as her eyes glared at the ceiling.

"So, I stabbed him right in the crotch, and my scissors were a lot bigger than his knife. He dropped the knife and grabbed his crotch with both hands, and fell backwards on the floor. He screamed, and I laughed while I cut off the top of his pants. He tried to cover his crotch, till I cut off his finger. He grabbed my left arm but he let go when I poked the scissors in his eyes. The back of his head hit the floor hard, and he covered his eyes and screamed again."

Marty watched Yan while she stared at the ceiling. Her face relaxed with an easy grin. Then the face grew hard and fierce. The grin turned evil. The beautiful dark eyes became those of a cobra, wicked and vicious, while she spoke again.

"I cut them off, Marty. I turned that ugly, filthy bastard from a bull to a steer. And I laughed the whole time while he screamed. I left him when he started throwing up."

Marty groaned and shivered as he remembered the big scissors, when he and Yan shared a pizza at her house. Now, he stared at her as she turned her head toward him and said, "That's the last thing I remember."

A nurse with *Stephanie* on her nametag entered and greeted Yan. "How we doing today?"

Yan smiled. "A lot better."

Stephanie performed the routine checks, and asked the patient if she needed anything.

Yan rolled her eyes at Marty. "I need more friends like him. But I guess there's only one."

Stephanie laughed and left.

Still shaking, Marty eased from the chair, pulled a phone from his pocket and placed it on the table. He walked to the end of Yan's bed and faced her, noticing her face now had more color. He jerked his head toward the table.

"I brought you a new phone. It's on my account, and my contact number's on there. If you need to call—"

"Why? Where's my old one?" She looked at the table.

"I stopped at the police station yesterday after I left here. They wouldn't tell me much, but they have your phone. For evidence, I guess."

She raised her hand and brushed aside his remark. "My smartphone? Evidence of what?"

"Do you remember calling me?" Marty brought out his phone and played the message she sent to him on the day of the crime.

She stared into nothingness. "Sorry, I don't remember any of that."

"Yesterday, you couldn't remember anything. Today, it seems you remember just about everything."

"I'm not sure I got all of it right, Marty. But I read that …" she rolled her eyes at the paper "and in a couple of hours, most of it came back to me."

"Did your nurse bring that in?"

"No. Some guy brought it in after you left yesterday and wanted to ask a lot of questions. I didn't want to talk to him, and told him to leave. He dropped that paper on the table and left. I read it this morning."

"Did he tell you his name?"

"I don't think so. He looked like he'd been in a fight. Had a big bandage on his nose."

Marty picked up the paper and found the byline.

Artie Covic.

Chapter Thirty-Three

Woody glanced up from the saddle tree as the barn door opened. He smiled big. "Kasey and Katy, my two favorite girls. What do you want to see in the barn?"

Katy stopped and rested her hands on her hips. "Daddy, we want to see *you*."

"Well, now, that's a very special reason." He hung his apron on a bull-horn hanger. "Do I get a hug?"

She ran to him. He picked her up. They hugged, and then he drew back his head and looked in her eyes. "You know what would be really special? If I could get a big hug from your mommy, too."

Katy wiggled, and Woody let her down. She grabbed her mother's hand and pulled her toward her daddy.

Kasey laughed, gave him a big hug, and stepped back. "Woody, you're such a great dad." Tiny tears came. "It's another reason I love you so much."

It was Woody's turn for tiny tears. "You and Katy are my reason for wanting to be a great dad. I love you both so very much."

Kasey smiled big as she wiped her eyes. "Okay but I have to break away from the melancholy stuff." She took a deep breath and dipped her head toward the saddle in progress. "I just love the smell of new leather." She took another deep breath. "Looks like it's coming along."

"Yeah. I guess I told you this one's for your dad. Hope I can finish it on time, so I can give it to him when he gets home."

"Woody, you amaze me sometimes. Have you ever found anything you *can't* do?"

He laughed and nodded. "A lot of stuff. But I think I can *learn* to do anything I want. Although … I couldn't have done this without your dad."

Kasey shrugged. "He didn't teach you that. You took all those saddle-making classes."

Woody nodded. "They were expensive, and your dad paid for everything, including my room while I was there at the school." He angled his head toward the half-done saddle. "This is the least I can do to thank him."

Kasey nodded. "Okay … what I really came to talk about is … what we talked about before. Did you have a chance to think it over?"

Woody made a slow nod toward Katy and rolled his eyes. Kasey grinned and nodded. She took Katy to a bench at the other end of the barn, picked up a barn kitten, and gave it to her daughter. "This little kitty needs lots of attention. So, sit right here and tell the kitty how much you like her. Daddy and I need to talk, and we'll be right over there."

Woody smiled and gave Kasey a thumbs-up as she came back. When she reached him, he picked her up. She squealed as he sat her on his worktable. He kissed her, stood back, and looked in her eyes. "Now, we can see eye to eye."

She angled her head. "Does that mean you're gonna talk to him?"

"I'll ask him … if you'll just … mention it to him first. He's *your* dad. Just tell him we want you, me, and Katy to live together. If he doesn't object, I'll ask him if it's okay for the three of us to share your room. I'll even offer to pay rent."

Kasey shrugged. "I don't want to do this on the phone, and I'm not sure when Dad will be back."

Woody glanced at a wall calendar. "He said ten days to two weeks. He's been gone five days."

Kasey's eyes lit up as she leaned toward him and grinned. "Maybe you could stay a couple of nights while he's gone. Nobody has to know."

Woody's eyes grew big as he shook his head, and then angled it toward the other end of the barn. "That would be the first words out of our daughter's mouth, the instant her grandpa returns."

Kasey rolled her eyes during a slow nod. She pushed herself off the table, and stood. "Mom should be back in a couple of days. I don't know what she would think about it. But I'll ask her. If she's okay with it, maybe Dad will agree."

Woody spread his hands. "What if she says *no*?"

"There's only one way to find out."

***

Two days later, Elly called Kasey to say she's home for a few days. "Why don't you, Woody, and Katy come for dinner tonight. I'll get takeout from the new Chinese place here in Taos. And bring your dad, too. He likes that stuff."

"Thanks, Mom, but after hours, Woody's working on a saddle for Dad. He won't leave the barn before eight o'clock. Besides, Dad's not back yet. However, I do want to talk to you when I get a chance but not on the phone. Thanks for the invitation, but I don't want to drive home after dark."

239

"Great, honey. You and Katy come and spend the night. You can drive home tomorrow. See you about six?"

Kasey and Katy enjoyed dinner and the evening at Grandma's. After breakfast next morning, while Katy napped, Kasey found the right time to talk to Mom. The two stood in the living room, and Kasey told her mom what she and Woody had talked about. Elly seemed surprised.

"Well, Kasey … I'm your mother, but you're a grown woman now, and I'm not your boss. Besides, I can't tell you what you can or can't do in your father's house."

"I'm not asking for your permission, Mom. I just want to know how you feel about it."

"You want just a short, straight answer?"

"Yes, I do."

Elly folded her arms, took a deep breath, and sighed. "Okay, fine." She leaned toward Kasey and looked in her eyes. "No. I don't think you should."

Chapter Thirty-Four

Detailed records were essential in the horse-training business. Marty recorded the progress for each horse after every training exercise and gave each horse a name to make the recordkeeping easier.

A name that fit a horse's personality was easier to remember. But he had not yet found a name to fit the last one he worked with today, a name for a cocky, young male too stubborn to train. Marty expected that behavior from stallions, but that young gelding had a lot of spunk. Today, that one wore him down.

No matter. Tomorrow, he would show the horse who's boss. Or … maybe he'd give the animal a day's rest. After all, for the middle of May, the day was warm enough to irritate a man, and Marty knew weather could also affect the moods of a horse.

Regardless, Marty was done for the day and rubbed his backside as he walked from the barn to the mailbox. It seemed that, for most of his life, he'd probably done more riding than walking. Nearly every day, he'd been on the back of a horse, or mule, or bull, or riding in an airplane, or in his pickup. Whatever … his butt still got sore sometimes. It made him smile. Just one of the hazards of the business.

As usual, he'd toss the junk mail in the outside trashcan and, if anything was left, he'd go through it in the house while he guzzled a cold beer.

After the first long swallow, he plopped on the easy chair and fanned apart the remaining mail. *A couple of bills and ... what's this?* He opened an envelope from Elly, and frowned. *Strange.*

Dear Cowboy: You probably think it's strange getting a letter from me instead of a phone call, but I need a bit of time to think about this as I say it. We've been together a long time, you and me, and I'm truly happy about that. I should have said this before. You and I talked around it more than once.

We've had our ups and downs. Things were rocky at times, but I guess that's how it is, because you've been a true rock in my life, and I've needed that more than you know. Yes, at times, I'm hard to put up with. I know that, but fortunately, you thought of me as someone worth putting up with.

You're not always easy to get along with either, just a bull-headed cowboy sometimes. Maybe that's why we need each other, because we recognize that to get the most from life, you have to be stubbornly strong and true to yourself. It seems funny now. Lots of times, you made me mad, but later it made me proud of you for being your own man and not caving in.

Even so, I'm sorry for any heartache I caused. I'm trying hard to learn from my past, to be a better person, a better mother, better woman, better friend, and a better sweetheart.

Okay, time to get to the point.

I don't know what you have scheduled for your business, but I'm hoping you'll consider coming to Albuquerque for the Independence Day rodeo. The

Lifetime Achievement Award is very special to me. But if you can't be there, I'll just ask them to reschedule it. Yes, I'm serious – it's that important to me. It doesn't seem possible that I've been doing rodeo performances for more than twenty years.

When the rodeo ends, there will be a party – don't know how big. A few people in charge at the arena are already planning it, and they promised not to say anything about the party until the night of the rodeo.

Kasey knows about the award, but I wanted to be the one to tell you, and she swore she wouldn't say a word. She's excited about it, and driving down to Albuquerque the day before.

I remember Son of Cyclone and your last bull ride a few years ago in Cimarron. It was the first Independence Day in a long time I did not perform at a rodeo. But I wanted to be there because I knew It was special to you, and that made it special to me.

Marty, I hope you'll be in Albuquerque at my big event. I don't want to do this if you're not. It means that much to me. *You* mean that much to me. If you can't be there, I'll put it off until you can. Just give me an answer soon, please.

You've been my one and only for 21 years.

Your green-eyed sweetie,

Elly

Marty dropped the letter on the coffee table and shook his head as he went to the kitchen. After two microwave burritos, a half bag of corn chips and another beer, he went back to his easy chair. Nothing on TV caught his interest. He switched it off and read the letter again, hoping he'd missed something.

He hadn't.

He took the letter outside and sat in the shade on the deck swing to talk it over with himself.

What would life be like afterwards? If she retired and moved in with me, would she finally want to get married? Would I? Every time I brought up marriage, she always found a reason, or excuse, to put it off. Maybe I should just tell her I want to put off going to this award thing for another year or two, or twelve, or whatever.

Elly knows a lot about horses. If she lived here, maybe we could run my business together. Or could we? We've never even run a household together.

Maybe she chose to forget I haven't missed the July fourth rodeo in Cimarron for more than twenty-five years. Now she wants me to skip that and join her in Albuquerque for some award. Hell, she's got lots of awards, and I didn't need to be there for any of them.

So ... who knows? Maybe I'll go to Albuquerque. But probably not.

The cellphone interrupted Marty's debate. He knew the ring.

"Kasey girl. What are you up to?"

"Hi, Dad. Just on my way home. You done for the day? Did you get the mail yet? And, oh yeah, is Mom there?"

Marty laughed. "Yes, yes, and no. Yes to your first two questions, and no to the third. And by the way, your mom doesn't live here."

Kasey gave a loud sigh. "I know, Dad. I just want to talk to you about something."

"Like what?"

"Like a letter from Mom. Did you get one?"

"Why would I get a letter from your mother? Did she move to Calcutta?"

"Dad, you're impossible. I'll be there in ten minutes."

Eight minutes later, Marty watched while Kasey took Katy out of the safety seat and led her toward the deck. She smiled big and waved. "Hi, Grandpa." Katy pulled loose from her mother and ran to Grandpa, who swept her up and hugged her. He sat on the deck swing with her in his lap.

"Oh, Katy, you're are so precious, and you're growing up so fast. How old are you now?"

Katy looked at her mother, and waited. Kasey nodded. "It's okay. Tell Grandpa how old you are."

Katy looked at Marty while she struggled to hold up three fingers. "I'm three."

Marty spent the next ten minutes holding his granddaughter, talking to her, and making funny faces while she laughed.

Kasey stood, took her daughter, and sat her on a rocking horse that Grandpa always kept on the deck. Kasey turned to Marty. "Now, it's my turn."

Marty laughed. "Okay, I'm guessing this is about your mom and a letter?"

She held her fists to her sides and leaned toward him. "You got the letter, didn't' you?"

"No." Marty took the letter from his back pocket. "Unless you mean ... this one?"

She snatched the letter, sat beside him, and shook it in his face. "You *are* going, right?"

Marty took a deep breath and blew it out. "I was hoping we could go to Cimarron, like always. You and me and Katy ... and Woody, if he wants to go. So, I don't know."

Kasey stood, turned away from him and shook her head. She turned back, biting her lip, tears in her eyes. "I love you, Daddy, but ... Mom has her heart set on all of us being there for her award ... Katy, me, and you. So ... Katy and I are going to Albuquerque, and Woody's going with us. So, he'll need a couple of days off, just so you know." She looked up, and her eyes filled with new tears. "If you don't show up, I'm going to be really hurt." Pain showed on her face as she turned away.

Marty stood, caught her arm and turned her back toward him. "Kasey, what is it? Why is this so important to you?"

She looked up at him, her eyes misty. "How many years have we struggled to bring Mom around? To get her to act like a woman who loves you and a mother who loves me? How long, Daddy? How long?"

Marty shrugged, and hung his head.

Kasey lifted his chin and talked while she cried. "It's been way too long. We both know that, but it's so much better than it used to be." She wagged her head. "We can't stop now, Daddy. Not *now*. It'll start going backwards if we do."

A tear made a slow trail down Marty's cheek as he looked at her. "It always ends up this way, doesn't it?"

Kasey wiped her face and frowned. "What do you mean?"

"I'm the father. You're the daughter. So how come you're right more often than I am?"

With a big grin on her face and tears in her eyes, Kasey left wet spots as she kissed him on the cheek. She pulled back, dropped her chin, and peered up at him. "It's not my fault, Daddy. It's just because you're a man."

From the corral, a horse let go a long whinny and tapped the ground three times with his front foot. Marty stared at the young gelding and wrinkled his face. "What the…"

Kasey looked at Marty, at the corral, and back again. "That's a horselaugh if I ever heard one."

"Yeah."

"What's his name?"

Marty glared. "Jackass."

Chapter Thirty-Five

Three-year-old Katy squirmed and complained, and pulled off her cowboy hat again. Without the hat, the breeze wrapped her blonde hair around the Popsicle that dripped red juice down the front of her dress. Marty dabbed at the little vagrant with his bandana, knowing he shouldn't give in to her so often. But she was a child, a precious little girl who wanted something cool, sweet, and wet. There was little a grandfather could do to keep her occupied.

In silence, he did his own squirming and complaining. The bleachers offered little comfort, and the late-afternoon sun in Albuquerque didn't make anything better. Now he knew he should have taken the box-seat tickets like always. The view was better and Katy and Marty would be in the shade. But there, he'd likely be recognized, maybe even called out by the announcer. Today, he wanted to be just part of the crowd. Or did he?

In her letter a few weeks ago, Elly said how much it would mean to her to have her family at this event. Marty wasn't sure he felt like part of her family and wondered if Elly ever really thought of him that way. After all these years, she still lived in Taos. He still lived in Cimarron.

Marty asked himself again why he was here instead of going to the rodeo in his hometown, Cimarron's biggest event of the year. He'd been a celebrity there every year since he rode Son of Cyclone years ago. But he was here because he'd promised Elly a couple of weeks back that he would show. Like his father, Marty Redman was a man of his word.

In all the years, Marty never tired of rodeos. To him, they were never routine. He was here because he loved it all, just like other people in the stands. The crowd loved the pageantry and spectacle, like the beautiful girls who rode out to start the show, wearing their white boots and hats that drew ooh's and aah's from the ladies in the stands. But a plunging neckline, bouncing boobs, and a million-dollar cleavage captured the attention of the men and left teenage boys chewing their tongues.

"Here she is, rodeo fans." In spite of a short echo, the announcer's voice came strong and clear from the speakers throughout the grounds. "Long known as the Sweetheart of the Rodeo, please welcome our beautiful and talented star, Miss Elly Kelly."

The crowd stood and applauded as she rode into the center on a golden palomino, its long mane and tail brushed and styled to perfection. Strapped to her stirrup, the flag boot held the pole for Old Glory, the American flag that flew behind Elly's head as her horse trotted in front of the crowd.

While the horse pranced around the loop of the oblong arena, Elly flashed her electric smile and waved to her fans. She pushed the stirrups forward to show off her white boots with red and blue trim to honor her country's birthday. Sunlight reflected off the long golden hair that spilled from under her white cowboy hat with the silver Concho band. And rhinestones lined the seams of her skin-tight, navy-blue jeans.

Elly had it all, and she knew how to use it all for the show. While the sunlight made a thousand flashing stars from the sequins on her red blouse, her tanned, perfect breasts danced with the horse's gait and flaunted almost enough cleavage to get her arrested.

"Ladies and gentlemen, boys and girls. In tribute to our great country, the United States of America, we ask you to stand for our National Anthem."

Boys and girls sprang to their feet. Parents stood and held the hands of young children or picked up those too young to stand on their own. Heavy people grunted as they pushed themselves off the bleachers. Older people struggled to maintain their balance. But, except for the fans in wheelchairs, everyone stood.

They didn't stand to please the announcer or to follow the crowd. They stood because it was the National Anthem, because it was the right thing to do. Rodeo fans were more than patriotic. They were proud of their patriotism and felt a strong emotional bond with their country and with other rodeo fans. An enormous flag flew above the crowd, and many saluted the flag until the anthem ended.

The breeze that waved Old Glory also shared the odor of urine and fresh manure from horses, bulls, calves, and steers. Noses wrinkled as music blared from the speakers. The animals made it all possible, but they were noisy, smelly, sometimes dangerous, and they kicked up clouds of dust that often choked the thousands of fans who paid to get in. This was the atmosphere of an event ruled by cowboys, the spectacle where they could show what they were made of, the feats they could perform better than all others – the world of championship rodeo.

The spectators did not enjoy the odors, dust, or afternoon heat, but they would ignore it, or at least, tolerate it all, and more, to watch trick riders, calf ropers, barrel racers, steer wrestlers, bronco busters, and bull riders. And always, the Sweetheart of the Rodeo.

They loved it all – bright banners and flags, crazy clowns, flashy costumes, the noise and energy of the crowd, and world-class athletes who risked entry fees, their safety, and their lives to entertain the fans. Cuts, scrapes, bruises, strains, black eyes, busted lips, and broken bones were routine injuries in the sport.

Marty sighed as Elly rode out of the arena. She was still the picture of poise, grace, and confidence. Her connection with the crowd was more than showmanship. She felt genuine and honest affection for those who adored her. And she was still the same gorgeous, green-eyed girl he fell in love with years ago.

Harmon gave his well-rehearsed, hardy laugh that never sounded rehearsed as Elly rode out of sight. Then he held up his hand to silence the crowd, but it was seldom necessary. That voice always commanded attention.

"For all our tremendous rodeo fans tonight …" he paused for effect, "we have a very special event planned for you when our rodeo competition ends this evening." Another pause. "I can tell you honestly, in all my years of broadcasting, I have never seen anything like this at a rodeo … never." He wore a giant grin and looked around at the crowd. "And I'm betting *you* never have." He waited while puzzled faces looked back and forth. "Never. So, make sure you stay for this event."

Marty shook his head. He was sure the event was connected with Elly. Most likely, she would announce her retirement, she would get an award, and the rodeo staff would host a party for her. She would stay an extra hour, sign autographs and pose for photos with her fans. But Harmon could always make any event sound like a much bigger affair.

****

Fans chewed their way through stale popcorn, cold hotdogs, and melting ice cream washed down with too many drinks, while cowboys and cowgirls suffered hard landings, twisted ankles, butt blisters, and busted noses to entertain them. Rodeos were seldom quiet. Between events, a clown would be on the field making everyone laugh. Or the announcer would talk about the stars of the show, introduce a celebrity, or plug the sponsors. But now, the competition was over, and a blanket of silence hung over the spectators, the kind of hush that often came when a

251

competitor could not get up after a hard fall or left the arena in an ambulance.

Low talk and whispers began to flow through the crowd as everyone waited for that special event promised to them by the announcer. They wanted someone to do something or at least break the silence.

An uneasy feeling gnawed in Marty's gut. *Was Kasey okay? Was Elly okay?* He knew Elly would not answer her phone. He called Kasey. No answer. Today, when Marty first arrived, she handed Katy to him. "Would you, please?"

She knew he would. But now Katy's clothes looked like she'd lost a food fight, and she was getting cranky. He did not see anyone leaving, but decided he wasn't curious enough to wait around for the special event. He picked up Katy, wiped her face again, and started down the bleachers.

The announcer broke the silence. "Attention all rodeo fans." After a short pause, he continued. "Ladies and gentlemen, we may have a champion bull rider in the crowd with us tonight. We all know Marty Redman."

A buzz flew through the crowd. Fans looked around. Many here knew the name Marty Redman, though most would not recognize the man without a bull under him.

"Marty Redman, if we're lucky enough to have you in the crowd tonight, would you make your way down here, please?"

Marty shook his head and looked down. Charmin' Harmon had never been one of his favorites, and he tried to tell himself his dislike had nothing to do with Harmon's affair with Elly before she and Marty got together. The man had all the character of a snake-oil salesman. If Marty and Elly ever got married, whether the wedding was big or small, that weasel would not be invited.

Many times, after Marty won a bull-riding competition, Harmon called him to the microphone for an interview. Marty didn't like standing next to him or pretending he liked the man, but he knew that was part of the broadcaster's job. For the sake of the show, Marty joined Harmon and talked to the fans.

That was then, when Marty competed. Now he found no good reason to accommodate *Vermin* Harmon. He held Katy in front of him and stepped faster on the way down. But a young woman turned, stared, and then pointed.

"Hey, that's him. That's Marty Redman."

People nearby stared. Marty knew he was busted. He turned toward the announcer, held up his hand and gave a big wave.

"It's him," a woman yelled, and pointed. Others joined in, and soon the whole crowd whistled, clapped, and cheered while Marty worked his way down.

"Here he comes, now. All you bull-rider fans, let's give Marty Redman a big round of applause for the true champion that he is."

"Marty, Marty, Marty." As he approached, fans cheered and clapped, and yelled, and gave Marty the biggest standing ovation he had ever seen. Elly stood beside Harmon. She clapped and cheered, and yelled Marty's name along with the fans.

Marty's eyes went wide and he made a sudden stop when his mother stepped in front of him. She gave Marty a big hug, and took Katy.

After the hug, he held her shoulders and stepped back. "Mom, what are you doing here? How did you get here?"

Behind a big smile, she said, "My granddaughter. I didn't want to miss the party."

Marty let go of Mom, and pushed his puzzled face toward her. "Why didn't you tell me you were coming?" She tapped her hearing aid as she walked away and sat on one of the folding chairs set up nearby.

Marty made a step toward Elly, but stopped when her father came toward him. "Mister Kelly, what a surprise. Good to see you."

"Hello, Marty." Ken Kelly extended his hand. "Happy to be here." He angled his head toward Elly. "I'm quite proud of that girl." He turned, walked to the chairs and sat beside Marty's mother. Now, Marty noticed Woody's parents, the Clarks, sitting on the other side of Mom.

For Marty, that erased all doubt. Elly wanted these people here for her retirement notice and for the sendoff party. She always enjoyed publicity and knew how to get it. Regardless, he was now glad to be a part of it as he walked toward Elly.

Elly took his hand, and turned to look behind him. Marty turned to see a young couple holding hands and coming toward them. Marty's face wrinkled in surprise. When he took the baby from her a couple of hours ago, Kasey was in jeans, boots, and a cowboy hat. He'd always thought of his daughter as a beautiful girl. He knew he was biased, but now he also knew he was right. Because now she was every bit a fully-grown woman in a gorgeous dress and a glowing face that said, *this may be life's finest hour.*

Woody, too, had changed. The handsome young man now wore an impressive suit and tie, and as the two came forward, Woody's face told everyone he was with the best woman he could ever meet. Marty started to speak but held back when Harmon spoke to the crowd.

"For our rodeo fans tonight, we have a special treat for all of you. This young couple" … with a wide grin, he turned and held his open hand toward the young couple, "are very much in love, and would like you to witness the wedding between Kasey and Woody right here and right now. Whaddaya say?"

The crowd applauded loud and long. Teenage girls stood and cried. When the applause faded and people sat again, a young man in a camo cowboy hat stood, cupped his hands around his mouth, and yelled, "No. You're too beautiful for him. Marry me."

While the crowd laughed, a man walked toward the microphone carrying a Bible. He stopped, accepted the mic from Harmon, and grinned big at the crowd.

"Ladies and gentlemen, boys and girls, this is a solemn occasion but a happy one. Kasey and Woody have expressed their love for each other, and wish to be united in Holy Matrimony." Kasey and Woody stopped beside the minister. He turned them to face each other.

"I am privileged to do the honors. Who gives this woman to be married to this man?"

Marty stared open-mouthed until Elly caught his wrist and stared at him. He swallowed hard. "Her mother and I."

The minister laughed. "I guess it's tough sometimes to give away such a beautiful daughter." The crowd giggled.

After a condensed version of the typical vows, Woody gave Kasey a passionate kiss while the crowd applauded. Elly and Marty congratulated them, and wished them a lifetime of happiness, but Marty stood puzzled as the newlyweds walked to the folding chairs and sat with the others.

The minister returned the mic to Harmon, shook hands with Marty and Elly, followed Kasey and Woody to the chairs and sat beside them. Marty turned to Elly and whispered.

"Why didn't you tell me about all this, Elly?" He looked down at his boots. "I would've dressed a little better."

Harmon handed Marty the microphone. Marty stood speechless until Harmon shouted, "Say hello to your fans, champ."

While the crowd applauded, Marty found his voice. "Thank you. Thank you all for such a tribute. The best reward for working your way to the top is all the friends you make along the way. I consider everyone here to be a friend." He held up his empty hand. "Are we friends?" Again, the crowd clapped, cheered, and whistled. He pointed at Harmon. "There's a reason people call this man *Charmin' Harmon*. Isn't he the greatest rodeo announcer you know?" The crowd cheered again as Marty returned the mic. Harmon handed it to Elly.

Elly beamed and pulled the mic close to her lips. "Ladies and gentlemen, most of you dear Marty Redman fans know I'm a big fan, too. Marty and I have been an item for a long time. What you may not know is that Marty asked me to marry him. And … I said yes!"

The crowd rose to its feet again. And again, people cheered, clapped, laughed, shouted, and whistled. As the applause died, the young man in the camo cowboy hat stood and cupped his hands around his mouth. He looked at Marty and yelled, "You lucky bastard." The crowd laughed, whistled, and clapped again. Marty chuckled and his face grew red. Elly grinned, and waited for quiet.

"I think we've waited long enough, don't you?" She extended her hand, palm up, and swept it around, spinning to include the fans behind her, and again the crowd went crazy. When the noise began to die, she reached for Marty's arm and looked up at him. "Marty Redman, will you marry me? Right here? Right now?" She pushed the microphone toward him.

Marty's face paled as he stared at her. His mouth opened but no words came. A man in a western suit carried a Bible toward them. Marty looked at him and back at Elly but still could not talk.

Elly brought the mic back to her face and yelled, "I love you, Marty Redman."

The newlyweds stood with their hands cupped, and yelled, "Yes, yes, yes." The crowd rose to its feet again and echoed, "Yes, yes, yes."

Marty took the microphone and yelled, "I love you, too, Elly Kelly. Yes, yes, yes."

He gave the mic to Harmon.

While Mister Kelly made his way toward the wedding spot, Harmon introduced the minister, and then held the microphone for him. The minister opened his Bible.

"Good evening, everyone. We have come here tonight to unite Elly Kelly and Marty Redman in holy matrimony, right here in front of God, cowboys and cowgirls, rodeo fans, bulls, calves, and horses, and everything and everybody. Everyone in favor?"

The crowd yelled, whistled, and applauded. When the applause died, the camo-hat cowboy stood again and cupped his mouth.

"No. Save her for me."

The crowd laughed, and Reverend Oso took the mic. "And … in front of the man in the camo cowboy hat." He laughed and the crowd cheered while that man, with a red-face grin, stood, nodded and clapped.

When silence returned, Reverend Oso asked, "Who gives this woman to be married to this man?"

Mister Kelly caught Elly's hand and stepped to the mic. "As her proud father, I do." He caught Marty's wrist, joined the groom's hand with Elly's, and walked back to the chairs.

The reverend smiled and nodded. "Marty, you're wearing such a silly grin, I think we'll start with you." Oso stabbed his finger toward Elly. "Marty Redman, do you really love this woman?" He pointed again. "This woman standing right here beside you? Because standing beside your spouse is exactly what a good marriage is made of." He pushed the mic toward Marty. "So, do you love her?"

"I do."

Oso leaned toward Marty. "C'mon, champ, say it with feeling."

After a nervous laugh, Marty yelled, "I do, Reverend, with all my heart."

The reverend laughed while he waited for the crowd's cheers to end. "Will you take her to be your lifelong soulmate, your wife, your sweetheart, your one and only, even when her hair is a mess and she's not wearing makeup?"

Marty's answer sounded weak. "I will."

With a twisted face, Oso leaned toward him. "Are you sure about that, Marty? I said, *with no makeup*." Marty laughed while Reverend Oso continued. "How about when she has a cold or fever? When she lays around the house all day in her pajamas? Will you understand when she has hot flashes? When she laughs one minute and cries the next? Will you keep her and love her even when she's cranky and ornery and seems to disagree with everything you say? When she's mad at you for no reason, and tells you to go sleep in the barn? Will you put up with that, and maybe more, as long as you both shall live? Well … will you, Marty?"

Marty shook his head as he laughed. He looked at Elly. "I will. That's a promise."

Oso faced Elly. "You heard what he said. I'm betting he means it. Now it's your turn."

Her eyes bulged. "O-oh my."

"Elly Kelly, do you love this cowboy standing next to you?"

"I do."

Oso glared at her and grinned. "Say it like you mean it."

"Oh, yes, I do. I love him very much."

"Do you promise to keep him, and cherish him even when you know he's wrong? When he won't listen or won't talk or won't shut up?"

"Yes, I will."

How about when he doesn't notice your new shoes or new hairdo?"

Elly shook as she tried not to laugh. "Yes, I will."

"How about when you tell him something a dozen times, and he doesn't hear you? When he trudges into the house smelling like a dead horse with bull droppings on his boots?"

Elly frowned. "Yuk. I mean, yes."

"Or when he's still mule-headed even after he had to spend the night in the barn?"

Elly laughed again. "I will."

"Do you really love this man that much?"

"I really do."

Oso pointed at Marty while he looked at Elly. "You told *me*. Now tell *him*."

She wrapped her arms around his waist. "I do and I will, because I love you so very much, Marty."

The minister pronounced them husband and wife, and turned to Marty. "Well, Mister Redman, I think you've got a good one here. So now you can do something you've probably never done before." He looked around and rolled his eyes while the crowd laughed. Then he turned back to Marty. "You may kiss the bride."

Marty planted a long, tender kiss on Elly. When he started to release her, she clamped the back of his head and held his lips to hers while the crowd went crazy one more time.

When the two released each other, they stood inches apart, her eyes consuming him, his eyes consuming her. As a tear rolled down Elly's cheek, Marty smiled. He'd waited a long time for this day.

With the weddings over, Marty said goodbye to the guests, and thanked the people involved. He congratulated his daughter and new son-in-law and hugged everyone in his family. Woody, Kasey, and Katy would take Grandma home. Then their family of three would spend a couple of nights at the Best Western in Albuquerque.

Minutes ago, Marty left Elly talking to the rodeo crew about her future plans, yet telling them nothing. Now, he turned to see her hand on the arm of a man he did not recognize as Elly approached him. The man reached for Marty's hand.

"Congratulations, Marty. You're the best friend I ever had and the brother I *never* had."

Sudden recognition filled Marty's mind and heart as he hugged his friend. "Billy, oh my God … it's so good to see you." Marty stepped back and stared. "You look great. So how the heck are you?"

"I've been through a lot, but it's over. I got married six months ago. Life is good."

"I'm happy for you, man. Didn't know you were here. How'd you find out about this?"

Billy jerked his head toward Elly. "She found me." He smiled big. "For my bull-rider friend, I wouldn't have missed this for a million *bucks*."

Elly rolled her eyes while Marty and Billy said goodbye.

The unexpected events tonight left Marty excited, but exhausted. Now, he wanted to go home. But fame often came with a price. He and Elly signed autographs at the arena and posed for pictures with fans and well-wishers. After more than a half-hour, Marty called it quits, and helped Elly load her horse into the trailer. She gave Marty a kiss and a big squeeze and looked at his puzzled face as she placed her keys in his hand.

"Would you take my horse home for me? I'll drive your truck and meet you at home. *Your* home." Her head tilted back and the big, soft green eyes looked into his again. "*Our* home."

"Did I tell you that you have the most beautiful green eyes I've ever seen?"

She cocked her head and smiled. "Does that mean you'll make breakfast for me?"

He smiled and nodded. "Scrambled or fried?" Marty gave his keys to Elly.

Chapter Thirty-Six

Elly approached the driveway of her new home, wondering if Marty would ever put up the garage he'd threatened to build for ten years. She often got mail at this address, and when she pulled a handful from the mailbox, she noticed the top envelope was addressed to her.

Inside the house, she dropped the mail on the kitchen counter and drew a glass of wine from the tapper in the fridge. Thoughts of the day filled Elly's head while she leaned against the counter and sipped the wine. The day and both weddings happened just the way she'd hoped. The thought brought a big smile. She felt happy, and tried to convince herself that her life wouldn't change much. But she knew it would.

She was now a married woman. She spent many nights in this house but never moved in. Now she would live here. Her name would be Elly Kelly Redman. She would be Marty's wife, a mother, a grandmother, and ... she swallowed hard ... a mother-in-law.

Most of those would be easy. Retiring from the rodeo ... that would be the challenge. But she would do it. She would announce her retirement *for real* after her next performance. Yet everything now seemed so *unreal*.

She refilled her glass from the tapper and picked up the mail again, but dropped it when she felt a sudden chill. Night skies in northern New Mexico often had no clouds and, as night arrived, the heat of the day made a fast escape. The new lady-of-the-house found the auto-igniter for the fireplace. A minute later, the room felt cozy.

A year ago, she complained about ashes, smoke, and odor from his wood-burning fireplace and, two weeks later, she found Marty had converted it to gas. *He was a real sweetie.*

Elly opened the top envelope on the counter, removed the letter, and sat in Marty's recliner in the living room. Today had been a long one, but after another sip of wine, she took a long, easy breath, let it go, and relaxed. She unfolded the letter.

Dear Mr. Redman:

> In regard to paternity test reports sent to you from our laboratory approximately three years ago, a recent routine review has exposed a reversed report.

Elly jerked her head and turned the letter face down on her lap. Earlier, the mail scattered when she dropped it on the countertop, and now she'd opened Marty's mail by mistake. An awful feeling gnawed in her gut. He was her husband now, but this felt like an intrusion. She had no right. Would he believe she opened it by accident?

Elly stared at the blank side of the letter on her lap. Was there anything in it that really matters? She turned the letter face up but, to avoid reading it, she kept her gaze at the top of the page on the red banner that announced *Error Report.*

She closed her eyes and shook her head. After another two sips of wine, her eyes eased open and her gaze drifted down to the DNA Report. Her forehead wrinkled as she looked at the meaningless list of letters and numbers. She skipped over them, and read the explanation below the list.

> The alleged father, Martin J. Redman, is <u>not</u> <u>excluded</u> as the biological father of the tested child,

Kasey Redman. Based on tested analyses of the DNA loci listed, the probability of paternity is 99.9998%.

Elly's forehead wrinkled again and she read the paragraph once more. Her mind needed a minute to put it together.

Does this mean the report Marty received three years ago excluded him from being Kasey's father?

She stared up at her husband's favorite photo that hung on the wall, a snapshot of Kasey and Marty side by side with his arm around her. They looked so much alike, and the picture captured a special moment where his face showed how proud he was of his darling daughter, his own flesh and blood. And Kasey's eyes told the world how much she adored her daddy.

Elly looked away from the photo. Her thoughts troubled her. *Had Marty believed for the past three years that Kasey was not his own daughter?* Her eyes misted. A lump formed in her throat. Her breath grew ragged, and a reality spread through her. For the first time, she knew how much she loved him. After all these years, Marty Redman was still the man of her dreams.

She set the wine glass on the chairside table, dabbed her eyes, and looked again at the paper on her lap. The next report showed the test results between Tested Child, *Martin J. Redman*, and Alleged Father, *Walter J. Redman*. She ignored the letters and numbers, and read the conclusion.

The alleged father is <u>excluded</u> as the biological father of the tested child. Based on tested analyses of the DNA loci listed, the probability of paternity is 00.0002%

"Oh, my God." Elly hid her face in her hands. Her chest grew tight again. She shook her head, hoping she'd misunderstood. She forced herself to read that last paragraph again, and she knew the new paternity test showed that Walter Redman was not Marty's biological father.

We have discovered those results were reversed on the report we sent you in the past. As an added measure, we tested the same samples again to confirm our recent findings. We are sorry for any —

"Oh, no." Elly covered her mouth and a gasp escaped as pain filled her chest. She pulled a wad of tissues from her purse, held it to her eyes, and cried for Marty. Her head wagged while she forced herself to read the report one more time.

No, no, no. It just couldn't be true. Why had Marty never told her about the tests? Elly knew for certain that he was Kasey's father, the only man who could have been.

The lump grew bigger in Elly's throat at a sudden realization. *If Marty believed the first report, how could he . . . how could he marry me? How could he love me?*

Elly's breath caught. Marty told her many times how he and his father had been so close, how much he loved his dad, how much he missed him.

Marty will be crushed. He will never recover from the loss. This was the happiest day of my life, but now ...

With her eyes closed, Elly could still see the bright red banner across the top of that page, with the words, *Error Report.*

Chapter Thirty-Seven

He did not hurry on the road to Elly's place, a two-hour drive from the rodeo. A thousand nights, maybe more, he'd driven this road and seldom saw another car. It gave him time to think, and tonight Marty had a lot of things and people to think about.

He was again a married man. But he did not feel the way he always assumed he would – settled and happy, at peace with the world and with himself. Instead, everything seemed unsettled. He drove to Albuquerque earlier today expecting Elly to retire. Would she ever? Would Elly be home more, now she was his wife? Could they sit together in the evenings? Babysit for their granddaughter? Watch concerts on TV and talk? Or enjoy watching *Tombstone* for the umpteenth time and recite the dialogue along with the characters? Questions stayed in his mind as he drove Elly's truck to her place.

His father would have been the best one to talk to about these matters. Dad always seemed to know how to approach such things, how to figure out what matters most, and what matters least.

Sometimes Marty woke up in the middle of the night with a problem that would not leave him alone. He'd send a thought message to Dad. In the morning, the answer would often be waiting in the back of his mind as if his father planted it there. Marty knew he would never stop missing him.

Yan too, had been a precious source of advice many times. Marty memorized the words of wisdom he heard from her two years ago on her patio. *The human brain cannot be trusted to make decisions about love. You have to let the heart be in charge of that.*

Three weeks ago, when he left her room at the hospital, he told Yan he would try to call her every day, and that he'd be back to see her in a week, two at the most. He hoped she would be resting at home by then, and he offered to pay for a visiting nurse if she needed one while she recovered.

He also wanted to talk to her about his crazy idea. Would she like to improve her life? Consider moving when she recovered? She could rent a home in Cimarron for much less than in Albuquerque. If necessary, Marty would buy a home and rent it to her. He wanted to hire her to train horses for barrel racing. The more he thought about it, the more he liked it. He would bring it up next time they talked.

Three days later, when his phone showed a call from Albuquerque, he assumed someone wanted to sell him insurance, or hearing aids, or would ask for a donation. But it could be a customer. He pressed the answer button, but waited for the caller to speak.

"Hello. Is this Marty Redman?"

The voice sounded familiar. "Who's calling please?"

"This is Elyse. I'm an ICU tech at Albuquerque General Hospital.

"Oh, yes, I remember. I gave you flowers and you gave them back. How are you, lady?"

"I'm fine, thank you. But I'm afraid I have some bad news for you."

"About my friend? Yan? Is she okay?"

"She developed an infection, and some complications set in. She was returned to ICU around midnight last night."

"Oh no. If I can get there tomorrow, will I be able to see her?"

"I'm so sorry, Marty. Your friend, Yan, died about two PM today."

"What? Oh, God, no." Marty's mind would not accept what the lady told him. There must be some mistake. Not Yan. It just couldn't be.

Four days later, Marty drove down for the memorial service. He rented a large car and, for the first time, Elly, Kasey and Katy rode with him to Albuquerque. On the way, Kasey commented that it was like having a real family. The thought troubled Marty. Too often, only tragedies brought families together. Still, that short time they spent together had been a true comfort when he needed it so much.

While they rode, Marty said he hoped for a large turnout for Yan. Maybe members of the Navajo nation would gather to honor her. But Yan was an only child, her parents left the reservation when she was just a baby. Both parents died several years ago, and Marty did not know any of Yan's relatives. Did they know about her death?

Other than those in Marty's car, only four people attended the service. Marty's mom, two longtime friends from Yan's rodeo career, and Arty Covic.

That sad memory brought another. When Billy showed up for the wedding tonight, Marty had every reason to be happy. And he was. But a nagging thought plagued him while they talked. One week after that awful fire that once again made Billy a true hero, the Zacharys died, both on the same day.

Now, with Elly's horse in the barn, Marty threw enough hay and oats in the stalls to keep both horses happy for a couple of days. That done, he swapped the truck and trailer for Elly's new white Mustang and headed for home, *their* home.

While he drove, he told himself, *I have it all, a family with Elly, Kasey, and little Katy. A comfortable home, a business, nice cars, horses to ride, and even a part-time rooster.* That thought made him smile.

More than one generation of roosters showed up over the years. To Marty, they all looked and acted the same, and he called each one *Hobo*. He laughed. His first encounter with the rooster would be hard to forget.

Following Marty's first night in his new home, the rooster crowed loud, proud, and much too long at the hint of sunrise, a bit past five in the morning. Half-dressed, but fully pissed-off, Marty stumbled into chilly air on the back deck, ready to hurl a Waffle House coffee mug at the rude intruder.

Bleary eyes began to adjust to dim light. Marty made out the backyard awning, and then the fountain and bird feeder. Then … there it was … a faint image, a silhouette of an over-grown chicken that stood erect on a small hill in the yard, his neck extended, his head held high.

In the early-morning haze, Marty pictured a magnificent bird with majestic feathers of red, gold, and royal blue, a pompous prince that strutted around his flock, commanding respect and envy.

Yes, the rooster's sunrise greeting had been well rehearsed and sincere. Regardless, Marty would not tolerate trespassers raising hell outside his bedroom window at ungodly hours.

A sliver of sunlight on the horizon behind Marty began to define the conceited cock of the hill in front of him. The red feathers Marty imagined were instead brown, a *dull* brown. Gold feathers had turned a dusty white, and royal blue became a drab gray splattered among the white and brown.

Marty blinked as the beak turned toward him. The rooster held his head high and clucked. He spread his wings and lowered them again while his tail stood at attention as if to show off his grace and dignity. But the comb drooped on his head like a battered crown, and the wattle on his throat jiggled with all the grace and dignity of a fly swatter hanging on a wind chime.

He dipped his head toward Marty and offered a *Good morning* cluck. Marty laughed. "Good morning to you. too."

The rooster stretched his neck, looked up and treated Marty to another loud, proud, and long, sunrise wake-up call. Marty laughed again and took that as a good omen and a hardy welcome to his new home. He held up his coffee mug to toast his strange, new visitor, and walked back into the house.

That rooster may dress like a hobo, but he knows how to make friends.

Marty's mind wandered through events of the last three years. The DNA test had been the toughest one to handle. But he resolved it in his own mind when they celebrated Kasey's most recent birthday. She was just like him in too many ways for that test to be accurate. He knew in his own mind and heart that she was truly his own. Now he was married to her mother and made a solemn vow to himself to never tell either of them about the tests. Could life be any better?

Thoughts of his new life and new wife, and hopes for a great future stayed with Marty until the Mustang's headlights reflected off the taillights of his pickup in the driveway and reminded him it's time to build a garage.

Finding his mailbox empty, he assumed Elly picked up the bills on her way in. And finding his house lights on, and the front door locked made Marty happy. He'd asked Elly and Kasey to keep the doors locked any time they were there when he was not.

He rang the bell, waited a minute, and rang again. No answer. He fished the spare key from his pocket and let himself in. The house felt cozy and he glanced at the fireplace. The usual blue flame showed a splash of orange. A half-burned sheet of paper with a red band across the top danced above the logs, and then the last charred remains floated up the chimney.

The heat on Marty's face was not from the fire. He had explained creosote buildup to Elly and Kasey, and asked them to never throw anything in the fireplace. But today was Kasey's wedding day, and his and Elly's. He shrugged off the issue about the fireplace as he thought about how long he waited to marry Elly. It took a lot of patience. Maybe now he could use some of that patience for other things.

"Elly, it's me. I'm home." Marty walked from room to room and called her.

"Elly, answer me, please. I'm getting worried." He stood still and waited, but not for long. He checked the closets. No Elly. He went back to the kitchen, found an empty wine glass in the sink, and then noticed the light was on outside the back door. He opened the door and started to call out to Elly, but a light in the barn got his attention. He reached the barn in a dead run, yanked open the door and yelled, "Elly, where are you?"

On the Jack Daniels barrel in the corner, Elly sat wrapped in a heavy wool blanket. Her eyebrows arched.

"Hello, Cowboy."

Marty spread his hands and glared at her. His face wrinkled.

"What are you doing out here?"

She slid off the barrel.

"Waiting."

"For what?"

"For my husband." Elly walked to him, caught his hands, and wrapped his arms around her waist. She cocked her head and licked her soft, pink lips. A faint smile formed as she looked up at him.

"When's the last time you had a good roll in the hay?"

***

Marty did not see, nor care about, the hint of daylight when it edged above the horizon. But a sound outside the bedroom window made him stir. The mind, still fuzzy from the champagne he and Elly shared in the barn a few hours ago, dragged him back to blissful sleep.

The sound came again. Marty stirred again. Images in his head tried to attach meaning to the sound. The mind wanted sleep, but someone lying next to him pounded on his back. He sat up, rubbed his face and groaned. That someone squeezed his arm.

"Don't you hear that, Marty?"

A rooster interrupted Marty's yawn, and crowed loud and long. Marty opened his eyes and grinned. He lay down, snuggled that someone close to him, and whispered, "It's a great life, my darling wife, and I love you more than life itself."

Other Outstanding Books by Frank Allan Rogers

Vagabond Blue

What is real freedom? True friendship? The value of life? And what impact would life make on a child forced to work like a man since age 11?

Blue Moon Bailey, son of a devoted God-fearing mother and useless alcoholic father grew up during the great depression in sharecropper shacks of the rural South, in a family so destitute that joining a hobo jungle would be considered social climbing. On his 16th birthday, Blue walked away with the only two things he'd ever owned; a guitar and a dream.

Vagabond Blue pulls the reader into a young man's heart and soul in his relentless pursuit of an elusive dream; and evokes sympathy for the middle-class young woman who can't stop loving him – a saga that spans more than 20 years.

Twice Upon a Time

Can a man from the 21st century survive in 1847? Murdered on his birthday, August Myles finds "crossing over" is nothing like he'd ever heard, read, or imagined, and learns he has not earned a ticket to Paradise. In a grand experiment, the members of the Divine Council gave August another chance. Or did they?

With all the limitations of a mortal, he is sent back in time to rescue an 11-year-old orphan girl, to get her safely from Missouri to Oregon. An impossible mission. An adventure filled with death and danger, courage and fear, love and hate, happiness and heartbreak - a grueling journey on the world's longest graveyard - with Bonner's Disciples on the Oregon Trail.

Yet, with all the needs and passions of a mortal man, August must also battle the advances of two gorgeous women during long months and close encounters. One woman just wants to seduce him. Another falls in love. But for August Myles, carnal knowledge is forbidden.

Upon a Crazy Horse

When Jack Brannigan whacked a stump with his knee, lost his breakfast down the horse's front leg and bruised his manhood on the saddle horn, all on the first morning of the ride, he knew the venture would play hell with his sense of humor. Without thinking twice, maybe not even once, he had ignored the elements of endurance warning in the brochure and flew to New Mexico for a week-long, 135-mile horseback ride.

On twenty-two horses and a mule named Molly, the riders would chase the ghost of Billy the Kid over the mountains and across the desert from Lincoln to Fort Sumner. Choking dust, scorching sun, freezing rain, and a blistered butt prove the brochure to be true. But elements become the least of Jack's concerns when tragedy strikes. The riders discover Bonita, a courageous and beautiful young woman, kidnapped and held as a slave on Paradise Mountain, and Jack Brannigan faces the biggest challenge of his life.

Follow Frank Allan Rogers at:

https://www.facebook.com › frankallanrogers

https://www.amazon.com › Frank-Allan-Rogers

https://twitter.com › frankarogers

Cover Art by Mary Rogers

Unique and beautiful fine-art oil paintings by Mary Rogers

www.mary-rogers.artistwebsites.com